HOT
FLASH

HOT FLASH

CARRIE H. JOHNSON

KENSINGTON PUBLISHING CORP.
www.kensingtonbooks.com

DAFINA BOOKS are published by

Kensington Publishing Corp.
119 West 40th Street
New York, NY 10018

All Kensington titles, imprints, and distributed lines are available at special quantity discounts for bulk purchases for sales promotion, premiums, fund-raising, and educational or institutional use.

Special book excerpts or customized printings can also be created to fit specific needs. For details, write or phone the office of the Kensington Sales Manager: Kensington Publishing Corp., 119 West 40th Street, New York, NY 10018. Attn. Sales Department. Phone: 1-800-221-2647.

Dafina and the Dafina logo Reg. U.S. Pat. & TM Off.

ISBN-13: 978-1-4967-0399-6
ISBN-10: 1-4967-0399-5
First Kensington Trade Paperback Printing: June 2016

eISBN-13: 978-1-4967-0400-9
eISBN-10: 1-4967-0400-2
First Kensington Electronic Edition: June 2016

10 9 8 7 6 5 4 3 2 1

Printed in the United States of America

Dedicated to my mom and dad,
Walter and Muriel Johnson

ACKNOWLEDGMENTS

To the following individuals I offer my thanks and appreciation for your support, thought-provoking comments, and editing: Roberta Johnson, my sister and best friend; Anika Nailah, editor and author of *Free: And Other Stories*; Connie Miles; Anita Beckett; and Alicia Silva.

Special thanks to Selena James, executive editor at Dafina Books, who believed in my story and was willing to take a chance on me; and Esi Sogah, senior editor at Kensington Publishing.

And a very special thanks and undying gratitude to Adrienne Lloyd, firearms examiner—retired, who helped me launch this project and has been there every step of the way.

CHAPTER 1

Our bodies arched, both of us reaching for that place of ultimate release we knew was coming. Yes! We screamed at the same time . . . except I kept screaming long after his moment had passed.

You've got to be kidding me, a cramp in my groin? The second time in the three times we had made love. Achieving pretzel positions these days came at a price, but man, how sweet the reward.

"What's the matter, baby? You cramping again?" he asked, looking down at me with genuine concern.

I was pissed, embarrassed, and in pain all at the same time. "Yeah," I answered meekly, grimacing.

"It's okay. It's okay, sugar," he said, sliding off me. He reached out and pulled me into the curvature of his body, leaving the wet spot to its own demise. I settled in. Gently, he massaged my thigh. His hands soothed me. Little by little, the cramp went away. Just as I dozed off, my cell phone rang.

"*Mph, mph, mph,*" I muttered. "Never a moment's peace."

Calvin stirred. "Huh?"

"Nothin', baby, shhhh," I whispered, easing from his grasp

and reaching for the phone from the bedside table. As quietly as I could, I answered the phone the same way I always did.

"Muriel Mabley."

"Did I get you at a bad time, partner?" Laughton chuckled. He used the same line whenever he called. He never thought twice about waking me, no matter the hour. I worked to live and lived to work—at least that's been my story for twenty years, the last seventeen as a firearms forensics expert for the Philadelphia Police Department. I had the dubious distinction of being the first woman in the unit and one of two minorities. The other was my partner, Laughton McNair.

At forty-nine, I was beginning to think I was blocking the blessing God intended for me. I felt like I had blown past any hope of a true love in pursuit of a damn suspect.

"You there?" Laughton said, laughing louder.

"Hee hee, hell. I finally find someone and you runnin' my ass ragged, like you don't *even* want it to last. What now?" I said.

"Speak up. I can hardly hear you."

"I said . . ."

"I heard you." More chuckles from Laughton. "You might want to rethink a relationship. Word is we've got another dead wife and again the husband swears he didn't do it. Says she offed herself. That makes three dead wives in three weeks. Hell, must be the season or something in the water."

Not wanting to move much or turn the light on, I let my fingers search blindly through my bag on the nightstand until they landed on paper and a pen. Pulling my hand out of my bag with paper and pen was another story. I knocked over the half-filled champagne glass also on the nightstand. "Damn it!" I was like a freaking circus act, trying to save the paper, keep the bubbly from getting on the bed, stop the glass from breaking, and keep from dropping the phone.

"Sounds like you're fighting a war over there," Laughton said.

"Just give me the address."

"If you can't get away . . ."

"Laughton, just . . ."

"You don't have to yell."

He let a moment of silence pass before he said, "Thirteen ninety-one Berkhoff. I'll meet you there."

"I'm coming," I said and clicked off.

"You okay?" Calvin reached out to recapture me. I let him and fell back into the warmth of his embrace. Then I caught myself, sat up, and clicked the light on—but not without a sigh of protest.

Calvin rose. He rested his head in his palm and flashed that gorgeous smile at me. "Can't blame a guy for trying," he said.

"It's a pity I can't do you any more lovin' right now. I can't sugarcoat it. This is my life," I complained on my way to the bathroom.

"So you keep telling me."

I felt uptight about leaving Calvin in the house alone. My son, Travis, would be home from college in the morning, his first spring break from Lincoln University. He and Calvin had not met. In all the years before this night, I had not brought a man home, except Laughton, and at least a decade had passed since I'd had any form of a romantic relationship. The memory chip filled with that information had almost disintegrated. Then along came Calvin.

When I came out, Calvin was up and dressed. He was five foot ten, two hundred pounds of muscle, the kind of muscle that flexed at his slightest move. Pure lovely. He pulled me close and pressed his wet lips to mine. His breath, mixed with a hint of citrus from his cologne, made every nerve in my body pulsate.

"Next time we'll do my place. You can sing to me while I make you dinner," he whispered. "Soft, slow melodies." He crooned, "You Must Be a Special Lady," as he rocked me back and forth, slow and steady. His gooey caramel voice touched my every nerve ending, head to toe. Calvin is a singer and owns a nightclub, which is how we met. I was at his club with friends and Calvin and I—or rather, Calvin and my alter ego, spurred on by my friends, of course—entertained the crowd with duets all night.

He held me snugly against his chest and buried his face in the hollow of my neck while brushing his fingertips down the length of my body.

"Mmm . . . sounds luscious," was all I could muster.

The interstate was deserted, unusual no matter what time, day or night.

In the darkness, I could easily picture Calvin's face, bright with a satisfied smile. I could still feel his hot breath on my neck, the soft strumming of his fingers on my back. I had it bad. But-terflies reached down to my navel and made me shiver. I felt like I was nineteen again, first love or some such foolishness.

Flashing lights from an oncoming police car brought my thoughts around to what was ahead, a possible suicide. How any-one could think life was so bad that they would kill themselves never settled with me. Life's stuff enters pit territory sometimes, but then tomorrow comes and anything is possible again. Of course, the idea that the husband could be the killer could take one even deeper into pit territory. The man you once loved, who made you scream during lovemaking, now not only wants you gone, moved out, but dead.

When I rounded the corner to Berkhoff Street, the scene

was chaotic, like the trappings of a major crime. I pulled curb-side and rolled to a stop behind a news truck. After I turned off Bertha, my 2000 Saab gray convertible, she rattled in protest for a few moments before going quiet. As I got out, local news anchor Sheridan Meriwether hustled from the front of the news truck and shoved a microphone in my face before I could shut the car door.

"Back off, Sheridan. You'll know when we know," I told her.

"True, it's a suicide?" Sheridan persisted.

"If you know that, then why the attack? You know we don't give out information in suicides."

"Confirmation. Especially since two other wives have been killed in the past few weeks."

"Won't be for a while. Not tonight anyway."

"Thanks, Muriel." She nodded toward Bertha. "Time you gave the old gray lady a permanent rest, don't you think?"

"Hey, she's dependable."

She chuckled her way back to the front of the news truck. Sheridan was the only newsperson I would give the time of day. We went back two decades, to rookie days when my mom and dad were killed in a car crash. Sheridan and several other newspeople had accompanied the police to inform me. She returned the next day, too, after the buzz had faded. A drunk driver sped through a red light and rammed my parents' car head-on. That was the story the police told the papers. The driver of the other car cooked to a crisp when his car exploded after hitting my parents' car, then a brick wall. My parents were on their way home from an Earth, Wind & Fire concert at the Tower Theater.

Sheridan produced a series on drunk drivers in Philadelphia, how their indiscretions affected families and children on both sides of the equation, which led to a national broadcast. Philadelphia police cracked down on drunk drivers and legislation passed with compulsory loss of licenses. Several other cities and states followed suit.

I showed my badge to the young cop guarding the front door and entered the small foyer. In front of me was a white-carpeted staircase. To the left was the living room. Laughton, his expression stonier than I expected, stood next to the detective questioning who I supposed was the husband. He sat on the couch, leaned forward with his elbows resting on his thighs, his head hanging down. Two girls clad in *Frozen* pajamas huddled next to him on the couch, one on either side.

The detective glanced at me, then back at the man. "Where were you?"

"I just got here, man," the man said. "Went upstairs and found her on the floor."

"And the kids?"

"My daughter spent the night with me. She had a sleepover at my house. This is Jeanne, lives a few blocks over. She got homesick and wouldn't stop crying, so I was bringing them back here. Marcy and I separated, but we're trying to work things out." He choked up, unable to speak any more.

"At three a.m."

"I told you, the child was having a fit. Wanted her mother."

A tank of a woman charged through the front door, "Oh my God. Baby, are you all right?" She pushed past the police officer there and clomped across the room, sending those close to look for cover. The red-striped flannel robe she wore and pink furry slippers, size thirteen at least, made her look like a giant candy cane with feet.

"Wade, what the hell is happenin' here?" She moved in and lifted the girl from the sofa by her arm. Without giving him a chance to answer, she continued, "C'mon, baby. You're coming with me."

An officer stepped sideways and blocked the way. "Ma'am, you can't take her—"

The woman's head snapped around like the devil possessed her, ready to spit out nasty words followed by green fluids. She never stopped stepping.

I expect she would have trampled the officer, but Laughton interceded. "It's all right, Jackson. Let her go," he said.

Jackson sidestepped out of the woman's way before Laughton's words settled.

Laughton nodded his head in my direction. "Body's upstairs."

The house was spotless. White was *the* color: white furniture, white walls, white drapes, white wall-to-wall carpet, white picture frames. The only real color came in the mass of throw pillows that adorned the couch and a wash of plants positioned around the room.

I went upstairs and headed to the right of the landing, into a bedroom where an officer I knew, Mark Hutchinson, was photographing the scene. Body funk permeated the air. I wrinkled my nose.

"Hey, M&M," Hutchinson said.

"That's Muriel to you." I hated when my colleagues took the liberty to call me that. Sometimes I wanted to nail Laughton with a front kick to the groin for starting the nickname.

He shook his head. "Ain't me or the victim. She smells like a violet." He tilted his head back, sniffed, and smiled.

Hutchinson waved his hand in another direction. "I'm about done here."

I stopped at the threshold of the bathroom and perused the scene. Marcy Taylor lay on the bathroom floor. A small hole in her temple still oozed blood. Her right arm was extended over her head, and she had a .22 pistol in that hand. Her fingernails and toenails looked freshly painted. When I bent over her body, the sulfur-like smell of hair relaxer backed me up a bit. Her hair was bone-straight. The white silk gown she wore flowed around her body as though staged. Her cocoa brown complexion looked ashen with a pasty, white film.

"Shame," Laughton said to my back. "She was a beautiful woman." I jerked around to see him standing in the doorway.

"Check this out," I said, pointing to the lay of the night-gown over the floor.

"I already did the scene. We'll talk later," he said.

"Damn it, Laughton. Come here and check this out." But when I turned my head, he was gone.

I finished checking out the scene and went outside for some fresh air. Laughton was on the front lawn talking to an officer. He beelined for his car when he saw me.

"What the hell is wrong with you?" I muttered, jogging to catch up with him. Louder. "Laughton, what the hell—"

He dropped anchor. Caught off guard, I plowed into him. He waited until I peeled myself off him and regained my foot-ing, then said, "Nothing. Wade says they separated a few months ago and were trying to get it together, so he came over for some making up. He used his key to enter and found her dead on the bathroom floor."

"No, he said he was bringing the little girl home because she was homesick."

"Yeah, well, then you heard it all."

He about-faced.

I grabbed his arm and attempted to spin him around. "You act like you know this one or something," I practically screeched at him.

"I do."

I cringed and softened my tone five octaves at least when I managed to speak again. "How?"

"I was married to her . . . a long time ago."

He might as well have backhanded me upside the head. "You never—"

"I have an errand to run. I'll see you back at the lab."

I stared after him long after he got in his car and sped off.

The sun was rising by the time the scene was secured: body and evidence bagged, husband and daughter gone back home. It spewed warm tropical hues over the city. By the time I reached the station, the hues had turned cold metallic gray. I pulled into a parking spot and answered the persistent ring of my cell phone. It was Nareece.

"Hey, sis. My babies got you up this early?" I said, feigning a light mood. My babies were Nareece's eight-year-old twin daughters.

Nareece groaned. "No. Everyone's still sleeping."

"You should be, too."

"Couldn't sleep."

"Oh, so you figured you'd wake me up at this ungodly hour in the morning. Sure, why not? We're talkin' sisterly love here, right?" I said. We chuckled. "I've been up since three anyway, working a case." I waited for her to say something, but she stayed silent. "Reece?" More silence. "C'mon, Reecey, we've been through this so many times. Please don't tell me you're trippin' again."

"A bell goes off in my head every time this date rolls around. I believe I'll die with it going off," Nareece confessed.

"Therapy isn't helping?"

"You mean the shrink? She ain't worth the paper she prints her bills on. I get more from talking to you every day. It's all you, Muriel. What would I do without you?"

"I'd say we've helped each other through, Reecey."

Silence filled the space again. Meanwhile, Laughton pulled his Audi Quattro in next to my Bertha and got out. I knocked on the window to get his attention. He glanced in my direction and moved on with his gangster swagger as though he didn't see me.

"I have to go to work, Reece. I just pulled into the parking lot after being at a scene."

"Okay."

"Reece, you've got a great husband, two beautiful daughters, and a gorgeous home, baby. Concentrate on all that and quit lookin' behind you."

Nareece and John had ten years of marriage. John is Vietnamese. The twins were striking, inheritors of almond-shaped eyes, "good" curly black hair, and amber skin. Rose and Helen, named after our mother and grandmother. John balked at their names because they did not reflect his heritage. But he was mush where Nareece was concerned.

"You're right. I'm good except for two days out of the year, today and on Travis's birthday. And you're probably tired of hearing me."

"I'll listen as long as you need me to. It's you and me, Reecey. Always has been, always will be. I'll call you back later today. I promise."

I clicked off and stayed put for a few minutes, bogged down by the realization of Reece's growing obsession with my son, way more than in past years, which conjured up ugly scenes for me. I prayed for a quick passing, though a hint of guilt pierced my gut. Did I pray for her sake, my sake, or Travis's? What scared me anyway?

CHAPTER 2

Forty years earlier, I attended the Mary Channing Wister Elementary School on the southwest corner of Eighth and Poplar Street in North Philly, the same spot where I now worked. Thirteen million dollars in renovations to the 1923 art deco building in the dilapidated neighborhood began a rehab project that improved the looks of the neighborhood, but nary a whisper of calm. Lush landscaping and a newly paved parking lot replaced the jungle gym, and the hopscotch and Four Squares outlines. The entryway was more elaborate than the heavy, double wooden doors of my school days, which kids burst through every morning—the entire student body at the same time. Now three tiers of cement stairs led up to a glass entrance that opened automatically when you neared. Inside the building, which housed the Forensic Science Center, there was no evidence a school ever existed.

Instead, the scent of gunpowder and hot metal wafted from the basement, where the Firearms Identification Unit, aka the lab, lived. The space was configured in a maze of cubicles whose occupants labored over bullets and firearms atop crowded desks.

We were firearms specialists. Our primary job was to examine, read, and organize evidence, mostly guns and bullets, so we could testify in court. It required examining all ballistic evidence, fired cartridge cases, and fired bullets to determine the caliber. Gun manufacturers use different rifling techniques that impact the class characteristics of a bullet—i.e., the number, width and depth of the lands and grooves, and the pitch and twist of the gun barrel.

In English, rifling is the process of cutting spiral grooves inside a gun barrel that gives the bullet a spinning motion. The metal between the grooves is called a "land." No two gun barrels have the exact same markings. Through careful microscopic examination, we can determine which bullets come from which firearms. The process begins with examining the scene and gathering evidence.

Parker, who sat in the cubicle adjacent to mine, stood and peered over the partition. His rosy face had a pimply nose and narrow eyes so close together he looked cross-eyed. "Hope it was good for you, because you look like shit," he said.

He was ignorant, not worth the effort. "Well, hello to you, too," I answered. I dropped my purse and notebook on the desktop, sending a spray of bullet fragments onto the floor and me scrambling on my knees to recover them. "Damn."

Parker laughed. The thought of loading the Smith & Wesson .38 Special on my desk and blowing his head clean off lingered longer than it should have.

Then Laughton arrived. He ogled, "*Really?*" at my failed effort to get up. He coddled a .22 in one hand and a .38 in the other, raised his arms, shrugged his shoulders, then took his seat. Our work cubicles connected with open access to each other, allowing collaborative conversation.

"You're in court today," Laughton said.

A gurgled grunt escaped me as I struggled to get off my knees. I swear God weighted my shoulders to keep me there in remembrance of all the time that had passed since I'd knelt for the right purpose. "Yeah. What're you doing?"

"Basics," he said, turning away.

"I think Marcy Taylor was murdered," I said.

He lifted his right hand, still holding the .22. "Me too."

I could only guess how he had gotten hold of the evidence from the scene so fast. It was part of the Laughton mystique. Usually it took a few days, and protocol would have us wait until all the evidence was in before we began examinations. The man had influence inside, outside, upside, and downside the department, and everywhere and anywhere else we went. I walked with grace next to his Sidney Poitier–looking-self, all six-foot-four of him.

Having Laughton as a partner made surviving seventeen years in the weapons unit possible. He had embraced me when I first arrived at the unit. He took me to gun, ammunitions, and partner school, the latter of his own creation. The lust was immediate, the love gradual, and the law ever-present, which was why we quickly set aside our affair, but not nearly quickly enough. Love slammed me like a WWE wrestler does his opponent. But either we broke off the love affair or we each got new partners, Laughton insisted. I hated to admit he was right. Ahhh, but the man could make me scream! God only knows what the outcome would have been had the department gotten a whiff.

"You need to learn everything about guns," he had said. "These guys want you to fail. That's not happening."

Looking at him now, I tried to see past his nonchalant exterior to an emotional spark; he had just gazed upon his dead wife. Ex-wife. The thought of Laughton being married blew my mind. I wanted to ask him about it but knew this was neither the time nor the place.

I grabbed hold of the desk edge for leverage, trying again to rise.

"Get off your knees so we can catch some bad guys." He flashed a smile and winked. "Actually, you need to go home and get ready for your testimony. Jesse Boone and his crew will be in that courtroom ready to demolish you."

I managed a *"Mm"* and felt my face flush. Just the mention of his name, Jesse Boone, knocked me off-kilter and sent a wave through my body that unnerved me. Boone was the suspected serial killer I was testifying against. I knew Laughton was testing my stamina.

"No worries. I got this," I assured him, shaking off my nervousness and seizing determination.

My brain stayed on Laughton as I made a right turn out of the parking lot, down Eighth to Brown Street, and stopped at the Wawa for a soda. When I left the Wawa, I turned left, then right, onto I-676 toward Route 1.

Laughton had never mentioned his marriage. His other claim to fame, besides knowing about guns, was his bachelor status. I tell you, women chased the man down, and every day a different one. He also volunteered much of his time at the Philadelphia Boys and Girls Club; you would think it a contradiction to his character, but if you knew him, it fit.

I mistakenly thought Laughton and I shared everything. It never occurred to me I might be the "other woman." I made a mental note to find out when he was married to Marcy Taylor. In seventeen years of being partners, he had never invited me to his house. He always came to mine. I never thought about it, mostly because of Travis, who was little more than a year old when Laughton and I became partners. Since I was away from him too much for work, any free time I had, I wanted to spend at home.

I lived in a middle-class neighborhood in North Philly on a

block lined with urban twin town houses built in the 1950s. Twin town houses means two town houses were connected and set on each lot on the street. They had three levels: the basement with a half bathroom was accessed from a driveway and garage at the back of the house; the first floor held the kitchen, dining, and living room: and the third floor had three bedrooms and a full bathroom. When I first moved in my unit, the place had holes in the walls, the kitchen counter was falling down and the cabinets were trashed, the basement was unfinished, and I could go on. It was a fixer-upper, but all I could afford. Laughton's hobby, I guess you could call it, was being a handyman.

He spent time every day at my house fixing whatever needed fixing, until he and Travis melded like father and son. Hearing Travis's silly laugh while the two tussled on the floor only heightened my attraction and bonded us even more. It was difficult resisting the physical aspect. Nobody since Laughton had twisted my pubic hairs. Until Calvin.

I had my idiosyncrasies when it came to relationships. I managed to muck 'em up every which way possible. A shrink might have said I was determined to be the first to bow out, the first to avoid heartbreak—what my mother termed "stupid logic." Now the thought of growing old alone churned up a ripple in my aorta and made me quiver. Timing was everything.

The loud ring and vibration against my hip brought my attention back to the road. Scary thought that for a few minutes I had driven blindly, off somewhere else, unaware of where or how I was driving. I checked the screen on the phone before tapping the button on my earpiece, because I was not ready to talk to Nareece again so soon. In times past, talking to Nareece every day calmed my brain, changed the rhythm to a slower beat, allowed us both to exhale and kept me sane. A day never passed without us having a heart-to-heart conversation after dispensing with the mumbo jumbo about the latest twin escapade or John's myriad projects, which all started with intense vigor and ended before completion. There were no heart-to-heart conversations of late.

My brain relaxed when I saw Dulcey's name on the phone screen. Dulcey is my other sister, as in my best friend.

"Hey, girlfriend," I said.

"Where you been?" she asked. "Seems like you got yourself all tied up in that new man of yours. Nothing wrong with that, I'm just sayin'." Dulcey cackled like she always did when she tickled herself. We have been best friends for near twenty years, since my parents died.

After the car accident that killed them, Dulcey and her Jehovah's Witness self came knocking and refused a closed door, a given since Dulcey was an Amazon—six feet, one and a half inches, one hundred ninety-six pounds' worth, ex-army sharpshooter, with giant-sized hands that would make Shaq blush. I really did not want to hear her nonsense. But I was all tangled up inside then and needed to hear it, I guess. So I let her in and started bawling until my eyes were slits and my nose, the size of a golf ball. I remember telling her about my parents' deaths and how the responsibility of raising Nareece seemed way huge and how the pressures of being a rookie on the force had my fingernails falling off, literally. Dulcey's touch and words soothed me, though I don't exactly remember what she said.

From then on, she came once a week for Bible study and Lord talking. She helped me decide which activities were appropriate for a sixteen-year-old Nareece, and how to handle the resulting fallout, as I straddled the line between sister and parent.

A few times, I went to Jehovah's Witness meetings at Dulcey's place, wishing, hoping, and praying for answers. Then she asked me to join, become a Jehovah's Witness.

"I don't know enough about God and religion to decide what I want to do, Dulcey," I confessed. "I don't believe I want to be a Jehovah's Witness, though. No disrespect. I'm just not there."

Dulcey stopped coming to the house, stopped calling, and would not return my phone calls. Two months passed before she showed up with a bottle of wine, some cheese and crackers, and her Bible. She said since I'd refused the faith of the Jehovah's Witnesses, she'd had to stop associating with me because Jehovah's Witnesses disassociate with outside folks. She lost focus over losing my friendship, given what we had shared. She said she knew God meant her to be in my life and me in hers, and that was all there was to that.

"Don't mean I'm giving up God. I'm still gonna do the Lord's work, but I know He did not mean for me to hate on my friends," Dulcey said.

She went to hairdressing school and soon after, opened D's Beauty Spot, a full-service hair, nail, foot, and facial salon that was now being renovated.

I slammed on my brakes and almost rear-ended the car in front of me, which had stopped for a red light. "Shit."

"What's that you're talking?" Dulcey said.

"Girl, I almost crashed listening to your nonsense."

"I know them knots in your head gotta be squeezin' your brain 'til you're simple 'bout now," she said, ignoring my rant.

I ran, or rather I tried to run, my fingers through my hair. The new growth of kinky hair barred the effort and tenderized my head. I felt cursed, unable to handle what I had inherited from my mother, which was more hair than Methuselah grew in his 969 years on God's earth with the might to mutilate a steel-toothed comb.

"Yeah, you're right," I said, massaging my scalp. "These roots are definitely snapping my neck back. And oooh, girl, my head is sore as hell. A manicure and pedicure are overdue, too."

"How you gonna keep that fine man?" Dulcey asked. "Lookin' like somebody's old-ass reject! Here, you got that fried chicken–brown complexion, them crazy green eyes, and smack-your-mama body, and you walkin' around with gorilla hair. Girl, you best bring your butt in here."

"Can't today. Got court."

"C'mon in tomorrow and I'll tighten you up. More to the point, I can't have no friend of mine walking around lookin' like a ho-come-lately." She cackled extra hard, then told me about the shop renovations and her plan for attracting more customers of the brighter persuasion. "Won't be another shop in Philly can run up against Ms. Dulcey." She hesitated a moment, then spat, "Nareece called" like it was burning her tongue. "Reecey hasn't spoken but two words to me in just about all the years since your parents passed. As I recall those two words were 'Fuck you' with extra emphasis on 'you' the day she left outta your house when you all argued about some boy she was seeing. You remember . . ."

"Yes, I remember. What'd she want?"

"Asked whether I thought she was wrong for wanting to talk to Baby Boy and tell him the truth and ask for his forgiveness. Muriel, she sounds like she's in a hard way. Why all of a sudden she want to mess with things? You should have told Travis a long time ago. I understand why you didn't but . . . Anyway, he's old enough now, girl. That boy loves you so much it won't matter to him a bit."

I hesitated, not wanting to get into another "what I shoulda done" conversation right then. "I always planned on telling him before he left for college. I want to be the one, though. Not Nareece."

"Close as you two are, you all need to talk and iron out the wrinkles before you involve him. He'll be fine with it and still love you both, you as his mother *and* Nareece. It wasn't her fault. Look, I gotta go. These guys are trying to install mirrors over the washing sinks instead of where they belong."

Saved by the mirror installers. "Yes. And I have to get ready for court."

"Hold on. Court? You're testifying today against that bastard killed that college student? The one almost killed you?"

"Yes."

"You okay with it? I mean, ain't easy going up against a demented individual the likes of Jesse Boone, up close and personal as you got to him."

"Whatever it takes to put him away, I'm good with."

"I got a feeling there's a whole lot more we're going to learn about Mr. Boone before his days in court are done. He's the kind of bastard that belongs in an insane asylum, lock him in a room and throw away the key. If I believed in it, I'd say kill him. Strap him in the chair and inject his behind. But that's God's place, not ours, I don't care if we do have the death penalty."

"Calm down, girl. They may not lock him up in an insane asylum, but you can bet he's going away for the rest of his life one way or another. No key necessary."

"Amen to that. Come by tomorrow, we'll talk more and I'll fix you up. Love you."

I clicked off as I turned to the right, down to my driveway. It ran between the three-story brick houses on my street, Longshore, and the houses one block over on Disston Street. Each home had a fenced-in driveway and garage. My kitchen window looked out on the driveway from the second level. I got out of the car and opened the gate to the driveway, then looked up, halfway expecting Travis to be at the window. He was supposed to be home that morning and I had not heard from him. I couldn't worry about that now, though. I had court to get ready for.

CHAPTER 3

I diverted my gaze from Jesse Boone and looked out over the courtroom from the witness stand. And yet I felt forced to look back at Boone, like he was magnetized. Did he just wink at me? The smirk he sported sizzled when our eyes locked, sending centipedes scurrying along my arms to my shoulders. He exuded charisma with a smidgeon of evil. The blue-gray Armani suit he wore hugged his biceps, which accented his chiseled physique. His eyes were black and sparkly, his nose small and pointy, his perfect hair blown out and back—a beastly variation on handsome.

My body twitched.

A heat boiled up inside me and lodged just beneath my skin. Not now, I prayed. Sweat trickled down from my left armpit, almost tickling. Of course. If I was holding a gun on a suspect who had a hostage in his grip and both our lives depended on me making the shot, *bam!* A damn hot flash would ravage my whole body.

I backhand swiped at my brow and forced my attention to the district attorney.

"Your Honor, I would like to offer Officer Muriel Mabley as an expert witness in the area of firearm identification."

"What qualifies this officer to be accepted as an expert witness in my court?" the judge said.

"Officer, please give your duties, responsibilities, and qualifications."

Boone's attorney sprang from his seat. "I will stipulate to the qualifications of this witness."

"Mr. Jameson, please take your seat. This is for my enlightenment also. I want to hear what Officer Mabley knows. She is new to my courtroom."

The DA nodded to me to speak.

"My duties are to accept all firearms and firearm-related material, such as fired bullets, cartridge cases that have been turned in or collected or confiscated within the city of Philadelphia. All evidence is examined and compared against all like evidence. I am trained in the microscopic comparison, photomicrography, which is photographing through the microscope, serial number restoration, tool mark comparison, distance determination through gunshot residue, wound ballistics, and crime scene reconstruction. I am also an armorer for Berretta, Smith & Wesson, SIG Sauer, Hi Point, Ruger, Colt, and have observed the manufacturing of these firearms from the beginning as raw steel to the finished product you see and identify as a firearm.

"I am an instructor at Widner School of Law, Philadelphia College of Osteopathic Medicine, and the Philadelphia Police Academy. I also instruct all the new DAs at the Philadelphia District Attorney's office."

The DA turned to the defense table and asked, "Are there any objections to this witness's qualifications as an expert witness?"

"No, Your Honor," Boone's attorney drawled as though bored with the specifics.

The district attorney walked across the floor and picked up the gun that killed Ms. Hodges. The gun had a plastic tie through the barrel and was locked in an open position. "Officer Mabley, can you tell me about this firearm, which was found at the scene of the defendant's place of residence?"

I took the gun from the DA and read the numbers from the property receipt. "Yes, this pistol was placed on property receipt #92714529338 and submitted to the Forensic Science Center through the normal procedures."

"What can you tell us about this firearm?"

"This is a semiautomatic pistol, manufactured by Sturm Ruger and Co. model P-ninety-five. It is nine-millimeter Luger in caliber, with six lands and grooves with a right-hand twist. The finish is stainless steel, three-and-seven-eighths-inch barrel, with rubber grips." I stopped and flipped the gun around so the serial number on the butt was visible. "Serial number 315-73198. The firearm was presented with gunshot residue in the barrel and found to be in operable condition. Also submitted were fourteen Remington cartridges, nine-millimeter Luger in caliber. However, this firearm has a magazine capacity of sixteen and one in the chamber."

"Was there any other evidence submitted that was found to be related to this firearm?"

The DA handed me an evidence envelope. I opened it and read numbers from the receipt that was inside along with the evidence.

"Submitted on Property Receipt #943673284309, received from the Medical Examiner's officer were two fired bullets."

"What, if anything, can you tell us about the relationship between this firearm and the fired bullets?"

"The bullets that were submitted were found to be nine-millimeter Luger in caliber with six lands and grooves and a right-hand twist."

"Is there anything else you can tell us?"

"Yes, the firearm was test fired into the water tank and those bullets were compared against the bullets submitted from the ME's office."

"What can you tell us about that comparison?"

"When these two specimens were compared against one another, it was determined that they were both fired from the same firearm."

"So, Officer Mabley, you are saying that the bullets that were taken from the victim were fired from the same firearm that was taken from the defendant's residence?"

"Yes."

"How can you be so sure?"

"During the manufacturing process, tools are used to put in the lands and grooves. Incidental to this process, microscopic markings are left in the barrel, which gives each barrel its own identifiable markings that are unique to that gun and that gun alone."

"You mean to say to the exclusion of all other nine-millimeter pistols out there, these marks are unique to this gun and this gun only."

"Yes. The bullet that killed Ms. Hodges was fired from the gun in evidence."

"Officer, where was this gun you're speaking about found?"

"It was found at the defendant's home, in the master bedroom, on the nightstand."

"Please tell the jury what led up to the gun being confiscated from the defendant's residence. What happened the night you found Ms. Hodges's body and the gun?"

"I received a call from who I thought was Officer Parker saying there had been a shooting at the defendant's address."

"What time did you get that call?"

"It was one twenty a.m."

"Go on."

"When I arrived at the address, the suspect came to the door covered in blood and pointing a gun at me. I had my gun pointed at him and told him to drop his weapon. Instead he rushed me, causing my gun to discharge. He hit me in the head with his gun, and I passed out. When I regained conscious-ness, I was on the bed with my hands tied to the bedposts. He was not in the room so I started trying to loosen the ties. When he came back, he climbed on the bed and unzipped his pants and said he intended to mess me up like the victim. I freed a hand and punched him. Luckily, I caught him off guard. He fell off the bed, hit his head on the nightstand, and knocked himself out. I finished freeing my hands, handcuffed him to some wall pipes, and called for backup."

"Did he rape you?"

"No." The answer echoed in my ears.

"Tell the jury when and where you found Ms. Hodges."

"I looked around the house while I waited for backup. There was blood on the floor near the basement door off the kitchen. When I went into the basement, I found Candace Hodges's body on the floor."

Gasps erupted from the audience into a continuous mur-mur. Again the judge slammed the gavel, this time threatening to clear the room if the audience did not remain quiet.

"Go on."

"I checked her breathing . . ." I stumbled on my words for a moment. Images of Candace Hodges's broken body flashed through my brain, before I forced myself back, readjusted, and continued. "She was cut up pretty badly. Her face was black and blue. She was naked. Her breasts were severed, and cuts went from her navel to her vaginal area." I swallowed, trying to moisten my throat and mouth. "She'd also been shot in the head. Defensive wounds on her wrists and hands indicated she fought back hard."

"Officer Mabley, do you usually go out to shootings without your partner?"

"No."

"Where was your partner the night in question?"

"My partner, Officer Laughton, was in Washington, D.C., on assignment."

"Do you know who it was that called you to the defendant's address?"

"No. Like I said, I thought it was Officer Parker."

"Was it?"

"No."

"Could it have been the defendant?"

"I don't know."

"Do you have any history with the defendant, Ms. Mabley?"

"No." The answer flew from my lips. Maybe too fast. I had worked undercover in the Black Mafia when I first started on the force. Now I wondered why I had not met Jesse Boone then.

Jesse Boone shifted in his seat, his eyes, bits of black onyx, drilled down on me.

"Thank you, Officer. I turn the witness over to the defense."

Boone's attorney swaggered up to the witness box and stopped in front of me. My hands sweated. I wiped them on my skirt. I noticed Laughton sitting behind and to the left of the attorney table where Boone sat. A slight nod, and the upturn of the left side of his mouth, allowed me a resurgence of confidence. I readjusted.

"Officer Mabley, isn't it true there are no universally accepted 'quality assurance' standards for firearms examination? That there are no objective criteria to govern what points of similarity or difference may be disregarded when evaluating whether a bullet or cartridge case came from a particular weapon? That my client is being held to your subjective judgment in making a match between the bullets that killed the victim and the gun found in my client's home?"

"Objection, Your Honor—" the DA asserted. A loud murmur from the audience challenged the judge's gavel.

Now my hands shook, though no one could see them. The witness box provided a veil of protection. I hated that Jesse Boone had me shaking as though I were a victim instead of testifying in the case. Everyone's eyes bore a hole in my temple—especially the students from Chestnut Hill University and their parents. They all wanted Boone, who had raped, mutilated, and shot a student, Candace Hodges, to be put away forever or better yet, dead by lethal injection.

He had come by his lethal persona legitimately. His father was Richard "The Pistol" Boone, a primary player in the Philadelphia Black Mafia, an organization that emerged in the 1960s and ruled over the city's underworld through the 1990s and into the early 2000s. Black Mafia members were vicious, both in their methods of controlling people and in their illegal activities of drug trafficking, loan sharking, numbers rackets, and extortion. I knew this from experience. I spent my first few years in the department undercover in their organization.

Boone spent fifteen years in prison for murdering his father. He beat and strangled him to death, stabbed him thirty-five times all over his body after he was dead, and shot him ten times, five in the head and five in his privates. Definitely a crime of passion and hate.

Since his release from prison in 2008, Boone had been the primary suspect in four murder cases. Candace Hodges, murdered six months ago to the day, January 29, 2013, made five. His last known victim, before Candace Hodges, was a thirty-year-old mother of three. She was found stuffed in a locker in an abandoned building in the Broad and Dauphin Street neighborhood, known as one of the twenty-five most dangerous neighborhoods in America. Her breasts were severed, her arms and legs were cut off, and she had gunshot wounds to her forehead, chest, and genital area.

Boone had escaped prosecution in the four previous cases

because of weak evidence or evidence that mysteriously disappeared, and witnesses who refused to appear in court fearing for their safety.

"I have no more questions at this time for this witness," Boone's attorney said.

The district attorney rose as Boone's attorney returned to his seat next to Boone. "Redirect, Your Honor," he said. "Officer Mabley, please tell the court how the Firearms Identification Unit is validated. That is, whether the practices used are accepted in the relevant scientific community, and please explain what that means."

"Yes, our practices are accredited. We use the National Integrated Ballistic Identification Network's computerized system, which assists in matching firearms-related evidence to other evidence entered into the system around the world. We also use ballistic comparison microscopes to conduct all levels of microscopic comparisons. Our practices are accredited by the American Society of Crime Laboratory Directors."

Laughton loitered outside the courtroom waiting for me. The elevator ride to the parking garage, the clicking of our shoes on the pavement, and the hollow sound of my car door opening soothed my nerves, though I sensed uneasiness between Laughton and me, something foreign to our relationship. I got in and started the engine.

"Thanks for showing up," I said. "I've testified in hundreds of cases before with no problem, but this guy, Boone, he freaks me out."

"What are partners for?" he shot back, automatically. Then he got heated. "No way is the son of a bitch getting off this time. He's outta here for good if I have any say."

"Well, you don't have any say. But thanks for helping me say my part."

"I wouldn't be so sure."

"Wouldn't be so sure about what?"

"You have a lot more testifying to do before this thing is over. Stay focused."

"Laughton, I've been testifying for fifteen years. I can handle whatever they throw at me. I'll say it again, I got this."

"Yeah, but by your own admission, you've never been up against a Jesse Boone."

He closed the door and thumped the car roof, a signal to take off. As I backed out and then straightened the wheel, I checked the rearview mirror and watched Laughton walk back to the doorway that led to the elevator. As I began to turn the corner to enter the down ramp, I looked in the rearview again and saw a man move out of the shadows and approach Laughton. Laughton looked in my direction, grabbed the guy's arm, and pushed him against the wall. I stopped in the entrance of the down ramp, got out, and ran back the few hundred yards to them.

"Laughton!" I yelled. He had the guy pinned up against a column and was punching him in the face full-force. I caught his arm on about the third or fourth punch, which lessened the blow, but didn't stop it.

"M, get outta here." Spit flew from his mouth as he talked. His face contorted, almost frightening me.

"What the hell's wrong with you? You can't beat this guy. And for what?"

"Get the fuck outta here. You don't know—"

"So, tell me." He yanked his arm from my grip and backed off.

I recognized the man as Wade Taylor, Laughton's dead ex-wife's husband.

"Are you all right?" I asked Taylor. I kept an eye toward

Laughton, expecting him to charge in again. Taylor nodded and wiped the spit and blood from his mouth with the back of his shirtsleeve. I leaned in some as he stumbled forward. Taylor looked to Laughton like he needed his permission to leave. Laughton breathed like a bull and paced back and forth. Five, six steps, turn.

A car approached and stopped behind mine, which blocked the way down the ramp. The driver leaned on his horn.

"Go ahead," Laughton told me.

I stayed put.

"I'm good now." He waved me on. "Go."

I hustled to my car, looking over my shoulder every few steps to make sure Laughton kept his fists from Wade's face. I got in and continued down the garage ramp, furious at Laughton. "Unbelievable. He just blew whatever case we might have built against Taylor if Taylor killed his wife."

That he might have beaten Wade to death the way he was going was unbelievable, as well. Laughton never lost control. His smooth operator demeanor confounded the brass and pissed off the rednecked Mother Hubbards who were unappreciative of minority representation in the firearms division to begin with.

As I exited the garage, my cell phone rang. Nareece. I had blown her off since the morning and still did not want to talk. She and I rode a collision course around Travis, the end undoubtedly being a major crash. My gut told me there was more to Nareece's sudden desire to confess all to Travis than she had shared.

"You didn't call back," she whined.

"I've been in court all day." I heard her husband, John, in the background reprimanding the twins for something. "The Twofer Detective Agency must be on another one of their crime-solving capers," I said, laughing lightly, not sure how Nareece would take it.

"They've taken over my third floor," she said. "You shouldn't be the least bit flattered that they want to be like you." Her voice intensified. "You should be horrified and steering them in another direction. It's always murder and mayhem and bad guys and never pink and dolls and dressing up."

"Crap," I mumbled. I had missed the turn onto I-95. I drove down a block and made a U-turn to get on the highway.

"I'm sorry if I messed up your day."

"I wasn't talking to you. I missed my turn. I'm glad you called," I lied.

"Muriel. I went out today and did some errands. When I got home I felt something, like someone had been in the house."

"You're always paranoid around this time of year. You just told me that this morning." I waited a moment, then thought better of negating her feelings altogether. "Did you lock the door when you left?"

"I always do," she whispered, her voice strained. "I called John. I thought maybe he came home for lunch, but he didn't. Then I found an envelope on the table by the telephone, you know, the table in the foyer. It's addressed to Carmella Ann Mabley."

I pulled onto the breakdown lane and stopped.

"Muriel? Are you there?"

"Yeah, I'm here. Did you open it?"

"No. I can't. I don't want to know . . ."

"Open it, Reece. Whatever it is, it can't hurt you. What's done is done. There's nothing else anyone can take from you."

"If they know about my life now, there's plenty they can take."

"Then all the more reason you need to open the envelope so we know what we're dealing with."

"You come. We'll open the envelope together," she whimpered like a little girl. "I can't, I don't want to open it by myself."

"Okay, I'll be there. Calm down. You don't want to upset the girls and John." I heard her blow her nose. The splashy, wet sound grossed me out. "I'll come this weekend," I said. My muscles tensed, bringing on the sweats again. I rolled the windows down and took a few deep breaths. I felt myself getting worked up with resentment. "Look. Sit tight and we'll talk more later."

I clicked off and pulled into oncoming traffic, causing a flurry of beeping horns, and sped toward the Harbison Avenue exit. I pulled up to the KFC/Taco Bell drive-up window across from the Fifteenth and Second district station and asked for a cup of ice, dumped a few cubes down the front of my blouse, and rubbed one against my cheeks. The woman at the window reacted as though I had three heads and six tits. Her destiny revealed and she did not have a clue.

I considered calling Dulcey, then brushed it away. Better to learn the contents of the envelope before getting girlfriend shook up over what might be nothing. That name, Carmella Ann Mabley, had not visited either of our lips for twenty years. Nareece often blew things out of proportion, and most of the time was incapable of rational thought. It seemed a trip to Boston was the only way to sort this out, whatever this was.

I arrived home to find every light in the house on. I drove up to the gate and saw Travis in the kitchen window chugging down a glass of something. He waved and disappeared from view. By the time I pulled the car in and was at the door fumbling for my keys, Travis whipped the door open.

"Hey, Moms. What's good?" he said and was on me doling out hugs like a mama bear. All squished up, lifted up, and unable to hug back without access to my arms, I reveled in the love. He put me down and backed into the doorway.

He bowed and gestured for me to enter—the queen, come home to her palace. The door from the driveway led down a hallway to a finished room, off of which was a stairway leading up to the kitchen. Travis slammed the door and rushed ahead of me down the hall and up the stairs. He paused at the top of the stairs. He flashed me a wide grin, pecked my cheek, and stepped aside from the doorway, allowing me entry to the kitchen. In simultaneous motion, he slid two fingers under the straps of my briefcase and purse straps and lifted them from my shoulder, then pulled a counter stool out for me.

The kitchen space is long and narrow so the wall that separated the kitchen from the dining room was cut down to counter level and ran three-quarters of the kitchen length to the entryway. It was a Laughton project.

I settled in the stool and marveled at the sight of my son as he took a wineglass from the cabinet and set it before me, then held a bottle of Massaya's Classic White, draped over his forearm for my approval, like a sommelier. He proceeded to uncork the goods.

Two years old had become ten years, now nineteen years old, and still I could not remember its passing, as much as it seemed a blur anyway. He pulled out the stool next to me and sat down. Then he filled my glass one-quarter full with wine.

"How's school going? 'Bout time for midterm grades, right?" I took a sip of wine.

"I don't get midterm grades. I mean, unless I'm doing bad. You haven't gotten any notices, I'm taking care of business. Only students who are failing get midterm grades, notices, whatever."

"Well, I haven't gotten any notices."

"Exactly."

"You know what happens if you don't take care of business."

"No. What?"

"Don't mess with me, boy."

He hesitated, then asked, "Laughton working on any new projects up in here?"

"I told you not to mess with me, boy," I said, punching him in his shoulder.

"I got your boy, alright."

"Sorry. Don't mess with me, man." I waited for whatever was coming, but not for long.

"Some of the guys are cruisin' up to New York this weekend. We're going to stay at Sam's aunt's place in Queens. Sam's moms is driving us. You know Sam's moms. She's a sociology professor at Chestnut Hill College. We're gonna catch Patrice in *Rent*, an off-off-Broadway number."

"Who's Patrice?"

"Sam's sister. Girl is a sexy . . ." The sudden remembrance that he was talking to his mother, not one of his boys, brightened his face. I gave him my sideways look, the one I inherited from Mom that had immobilized me whenever I had carried a moment too far.

"I'm saying she's dope. You know she went to New York after high school. Her moms was pissed that she skipped college. Moms is cool with it now, though, cuz girlfriend is doing it."

"Shareen."

"What?"

"Sam's mother's name. Nice lady." I took a sip and savored the crisp semisweet flavor of melons, citrus, and dried herbs that made Massaya's Classic White one of my favorites. For a moment, I closed my eyes and went away.

"She says the same about you, then goes into how you helped her father beat some kinda altercation with the po po. Heard it a hundred times at least, but she never gives us the scoop, just that you helped her out, end of story." Travis pulled a box of Carr's water crackers from the cupboard and Brie from the fridge.

I smiled. "Some things are better left where they lie."

"You aren't going to fill me in? That's cold, Ma." He stood beside me at the counter and methodically placed water crackers in a circle on a saucer and slices of cheese in the center, then set the saucer in front of me. I scooped up a cracker as he slid into the stool across the counter from me.

"Police business, end of story."

I remembered Shareen's father had been stopped while driving erratically down I-95. Police found an unregistered .38 pistol under the car seat. I called in a few favors, kept him out of jail.

"Good explanation at ten. I'm a man now." He punched his chest once with both fists, King Kong–like, groaned, and fell forward ending with his head on the counter.

I patted his tousled hair. "A haircut and a shave would do you good."

"Yeah," he said, sitting up, "So can I go?"

He badgered me until I agreed, then left to hang out with his friends.

My muscles resisted the hot water. I got out of the shower as strained as I entered, my fingertips wrinkled and mushy. I wiped the mirror and studied my reflection. "He'll be fine. 'Bout time you gave the boy some room to move," I said out loud. Poor Travis had endured my overprotective antics all of his life without protest, mostly. He was nineteen and a freshman in college and I still treated him like he was fourteen.

Nareece needed overprotective; Travis, not so much. A hint of anxiety fluttered through my chest at the thought of her and the letter. I forced it back. There was not a thing I could do about it until the weekend. I shuddered at the thought of having to drive to Massachusetts for what was probably nothing. Nareece lives in Milton to be exact, a pretty wealthy suburb of Boston. It would be good to see the twins and John. It would be good to see Nareece, too. I sighed at the image in the mirror. It had been a year since I visited.

The ring of the phone gave me escape from my guilt. I rushed to the bedside and checked the caller ID, then flopped down on the bed.

"Hey, sugar. I'm betting you just got out of the shower. Wish I was there."

"Calvin, stop with your foolishness." Stupid. I sat up and wrapped myself with the towel.

"I do believe we have some unfinished business."

"Mmmm."

"Dinner tonight?"

"I'm there."

I sat on the edge of the bed, smoothing lotion over my body, the phone lodged in the crook of my neck and ear. A loud *bang* shook the house. I dropped the phone, grabbed my gun from the top drawer of my nightstand, and hit the stairs, calling out to Travis on my way down. No answer. The front door was wide open. A car sped down the otherwise empty street. I slammed the door shut and turned the dead bolt. I continued to make my way through the living room, through the dining room, gun extended straight out, holding on with both hands except when flicking lights on as I went, moving from side to side. To the kitchen. Clear. Down the basement stairs, around each corner, in the closet, in the bathroom. Clear.

The sound of the front doorbell seized my heart.

CHAPTER 4

"Muriel, are you here? Miss Mabley?" Mr. Kim, my neighbor, pushed the door open wider than I offered. "Miss Mabley, are you in need of assistance?"

I pulled the towel tighter around me. "I'm fine, Mr. Kim."

"I was just coming home from my evening walk and noticed a young man running from your house. He jumped into a blue Camry with a woman driving. It had New Jersey plates, though I could not see the number except the first two letters, *JH*."

Mr. Kim manned the neighborhood watch. A martial arts wonder, he was fit for the position, all five feet two inches of him. Tinker Bell meets Hurricane Katrina.

I released my hold on the door and allowed him into the foyer. "Thanks, Mr. Kim."

"Your teaching skills are impeccable, Miss Mabley."

"And yours as well, Mr. Kim."

I had studied tae kwon do with Mr. Kim going on twelve years, since I moved in, though my attendance had fallen off lately. To tell the truth, the amount of time I had spent over the years maybe added up to four years of training, maybe four and a half.

"The man who fled from here was African American, very tall." He raised his arm and stood on his tiptoes, reminding me of a little boy trying to reach the forbidden cookie jar. "He resembled Mr. Laughton, but with long hair, dreads I believe you call them." He made his fingers dance on his hair.

I was somewhat relieved, as Mr. Kim's description fit Travis's friend, Fortune, to a tee. "You saw all that in a matter of seconds."

"Miss Mabley, I am a keen observer. It is an invaluable skill in the world of martial arts. Have I not expressed that to you many times?"

"Indeed, you have." We laughed lightly.

"Where were you at when he got in the vehicle?"

"Behind the preposition, Miss Mabley." He hesitated to allow me time to absorb his correction. Mr. Kim also teaches English at Northeast High School, one of the city's oldest high schools. "About a hundred feet in that direction," he said, turning and pointing right. "Well, as long as my services are not needed, I will leave you now," he said, bowing his way out of the foyer, I suspected embarrassed by my dress. "You have a wonderful evening."

"Thanks for looking out, Mr. Kim. You have a good evening, too." I watched him tiptoe down the flower-lined walkway. Flowers he had planted. As he picked his way down the steps and turned left to his house, I realized that in the twelve years of being neighbors that was the most conversation we had ever had. I did not even know where Mr. Kim was from or whether he was born in the United States, never mind how he became a martial arts expert or knew so much about plants, or came to teach English. I had a key to his house so I could use the dojo anytime I wanted. Yet I hardly knew the man. I promised myself I would visit Kim in the very near future and have a real conversation.

I closed the door and started upstairs to call Calvin, when the doorbell rang and there was a flurry of banging.

"Muriel, it's Calvin!"

I rushed down to rescue my door. He burst in.

"What happened?" he asked. "You left me hanging on the phone. First a loud noise, then the phone went dead."

"I'm fine, Calvin, I'm fine. The door flew open is all. Travis must have left it open when he went out. Scared the hell outta me, though." The explanation sounded plausible, but my tongue felt pasty saying it. I liked Calvin, a lot, but he had not reached the share-all level yet. It occurred to me how quickly he had arrived at my home.

Calvin closed the door and moved closer.

"I was on my way up to call you." I gestured upward and realized I had my gun in hand. No wonder Kim had hurried away. I set the gun on the end table. In a single motion, Calvin kissed me, scooped me up, and carried me upstairs like Richard Gere scooped up Debra Winger at the end of *An Officer and a Gentleman*. Top of the stairs, straight ahead. I shook my head and groaned when my cell phone rang. Calvin held me captive for a few rings, then succumbed to my downturned lips and sent me hustling.

"Did I get you at a bad time, my dear?" Laughton.

"Are you spying on me?"

"We got another dead body."

"Please tell me this isn't happening. Not now."

"Now, partner. Wade Taylor, shot in the back of the head at his pad. Looks like a professional hit."

"So why do we need to be at the scene?"

"So far I see three holes in the wall in the bedroom and hall that appear to be bullet holes and two fired cartridge cases across the room."

"Give me a half hour. I'll be there."

Marcy Taylor dead in the a.m. and Wade Taylor in the p.m. produced the makings of a bad movie, I thought. Laughton's voice had no play in it this time. Postponing my trip to Nareece's house in Boston for the weekend seemed a must-do, considering Laughton's closeness to the case. I also figured Marcy and Wade's deaths had just jumped to the front of our caseload.

This time, when I arrived at the scene, there were no reporters, no police lights, no commotion except what was going on inside the house. Chestnut Hill was a wealthy neighborhood in Northwest Philly. Folks here would not stand for the smear. The location on Germantown Avenue in Northwest Philly was a beautiful, old, three-story brick house, built around the early 1900s and worth half a million dollars, I guessed. Chestnut Hill was one of Philly's oldest settlements with many historic homes. I would say it was about the only wealthy neighborhood left inside the city besides its abutters, Mount Airy and Manayunk. I wondered what Wade Taylor did for a living.

When I went inside, I was directed to the basement. It was like descending into a dungeon; dirt floor, protruding stone walls, and a low ceiling, low enough for me to check the danger to my head at the bottom of the stairs. A section of the floor was dug up. Dirt, rocks, and rumble were piled beside a human-sized hole. Wade Taylor was sideways on the floor in the center of the room, with his hands tied behind his back and his feet tied to a chair, which had fallen with him. A rag protruded from his mouth. And, just as Laughton reported, he had one shot to the back of his head.

"Close up and personal," Medical Examiner Robert Hayes said, as he rose from inspecting the body and snapped off his latex gloves. Officers moved in to remove the body. "You're all set, Ms. M. Your partner did the preliminaries." Hayes was creepy in a bone-chilling sense, with his sculpted widow's peak and long, pointy nose, looking like Vincent Price complete with the deep, crackly voice. He continued, "Said he'd meet you at the lab." He waved his long, skeletal finger, pointing toward the stairway.

"Where's the daughter? He has a daughter."

"I don't know anything about a daughter."

No doubt. I could not imagine Hayes a daddy.

"No one was here when we arrived, except, of course, the deceased." His weak try at humor. His smile revealed scraggly, discolored teeth, completing his "Doctor Death" image.

Laughton's phone went straight to voice mail and his car was not in the parking lot when I arrived at the station. The lab was dark except for Parker's cubicle. He hunched over his desk disassembling a Beretta. I braced for an inappropriate remark as I passed and got a "Hey, M" instead.

"Hi, Parker. Laughton been here?"

"Nope. Nobody here but us." He raised the Beretta. "Heard about Taylor getting popped. I'm bettin' he did the missus."

I dropped my purse on my desk, moved over to Laughton's desk, and clicked on his lamp. At first I just looked, trying to discover something among the debris of guns, bullets, and folders.

I never doubted Laughton. Hell, like I said, we were lovers . . . once upon a time. We were friends, but most of all, we were partners. In life and near-death experiences, we protected each other's backs. We handled crime scenes together, tag-teamed possible scenarios, and worked the evidence.

I flashbacked on the garage scene . . .

Laughton had asked Taylor what was wrong with him, and Taylor had said something I could not decipher before Laughton punched him. I pulled open the top drawer of his desk, then the side drawers. The bottom side drawer would not open.

"Looking for something, are we?" Laughton spun his chair around with me in it, nudged me out, and sat down. I felt caught, hand stuck in the proverbial cookie jar.

"Where've you been?" I said, innocence oozing.

"Chasing down Wade's daughter. She's been with his parents since Marcy's murder."

"We know she was murdered? Wait a minute, what the hell are you doing? We don't chase down murder victims' children. We do weapons, remember?"

"Looks like she was murdered, but we still have work to do before that conclusion is proven," he said, ignoring my comments.

"And Wade Taylor?"

"Somebody executed him."

"Laughton, what's going on with you? You okay? You're running with this solo, like I'm not a part of this team. You call me to the crime scenes late—"

Laughton popped up from his chair, grabbed my arm, and guided me to the back, where the microscope lab was located, empty at this time of night. He opened the door and nudged me inside the room in front of him, then closed and locked the door. He ran his hands over his head, walked to the rear of the lab and back, stopping in front of me, nose close.

"M, do me this favor—back off. This one's personal. I'll keep you informed, make it like we're working together."

I took a half step back. "Laughton, what are you doing?

We're partners. That's what we do, work together. I need to do my job."

"Go home, M. Be with your new boyfriend. What's his name, Calvin? Make it work for a change. Take a trip for the weekend. Go."

I shot back, "You're too close to this one, Laughton."

He turned away, then came back and got up close. "I don't need you on this one. I don't *want* you on this one." He stepped away and turned his back to me, then turned back and got up close again. "I want to . . . Just trust me on this one."

The hotbed inside me exploded. Sweat dripped off my nose. I opened my mouth to speak as the door closed. A few seconds of stunned disbelief squeezed me before I regained my senses and followed him out. By then I saw him race up the stairs two at a time and then he was gone. Parker was gone, too. There were three other members of the division. All gone. I checked my watch. No wonder, since it was 8 p.m.

My cell phone buzzed. "Muriel Mabley."

"Muriel. John."

"John?" In ten years of marriage to Nareece, John had never called me before.

"Nareece is gone."

I returned to my cubicle, as John went on, agitated.

"She supposedly went out to do errands earlier, much earlier today, and she hasn't returned home yet. I've tried her cell, but she's not answering. The girls keep asking, 'Where's Mommy?' and I don't know what to say anymore. I'm about to call the police."

"John, calm down. I'm sure she's fine. Hold off on the police. Let me make some calls, and I'll get back to you. Stay at the house in case she comes back." This was not Reece's first disappearance episode.

"Muriel, she's getting worse. I keep telling her she needs to see a therapist. All right, another therapist, cuz truly the one she's jawing to isn't doing a damn thing to help her. She won't talk to me. I don't even know what's wrong with her, why she acts the way she does."

"I'm coming this weekend. We'll talk about getting her more help when I'm there. Let's just find her first. I'll get back to you."

After I hung up from John, I moved to Laughton's desk. My locked-drawer curiosity ratcheted up to near-execution before I abandoned the idea and punched Reece's number into my cell phone. It took five rings before she answered.

"Reece, you alright? John is worried sick."

"I want to open it, M. I want to but I can't."

"Where are you?" Silence. "Reece, answer me." More silence.

"Remember when you said everything would go away? That one day it'd be so far away that it would seem like a dream? I was almost there."

"You *are* almost there, Reecey."

"It was almost just a bad dream."

"Nothing can bring that night back. It's so far behind us, baby girl."

"If they'd only been caught, put in jail. But they're still out there."

Silence.

"Look, I'm coming in two days. I'll be there on Saturday. I promise. We'll open the letter together and you'll see that there's nothing to worry about. Please just go home. I'll call John, tell him you're safe and on your way."

I could hear her sniffling and sucking back tears.

"Travis. Are you bringing Travis with you?" Her tone switched up as though nothing was wrong, as if there was no envelope or note and everything was right with the world.

I struggled to contain my irritation. "No, he's only home for spring break, and you know college kids. He's going to New York for the weekend. Now, go home. Please."

Travis had not visited Boston since he was ten. I always feigned a sleepover or sporting event, some reason for his absence. Nareece had made him hate going there. She had acted like he was the devil child from *The Omen* the few times we visited together. I shielded him when he was a baby. As a rambling and roving two-year-old, everything he touched, every word out of his mouth, he heard, "Bad, bad, boy," which often resulted in arguing the likes of which totally exposed our communication incompetence. Travis always came away asking why Auntie Reece did not like him. All I could say was that Auntie Reece loved him and her issues had nothing to do with him. After the twins' birth, she changed, though. She started asking about Travis. She drilled for things, like how he was doing in school, what sports he played and whether he was the star player, whether he liked vegetables, whether he was smart, and then when was he coming to visit, spend a week with her, and meet his cousins? Travis and the twins, Rose and Helen, were acquainted by phone only.

"Does he like the college he's going to? What is it, Lincoln University?"

"Yeah, he likes it. Look Reecey, I'm at work, I gotta go. Please just go home. I'll call you later to check on you."

She rambled on about how fast time passed before finally acknowledging that she would go home and then clicked off. I called John to relay that Nareece was fine and on her way home. Then I tried Laughton's cell. His final words were unacceptable. When his phone went to voice mail, I hesitated, then left a message that we needed to talk before I went to Boston for the weekend. I didn't like the idea of letting him investigate his ex-wife's death on his own, and I had no intention of doing so. I figured he would be more apt to return my call if I seemingly agreed to his request to back off for a bit. I definitely had to go to Boston anyway, and I expected Laughton could handle that much time without me.

The black glint behind his eyes when he told me he didn't need me made me think that something more than Marcy Taylor's death had him twisted up. As close as we were, that much I knew. I was unsure who had me more twisted, Laughton or Nareece. Fact was, it did not matter. Between the two I would end up checking in to the senseless bureau in a minute.

I started out the door, then went back. Laughton's locked drawer opened easily with a gun-cleaning pick. As soon as it popped open, I felt guilty, rifling through his files like he was the enemy. I flipped through the file tabs. Then I pushed them back, revealing a manila folder lying flat at the bottom. On the tab was *Mabley—Case #92-22-82965. COLD CASE* was stamped across the jacket. Emotional walls that had held steady for twenty years crashed down around me.

CHAPTER 5

After I made a copy of the file, I debated driving to Laughton's house and confronting him, but I was beyond exhausted from the day, and I decided on sleep first. Two murders in one day, Nareece losing her ever-loving mind, Laughton following close behind her, old wounds coming to roost—and it was only Wednesday.

It was 9:00 p.m. when I finally turned the corner onto my block. I pulled up in front of the house rather than down the driveway and into the garage as I usually did. A noisy gaggle of teenagers swooped down on the otherwise quiet block, half in the street, the other on the sidewalk. I stayed in the car until they passed, too tired to act, praying for nothing happening that I'd need to act on.

When I got in the house, I started up the stairs, my bed screaming for my attention, but then I paused midway, backtracked to the dining room table, took the file out of my briefcase, and dropped into the chair.

I flipped open the file and fingered its contents, then dove in. This whole time I'd thought my sister was the only fragment of my life I had kept from Laughton. How did he learn about the file? Carmella Ann Mabley disappeared twenty years ago. She was now Nareece Troung. Before marrying John, she was Nareece Dotson. Why had *Carmella* resurfaced now? Nareece's rants were too vague to determine what the envelope she received might be about. She made it sound like there were goings-on I was not privy to, that someone who had known her twenty years ago was threatening her new life.

I shuffled through the photographs. The photographs' borders blurred when my brain took over and streamed images in front of my eyes like a flip book. I fast-forwarded and replayed the images in my head, searching for anything meaningful. Nothing. I drilled my memory pack, but a lobotomy would have served me better, I thought, waving a tearstained photograph of a battered Nareece from the cold case file.

I dug my cell out of my briefcase and called Laughton again. Rather than make a lot of assumptions, I would ask questions. No answer made me crazy. I left a tenth message on his cell and home phones, refusing a pleading tone. I checked the clock on the cable box set on top of the television: 9:45. A moment of desperation attacked my gut. The pangs surrendered to Dulcey leaning on the bell as only she could. When I got up to answer the door, I realized I still had my coat on. I took it off on my way to the door and threw it on the couch.

When I opened the door, Dulcey blew past me saying, "I know, I know, it's late, and you're working, you're always working, so it's time to take a break and sit with me. I can't listen any more to them ladies at the shop talking up a storm about anything and everybody. Lord should deliver down a lightnin' bolt, burn up all their behinds, and send 'em hollering for cover, gossiping and carrying on like ain't no savin' souls mornin' comin'. They shoulda been long gone anyway. Acting like they don't have homes to go to, families to care for."

I followed her in. The windstorm she made sent the contents of the file that were spread across the dining room table flying, her butt swaying like a giant pendulum. She caught sight of a photo on the table, stopped short, and backed up. She had her hairdressing case hanging on her back from a wide strap that lay across her chest and a shopping bag in her arms. She shifted the shopping bag and picked up the picture of Nareece, unconscious, beaten and bloodied, sprawled across her bed.

"Girl, you told me about this before," she said. "But I never imagined anything this bad."

I snatched the photo from her and gathered the papers from the floor and the table, shuffling them into a pile. "Don't even go there. Bad enough I have to relive this nightmare, without you getting dragged in."

"What kind of mess you talkin'? Relive the nightmare? What's that about?" She gave me about a second to respond, then said, "I've been in this from the git-go, so don't start blocking me out now. I want to know what we've been talking about all these years. I want a full understanding."

"Trust me. You understand enough," I said, stuffing the papers into my briefcase, avoiding her stare. She allowed me a smidgeon of latitude.

"You look like you need a little somethin' somethin', honey," she crooned, moving on to the kitchen. I plopped into the chair. The opening and closing of drawers and cabinets and her ramblings echoed in my ears until no sound penetrated them.

Next thing I knew, Dulcey was talking to me like I was deaf. "M, where are you?" She stood in front of me with a glass of wine. In a softer tone she said, "Here, honey, your favorite, or one of them anyway." She cackled a bit. "I'm clueless since you've become such a wine *connoisseur*." Then she examined my hair, running her fingers up under my kitchen, you know that place at the nape of the neck where the nappiest and most resistant to change hair resides. "Looks like a sister didn't come a moment too soon." More cackling. She pulled out a chair opposite me and folded her legs under her with the grace of a gazelle, then lifted her glass. "Soon as I settle my brain with a few swigs, I'ma hook you up. To the evening." Dulcey took a few sips and set her glass on the table.

I gulped and let the sweet, aromatic Sancerre warm my insides. Second go 'round I sipped and savored.

"Now, spill it," she said.

I unloaded the happenings of the past few days: my testimony at Boone's trial and how I felt like a victim, Laughton's weird behavior and his ex-wife, my sneaking around behind him, and Nareece's neurotic behavior and desire to confess all to Travis. I held back the part about the letter Nareece had received. There was no sense getting Dulcey in a tizzy until I knew what was in the damn thing.

"You and Laughton ain't nothing but a minute. You all will work that stuff out and move on like nothing happened. Too much glue in you all's relationship for anything different. Now this thing with Nareece, that's another story."

Silence fell between us as she readjusted her legs, one over the other in the opposite direction, and jerked her head back to empty her glass. Then she got up and went for refills.

"She got a letter today addressed to Carmella Ann Mabley." I don't know what made me say it, but suddenly I needed Dulcey to know exactly what was going on.

Dulcey stopped her steps, spun around, and made her way back, almost tripping over rather than into the chair. "Nobody knows she's who she is. I mean, nobody knows who she was."

"Somebody knows."

She returned to the table and sat down, empty glasses in hand. "What are you gonna do? What did the letter say?"

"She wouldn't tell me. Rather, she wouldn't open the envelope. Said she won't open it until I'm with her. She just started talking crazy. Said something about they know what she did. You know how Reecey can get."

Dulcey got up again and went to the kitchen. "Then we need to take a road trip," she called over her shoulder. She must have had second thoughts about more wine before doing my hair because the next thing that came out of her mouth was, "C'mon in here, girl, let me fix those numbers you got invading your head."

I obeyed her command. I sat in the chair Dulcey had set up at the kitchen sink and let her wrap a cape around my shoulders, before I commented on the road trip comment. "Yeah, I was planning on going to Boston this weekend, see what's in the envelope." I hesitated. "I should have been there, Dulce."

"Don't go there, girl." Dulcey snapped on some rubber gloves and began parting and retouching the roots of my hair. Part, dab, rub. The mercaptan smell of the perm made me pinch my nose and breathe through my mouth to survive. She moved through my head like gangbusters, yapping all the way. "You *were* there or the girl might not be with us now. You been carryin' guilt around in your briefcase all these years blockin' you from livin' life the way God intended."

"I'm ready to retire from the job, Dulcey. Do something more . . . sane. I'm forty-nine years old, no man, change coming on, Travis in college, and then there's Reecey."

"Long as you do what you do for you, Muriel. Reece got her life. And what you mean, no man? You got that fine Calvin dotin' on you now. Nothing like a good man to soothe what ails ya. And if he's fine, then all the better, and Calvin is fiiine!"

"And you know about a good man soothing ailments how?"

"Honey, Hampton is a good husband and fine as they come. Hamp got issues for sure, but what man doesn't?"

"Exactly." I huffed for air, then jumped up, grabbed the day's newspaper from the counter, and waved it for a breeze.

"What the hell is wrong with you? I mean, I know what's wrong with you, but you must be out of your mind right now." Dulcey waved her gloved hands, which were covered in relaxer. "You better sit your behind down here before you burn all that hair off your head, hoppin' around with this perm on your head. First thing you'll do is curse me for leaving scabs in your scalp. Never mind it's your behind acting the fool."

"Yeah, yeah." I sat down, and Dulcey immediately laid me back and rinsed the perm out of my hair. "Calvin's no different. I'm positive he has issues," I said. "I haven't figured him out yet is all." I struggled to sit still and let Dulcey finish rinsing my hair before I lost it and jumped up again. I felt like I was being suffocated and strangled by the plastic cape she had wrapped around my body and tied at the neck.

"You're the one with issues, honey," Dulcey said, wrapping a towel around my head. She snapped off the gloves and cackled her way through getting some ice cubes and wrapping them in a dish towel, as I labored through the fire that welled up from my insides. "Breathe, girl, deep breaths," she instructed, wrapping the cold towel around my neck and rubbing ice cubes on my cheeks. "Gotta go with it. It's your initiation, preparing you for the second half of your life." She put on more gloves and worked some conditioner through my hair, then put a plastic cap over it.

Dulcey pulled off her gloves again and refilled our wineglasses. "It's a shame you dealing with so much drama on top of gettin' the hot spells. At least when I thought I was losing my mind I didn't have anything or anybody to deal with but me. Poor Hamp thought he was gonna have to sign me in the looney house for real." We laughed. "You'll make it through. Just knowing there's an end to it right around that corner you keep bumping into, oughtta keep you straight. Like I said, preparation for the second half of your life—the best half."

"Yeah, providing it doesn't fry my brain or kill me. Or worse, make me kill somebody else first. Hell, I'm still dealing with the first half of my life, never mind the second half."

"How that little girl sing—'what doesn't kill ya makes you stronger'?" Dulcey crooned.

An hour later Dulcey pulled down on the last curl. It was then I heard the basement door open. Travis. I jumped up like a jack-in-the-box and rushed to gather the rest of the file papers and stuff them into my briefcase. With everything popping, I'd forgotten he'd called earlier to say he wouldn't be home until late. I was back in my chair before Travis and his girlfriend graced the top step from the basement.

"Hello, Miss Mabley," Kenyetta said, gliding from the basement door over to me. At five-eleven, she was statuesque with creamy dark skin and bold eyes, her hair braided into a spiraled updo intertwined with gold strands. Elegant. Almost. Her size twelves didn't clear the corner of the counter. She tripped and fell forward, so her head grazed my cheek, rather than her giving me an intended kiss.

Travis bounded over to Dulcey, who wrapped the cord around her curling iron and put it in her case.

"Hi, Auntie."

"Hey, baby. How's my favorite godchild?"

"Your *only* godchild is right," Travis kidded and lifted Dulcey off the floor in a bear hug.

I noticed I'd missed a photograph that had fallen on the floor under the dining table. I went for it and stuffed it into my briefcase in one swoop.

"Working on something murderous, huh?" Travis said, shaking his head, as he put Dulcey down and headed for me.

"Like I keep telling you, you have a lifetime to experience

awful things, as much as I hate the thought. You can't escape, but there's no need rushin'." He hugged me and headed back down to the basement. Kenyetta followed on his heels.

"We're going to New York this weekend, remember?" he called back. "We're leaving tomorrow morning. Ms. Nelson is rollin' through at eight."

"New York. You mean to tell me your mama is letting you go to New York by yo'self?" Dulcey hollered down the stairs. "*Hmm, hmm, hmm,* she really is growing up." Dulcey cackled some more.

"I know that's right," Travis said. You could hear him whispering to Kenyetta and laughing.

Dulcey closed the basement door and said, "You sure he's gonna be all right in New York alone?"

"Oh, and I worry too much?"

We moved into the living room and stretched out across the sectional sofa that occupied three-quarters of the room. By the time we killed the bottle of Sancerre, we had solved the immediate problems of the world: hunger, homelessness, and age-old discrimination against gays and blacks. Then we moved on to the more delicate, sweeter blend of a Vouvray and softer issues: rising food and gas prices, rising irritation with aging men, and grandchildren, which neither of us had. Dulcey's forty-year-old-daughter, Macey, was gay and lived in Nova Scotia with her now wife of fifteen years. They did not want children. I had no problem waiting for Travis to do his education thing before becoming a baby daddy. So ours was a dreamscape conversation of Nana's little darlings.

Dulcey left at 2:00 a.m. An evening with Dulcey always made me feel like I had experienced a full body massage and was ready for whatever came at me.

The orange numbers glared 4:41 when I woke up, dry-mouthed and woozy. I rolled over like a roast on a rotisserie for an hour before I surrendered, clicked on the light, and recovered the file from the briefcase at my bedside and began reading.

The report noted that Nareece had little memory of the attack when she woke from being in a coma for two weeks. The coma was caused by a severe concussion. She told police she had been in her bedroom lying on her bed with earphones on, listening to music, when three men attacked her. No, two men. She was unsure. One punched her in the face. "*They were all over me. They kept punching me and tearing my clothes and punching me, and cutting me and spreading shit over me.*" The attackers had slashed her arms, legs, stomach, and face with a hunting knife.

I hugged the papers to my chest, fighting against the memory as my eyes filled with tears.

> *I pulled into the driveway and groaned at the first tingle of apprehension. The house was dark. Since Mom and Pops had died six months earlier, Carmella kept every light on when she was home alone. The tingle became a bear skittering around in my stomach. I knew she was home. I'd just talked with her on the phone during the drive.*
>
> *I peered through the windshield, craning my neck to see the whole house. What was wrong with that girl? Lights out. Windows closed. "It's going to be hot as hell in there." Did the curtain just move? I squinted more. A few hours of sleep would do wonders for my eyesight, I thought. I looked away and tried shaking off my anxiety. Carmella was fine.*
>
> *She was sixteen going on thirty-six. Girl was always telling me, "You're worse than an old mama. You need*

to find yourself a man so you can get a life and let me get on with mine." Hmph. I chuckled to myself. I had plenty of time for the man thang. First things first—getting her through senior year to graduation and into college took priority.

I considered putting the car in the garage, then decided against it since I would be leaving in a few hours to go back to work. While working undercover, sneaking home to check on Carmella was necessary, though it wasn't wise nor in the job description.

"Carmella," I yelled going in.

I dropped my stuff on the kitchen counter and flipped the light switch next to the door. Then toe-to-heel slid my shoes off and went for the refrigerator. I hadn't eaten since the Lots O' Chocolate cookie from Dunkin' Donuts I'd had for breakfast. "Mmmm."

"Ca—" A blow to the mouth sucked my words away. Every muscle in my body tensed as I spun around with raised arms, knocking away the arm that reached for me. I knocked the man aside and tried to bolt. "No! No! No!" I shook my head furiously, kicking and screaming and scratching and pulling at the hands that covered my mouth and kept my feet off the floor. Then I was flying, stopped by the maple cabinets lining the walls above the sink. I hit the stone tile floor face-first. Don't pass out, get up, get up, get up. I was a rag doll when he lifted me off the floor and banged me down on the island countertop. My back cracked like a two-by-four. My head ricocheted from the force. Blood pulsed through my veins and slammed against my temples.

I gulped a breath and thrust my leg out, kicking the man at my front in the face, and went for my ankle pistol. The second man tried to knock it away, causing a bullet to discharge and hit the ceiling light, which then crashed down on his head. Move! I rolled off the counter and stumbled backward, holding on to the gun with both hands, waving more than pointing it at them. "Carmella! Where are you, baby girl? Answer me! Mel!" I backed up to the hall staircase and looked away for a second. The men bolted out the door as my pistol exploded again and again.

Pain shattered my body each time I raised a foot to take another step, shoving me to my knees at the top of the stairs. Tears and mucus blinded me as I struggled to stay conscious. "Mel." I pulled myself up by the railing and stumbled up the last steps to the bedroom door. "Don't be . . ."

In the shadows, I could see Mel's silhouette. She was facedown across her bed. I flicked the wall switch and went to her. Carmella's ninety pounds felt like nine hundred as I struggled to turn her over and leaned in close to feel for her breath. "Please, dear God, please." I pushed the hair from her bloodied face and rubbed her cheeks. My insides tried to force their way to the surface. Black and blue handprints peppered her thighs. Blood trickled from her groin. "Come on, girl, wake up. You're all right. Come on now. It's just me and you now. You have to be all right." I pulled the soiled bedsheets around her half-naked body and rocked her. "It's going to be okay, Mel. I'm here."

The vision forced me over the side of the bed with the dry heaves. The file contents nearly dumped out, but only a slip of notepaper escaped my grasp. I picked it up and almost slid it back in the file, but took notice instead. *FMJ 732-5697.* Who was *FMJ?*

The thought was interrupted by Travis's knock on the door before he opened it and stuck his head in, then rushed to my bedside.

"I'm out," he said and kissed my forehead. "You good? You look like you seen a ghost."

"Long night trying to solve crime is all," I said.

He handed me a piece of paper. "Here's where we're holdin' up, and Ms. Nelson's cell number. See you Monday." He danced to the door, singing, "Who you gonna call? Crime busters."

"Get out of here, boy. Have fun and be careful."

He stuck his head back in the door and said, "Yeah, yeah, I'll be very, very careful." He e-nun-ci-a-ted the *very, very* part. I threw a pillow at the door he slammed shut.

Back to FMJ. Assuming it was a phone number, I pressed in the number with a 215 area code. It went right to a generic recording saying that the number was not available and to leave a message after the beep. I hung up without leaving one. Then I tried Laughton's number. No answer. His voice-mail recording said there was no room to leave a new message. I tried his home landline. After ten rings and no appeal to leave a message, I hung up.

I showered and put on clean khaki pants and a blue polo shirt—our lab uniform—and accessories, which included gun belt, handcuffs, and baton. The whole police outfit was unflattering, and with accessories added at least ten pounds to my already weight-sensitive parts. You would think hoisting around the extra weight would help melt away some poundage. Not happening.

I tried Laughton again before leaving the house.

Still no answer, so I decided to drive over to his place before going to the station. My first-ever visit to his place of residence. *Ahem.*

Laughton lived in Old City on cobblestoned Church Street.

Old City is a neighborhood of Center City bounded by Vine Street to the north and Walnut Street to the south. It is one of Philly's most popular nightlife destinations, with an artsy aura. His condo was the only one with a private entrance street side. His Audi Quattro manned the entrance. It took me leaning on the doorbell Dulcey-style and banging on the door Calvin-style, which brought neighbors to their windows spewing obscenities at me, before he answered.

Surprise lost, he droned, "I thought you were going to Boston." He was shirtless and rumpled-looking, and he squinted to lessen the effect of sunlight in his eyes. "You shoulda called first," he said, turning back into the town house. "If I'd known you were coming, I would've had Jemima clean the place."

I shuddered down to my core at this new feeling between us. A wave of pain and sadness slid through my body, leaving goose bumps behind.

I stepped over the threshold, holding the wall to steady myself. When I got inside I hesitated, letting my eyes adjust to the darkness, then closed the door and followed Laughton down a short hallway. It felt like ten o'clock at night in the apartment rather than the bright morning hour of 10 a.m. that it was. The hallway opened into a living space with high, beamed ceilings and dark wood floors, accented with muted-colored orientals. A giant Robert Freeman painting hung on one wall. To the left were a kitchen and a short hallway, which I guessed led to his bedroom.

I closed the door and followed him farther into the room, completely dark save for a sliver of sunlight through an open fold of the floor-to-ceiling drapes that covered two walls, as well as the light from the television. The room reeked of cigarettes accented by the morning after a party boozy smell. A cigarette burned in an ashtray on the coffee table. The smoke settled in the sliver of sunlight and swirled in the air like a fog.

I could handle the smoke. I had smoked for thirty years myself before quitting two years ago. But the stench of old beer and stale butts that overflowed several ashtrays around the room permeated the air and challenged my breathing.

"What's going on, Laughton? Talk to me," I said. I dropped the file on the table in front of him. "What about this? And why didn't you ever tell me you were once a married man?"

He ignored me for a few moments before saying, "You tell me. All these years we've been partners and you never mentioned you had a sister." The words, laden with sarcasm, spilled from his mouth.

Guilt and betrayal blew through me. "You never asked. I had no reason to mention it." My voice intensified. "Why do you have this file?"

His face looked ashen in the glow from the television. I followed his gaze.

"Laughton!" I yelled in frustration.

The words I was about to say lodged in the back of my throat. On the television, Jesse Boone stood on the stairs of the Criminal Justice Center, reporters' microphones shoved in his face. Laughton reached for the remote and turned up the volume.

"I been telling you all I was innocent. They had to let me go," Boone said, laughing as he pushed his way through the hungry reporters who heaped questions on his back, until he escaped into the backseat of a black Range Rover and was driven away.

CHAPTER 6

I sped down I-95 cursing and pounding the steering wheel throughout the twenty-minute drive to the station. When I arrived, I blew past Parker and another of his stupid remarks, something about me looking like Cruella de Vil. I destroyed the hinges and almost shattered the glass window on Captain Butler's office door, causing it to bang into the wall and bounce back to slam shut behind me.

"How'd this happen, Cap?" My voice squeaked.

"What the hell is wrong with you, Mabley? Knocking is out of the question now?"

I fell into the chair in front of Cap's desk and rested my forehead in my palms to stave off a throbbing headache.

"Look, Mabley. It's out of our hands."

I sat up and snapped, "What the hell does that mean, 'it's out of our hands'?"

Laughton stormed in a moment later. He sat down in the chair next to mine. I resumed my position trying to lessen the pain of my headache.

The creaking of both Cap's and Laughton's chairs and the silence between them made me look up again. Laughton got up and leaned over the captain's desk, his fists balled on the desktop as anchors for his taut arms. They glared at each other like boys crazed with proving whose testosterone level was mightier.

The captain said, "Bastard's skippin' on some technicality, or at least that's what they're saying went down. Something about prosecutors let too much time pass between arresting him and taking him to trial. He's got one shrewd attorney. Got a call in to Bandizzi, the lead on the case. Don't expect things will change. But for now, Boone's a free man. Fact is, he may stay a free man. Word is they may have to drop the charges altogether, including assault. Then we're back to square one."

There was more silence while the staring duel continued.

"Okay, so what am I missing? I definitely get the feeling there is something more to this episode than I'm privy to. Cap?" My stomach growled loud enough to disturb the dander contaminating the air. "Laughton?"

"Damn," Laughton said, pounding his fist on the desktop, then he stormed out. When the door slammed shut, a photograph of Cap's wife and two daughters that hung on a side wall crashed to the floor. I resumed the headache position.

"I'm sorry, Mabley," Cap said. "You did your job. No fault of yours. Take a few days. You got plenty on the books. Laughton can handle the lead on the Taylor business."

I lifted my head and sat straight up in the chair. "That's it? That's all you're going to tell me to take a few days off?"

"That's all there is to tell you."

"I'm no damn victim," I squealed. "God knows I know the drill. 'Don't worry, we'll get the guy,'" I mimicked Cap's baritone voice. "I've said it at least a thousand times to victims. But how do you tell the parents that their daughter's killer is free because the police messed up?"

"Not your call, that's Homicide's job." He got up and came around to sit on the desk facing me. "Are you okay?"

I hung on to his question. "This whole thing doesn't feel

right. Boone's killed at least four people that we're sure of, but we can't seem to prove it and he's out there, fancy-free. A technicality, my ass."

"They'll get him."

"There's something about this guy, Cap. He's so sure of himself. Cocky, even."

"Why'd he call you that night? Or was it just that you were the one who answered the call?" He hesitated, then continued. "You know you need to be clear on what happened that night and how you ended up at Boone's house without backup."

"Yeah, I know. Internal Affairs contacted me."

"Not much to worry about right now anyway, with the case against him dropped for the moment."

"Doesn't feel right, Cap. He's guilty and we know he's guilty of way more than we had him on. Someone's giving the man a hand up. Laughton's right, it has to be someone in the department. Why doesn't anyone else in the department get that?"

The captain shifted his weight so his right leg was the anchor and his left knee dangled and crammed my personal space. I leaned back in the chair and sighed.

"What else is on your mind, Muriel?"

My intention was to tell Cap about the letter after I knew what was in it and then only if it was warranted, but then I considered he might have some good insight. At the very least I wanted to catch his reaction. "Cap, Reecey got a letter addressed to Carmella Ann Mabley."

Cap is a five-foot-eight Irish-Catholic, with red hair and a red complexion from all the freckles fighting for space on his face. Now the color drained from Cap's face; it almost reached transparency, his freckles seemingly floating unattached.

In a hushed tone, he asked, "What'd it say?"

I masked my alarm at his reaction by getting up to leave, not sure why I felt the need to pretend. Reece was living because of

Cap. He'd helped me get her out of Philly after her attack, and into an unofficial version of the witness protection program. "She won't open it without me. I'm driving down this weekend."

He shifted his weight again so his left leg was now the anchor, and cleared his throat. "I'm sure it's nothing. After twenty years, it has to be nothing," he said. Cap got up and went back to sit in his chair. "She's been doing real well for herself. Husband, two kids, big house. Her husband . . . what's his name, James? John? What's he do for a living anyway?"

"His name is John. I can never get a straight answer, or I'm too much of a flat foot to understand exactly." It was a lame attempt at humor that got my lone chuckle. "He does something with computers, technology. As long as he's taking good care of Reecey and those babies, and it's legal . . ." I shrugged my shoulders.

"When you find out what's in the letter, call me. Let me know what's going on." Cap flipped open a folder and picked up his phone, my cue to leave.

Laughton was gone when I came out of Cap's office. He was good at that lately, disappearing. I sat at my cubicle and sighed at the array of cases assigned to me that covered my desktop.

Bullets from an automatic handgun used in a drive-by in Germantown that left an eight-year-old girl paralyzed, bullets from a .38 that killed two teens outside of a graduation party in North Philly, bullets and a .22 from a shooting in a Nicetown bar by a patron who had been kicked out because he wouldn't stop smoking. Nicetown is a not-so-nice neighborhood in North Philly. The smoker, James Waller, came back and opened fire. He was the only shooter who had been caught, and a trial date was set for September 26. I had time. The bullets that killed two men and injured four others definitely came from Waller's gun, but nothing is ever that pat. Shooters got off despite the certainty of the testimony our unit provided, and oftentimes they killed again before justice finally reigned. I spent a few hours organizing the contents on my desk, then clicked off my desk lamp and left.

I landed a flurry of kicks into the punching bag and countered with several punches, back kicks, then more punches, unable to stop the pounding in my head. The face of my unmoved opponent flashed the maniacal grin of Jesse Boone. It remained undeterred by more punches and kicks until I fell into the bag, taken down by the force of my own punch that grazed the side of the bag and pulled me forward.

"You are defeating yourself with no focus." It was Kim. He surprised me. He hadn't been home when I entered using the key he'd given me.

"Yes, I'm doing a fine job at defeating myself lately," I agreed.

"Focus," Kim commanded.

"Too much going on to focus on this freakin' bag, Mr. Kim."

"If you focus on what you are doing, the rest will come."

Kim squatted on the sidelines and nodded for me to continue. Thirty minutes later, sweaty and sucking air, I hugged the bag for support, expecting another "Focus" from Kim, but he was gone. When I left, he was nowhere in the house, or at least he didn't answer my call.

There was a voice mail from Calvin when I got home. I called back.

"Ms. Mabley. Good to hear your sweet voice," he said.

"I'm sorry I've been AWOL lately. Work is consuming me as usual."

"I can help soothe that if you'll allow me to dazzle you with dinner at Bistrot La Minette, French wine, soft music, kneading of your most tender spots."

I laughed at his attempt to pronounce the restaurant name with a French accent. I'd never been to La Minette, as it was way out of my league. I told Calvin I would be ready in an hour. I showered and went the distance to make the mess on my head presentable. I already knew what I would wear—a Red Valentino, a black slinky number I had scooped up on sale at Banje's last year, along with black velvet pumps to match. I had agreed to a blind date orchestrated by Travis's friend's mother's sister, whom I barely knew. I know, sounds desperate. Rather it was just me trying to accommodate my son and everyone else in my world. Maybe a little part of me was hopeful. Anyway, the dress was the bomb; the blind date needed bombing.

Calvin came with corsage in hand and thugged out, wearing a black shirt against a black two-button vested suit with peak lapels and accented with a lavender tie. The presentation was a little overstated for my taste, but there was that charisma thing going on that gave me a hard-on, and the gentleman thing, and the "I'm the queen for the evening" thing, and the "I'm the most beautiful and sexiest woman on the planet" thing. All of which was slathered on, none overstated.

He held the door to a late-model silver Porsche 911, black interior with red trim. Nice. Midlife-crisis car, no doubt. Calvin's other car was an older Mercedes S430, white with black interior. Not too shabby by any means.

He closed the door and scooted around to the driver's side.

"Nice," I said when we pulled away from the curb.

"Just a little something I picked up for special occasions."

"Special occasions, huh." We chuckled.

"Tell me again what you do."

"That would take a while, when I'd much rather talk about you, what you do, and what I would like to do to you and with you."

"Really, Calvin. It's been what, three months? And all I know about you is that you own the club and you can sing. Oh yeah, you live over the club, you've never been married—or so you say—and you don't have any children. You're a Philly boy by way of Alabama and . . ."

"I'd say you know quite a bit."

"Sooner or later you're going to have to spill it. All of it."

"So be it," he whispered. He reached over and took my hand, kissed it, and held it next to his chest while he drove the rest of the way to the restaurant and Etta James crooned from the car stereo how she'd rather be a blind girl than watch her man leave.

When we arrived at the restaurant, everyone, from the parking attendant to the hostess and the wait staff, lionized Calvin, and since I was on his arm, me too. I won't say I did not get caught up in the attention from the get-go. It was mesmerizing. I was spellbound—until the first time my phone buzzed.

It was Nareece.

We nibbled on the appetizer of escargot with butter, garlic and parsley and made goo-goo eyes at each other like a scene from a sweet-sixteen-and-never-been-kissed movie. No direction needed. By the sixth Nareece disturbance, I was sufficiently stupefied and needed a break to shake off the trance anyway. After one heavenly bite of the entrée, poulet—French for chicken—with aligot potatoes, I excused myself and went to the ladies' room to take the call.

Before I could say a word, Nareece pounced. "What happened? Where are you?" She was teetering on hysterical, her voice piercing my ear.

"Is everything all right?"

"No. Everything is not all right. I'm scared, Muriel. I'm scared for my life and my family's life. Why aren't you here? I need you here so we can open the envelope and fix things."

"Nareece, did something happen? What do you mean, you're scared for your life? Did someone threaten you?"

"No, not exactly."

"Then what are you talking about? You just sent my blood pressure through the roof." I struggled to keep my voice in check. "You're taking this thing to someplace it doesn't need to be. We don't even know what's in the envelope. It could be somebody playing some kind of a joke."

"Yeah, right." She snorted with sarcastic laughter. "Who the hell do you know that can make that kind of joke or even knows that much about me to make that kind of joke? Who?"

For a moment I listened to the hollowness of her heavy, fast breathing in the phone.

"I'll be there tomorrow, Reece. I promise. I'll call you when I get on the road."

She clicked off without even a grunt of acknowledgment. It seemed her regular modus operandi of late.

I rang her back, but it went straight to her voice mail. I left a message. "Reecey, I love you. Whatever it is, we'll work it out. I'll call you tomorrow when I get on the road." I hung up and called back again just in case, but it went to voice mail again.

When I returned to the table, Calvin stood and pulled out my chair for me, a gesture I thought long retired from all existing etiquette teachings. On second thought, it probably *was* gone from existing etiquette teachings. Calvin was old school.

"You good, babe?" he asked, scooting his chair in. When he was done, he reached out and covered my hand with his. "Anything you want to talk about?"

"No. I mean, it's my sister." I sighed. "I'm going to visit her for a few days. There are . . . issues."

"Can I help?"

"Believe me, you are helping right now."

A pretty salad of persimmon, pear, and avocado followed the entrée. Calvin explained that while Americans tend to eat salad before the entrée, it was customary in many European countries to eat it after.

The best part was the wine, Four Bears Sauvignon Blanc

2010, that accompanied the appetizer and the Byron Pinot Noir 1996 that complemented the entrée. It was the effect of the wine I'd say that would not let me leave our getting-to-know-each-other conversation alone.

"Calvin, this is lovely. Thank you."

"Muriel, I would love to spoil you for the rest of your life." He leaned in. "I get the most pleasure out of pleasing you, seeing that smile of yours light up your beautiful face. And best of all, that ugly face you make when you come."

"Ugly face! I make an ugly face, huh? So you're saying you have a problem with the way I look when I'm—"

We laughed. I probably could have been embarrassed or insulted or something in one of those corners. Instead it felt right, a quirk of mine that only he knew about and loved.

Over dessert, pot de crème, or custard, that was orgasmic, Calvin talked about his singing days and how he'd almost recorded an album and made it to overnight stardom. He and his band were famous in Europe, Japan, and Korea in the sixties and seventies. It was then that they were offered a record deal by a label out of London. At the same time, he received word that his mother was ill and he rushed back to America—Philadelphia, to be exact. He took care of his mother for ten years before she passed away, and here he'd stayed.

Something signaled me that Calvin was holding back. I made a note to check him out more, then wiped it away thinking I was overreacting or worse, acting like a police officer.

We left the restaurant and drove down Sixteenth to Market Street to Fifteenth and around Penn Square. Calvin bypassed I-95 and drove the streets, the long way home. A sweet, comfortable silence settled between us. I gazed at him in adoration. Bright lights flashed. I screamed and then nothing.

CHAPTER 7

The dark was peaceful. An ugly gurgle crept up and back down my throat, causing a fit of coughs and dragging the pain through every part of my body. A shadow propped up my head and offered me a sip of water. More darkness.

When I opened my eyes, the dark hung on, but the peaceful feeling became more like the garden of evil. Afraid to move any part of me, I tried to focus on my surroundings until my vision cleared on Travis and Laughton, both sleeping in chairs next to my bed. My head spun with the memory of my last moments with Calvin. Tears trickled down the side of my face, causing an itch I was helpless to scratch. Was Calvin alive? I lay in silent agony waiting for someone to notice.

Laughton stirred and came to me, then Travis, then darkness.

A soft, melodious voice pulled me back. "Muriel, wake up, Muriel. It's okay. You're just having a dream. Wake up, dear." The nurse rubbed my arms with a cool cloth. "That's it, wake up. That must have been some dream you were having. I thought for sure you would leap out of this bed." She lifted my head, put a pill on my tongue, and stuck a straw in my mouth.

I sipped. I was afraid to move for fear of pain, but then I panicked. I lifted a finger and wiggled my toes to check.

"Everything works," the nurse assured me. She was plump with a skinny face and wide eyes. "You've been in and out of consciousness going on five days now. Today is Wednesday. You were brought in Friday night." She moved around the bed, tucking in my sheets and checking the bag of fluid hanging from a hook suspended above my head. A tube from the bag attached to an IV in the back of my left hand. I lifted my hand and spread my fingers to test the degree of pain. The nurse gently pressed my hand back down and pulled the covers up. She slid a thermometer in my mouth and took my blood pressure and pulse.

"You're going to be fine, young lady," she said. "Your son, sister, and police friend visited every day. Your son and sister never left your side until I sent them home today. They'll be back in the morning."

It took a minute before I gathered that "my sister" was Dulcey.

"You have questions, but they'll wait until the morning when the doctor comes. You rest now." She scurried out.

Wake up, go to sleep, was all I could think. Protest did not register. Once again, darkness ruled. I woke before dawn feeling like I had to use the bathroom, but was unable to move enough to escape the confines of the hospital bed. I pressed the button for the nurse, but no one responded. I cried, not so much feeling sorry for myself, but trying to remember what had happened and afraid that Calvin was dead. I pressed the button again. It seemed an eternity before a nurse came, by which time I recognized I had a catheter. I cried some more from the frustration of not knowing what was happening, if Calvin was alive or dead, if I had all my parts and they worked. Somehow the nurse's words of reassurance did not feel true.

The next morning, Dr. Lebowitz ran down my ailments, the

worst of which was a severe concussion. I also had multiple cuts and bruises, a busted lip, three cracked ribs, and a broken toe. Complete recovery was certain in time. The doctor said a Jeep broadsided us on Calvin's side—a drunk driver ran a red light.

I managed a few more hours of sleep before the onslaught of voices humming, phones ringing, machines whirring, dishes clanging, and the groans and moans and wailing of patients woke me. My eyes were still sticky and my vision blurred when Laughton arrived.

"Tried to check out on me, huh?" he said. "You're damn lucky, M. Scared the hell outta me. Scared the hell outta everyone."

"Travis," I managed. My voice sounded foreign to me, thick and raspy.

"He damn near chewed his thumb off, but he's good. I've been keeping an eye on him. He should be coming around in a minute."

"Calvin."

Laughton did not answer.

"Calvin."

"I'm not going to bullshit you, M." He hesitated before continuing, "Calvin's in a coma. They still don't know if he's going to pull through."

I closed my eyes against a jagged pain. Laughton pulled a tissue from the box on my side table and dabbed at the sides of my face. "He's a fighter, M. Got to be if he's in your sights." He grunted and smiled, then got serious again. "He'll make it."

His expression told me he wanted to say more, but I did not want to hear more. He tried to talk, but Travis and Dulcey rushed in and rescued me. After hugs and kisses and Travis assuring me that he knew I would come through because "Nothing and no one can defeat Moms." Dulcey dismissed him to the cafeteria for coffee. Laughton went with him.

"Girl, you gave us all a scare," Dulcey said. "Living without you is just not an option." She bowed her head and mumbled, "Thank You, Lord."

"Dulcey, Calvin . . ."

"The Lord has His hand on him, Muriel. You worry about getting on your own feet and outta here."

"Nareece."

"She disappeared again. John called me when you didn't show up this past weekend and his phone calls to you went unanswered. Baby girl took off. I've called her cell a thousand times, but she won't answer. John's been beatin' up my phone. I finally told him to call the police."

Dulcey smoothed my covers and fixed the pillow under my head for more comfort—unattainable comfort. The throbbing was building in my head again. I closed my eyes.

"There's more, Muriel." She pressed her fingers against my temples and moved them in a circular motion. The throbbing retreated. "Someone broke into your house over the weekend. When Travis got home, the place looked like a bomb had blasted through. The boy was petrified, especially since he couldn't get you on your cell. He's staying with me for now."

"Mr. Kim."

She worked her fingers to my widow's peak with the same circular motion. "I talked with Mr. Kim. He wasn't there. He visited his daughter in D.C. for the weekend and didn't get back 'til Monday. He's a good man. Said he'd keep an eye out 'til you got home."

"Twins."

"Honey, they're fine. John is taking good care of God's little angels. I told him you'd call soon as you're able."

"Reecey."

"I keep telling you, Reecey is stronger than you think." Dulcey's voice deepened. "You think she'd be here or would have called me or something to find out if you're okay. Girl doesn't think about nobody but herself." She hesitated before she spoke again, her manner more tender. "She'll figure it out. Besides, ain't nothing you can do now 'cept get yourself well." She walked around the bed and cleared tissues and empty plastic cups from the table situated in front of me. Then she went for the matted hive my hair had become and started to work her magic. Twenty minutes later, she handed me a mirror and stepped back, waiting for my approval. I shared a strong likeness to Frankenstein, or rather, Frankenstein's mistress. I started to cry, which sent Dulcey hustling for tissues and dabbing at my cheeks to stop the flow.

"Honey, you're looking good now. You looked dead for sure when I first saw you. Made *me* want to scream."

"Scream about what?" Travis said, reentering the room. Laughton was not with him.

"Where's Laughton?"

"We ate lunch and he took off. Said he'd be back. Scream about what?" he repeated.

"The way your mama looked when we first saw her."

"That's only the half of it. I freaked out after going home to the place all jacked up and you didn't answer your cell. Laughton didn't answer his cell. If Auntie hadn't answered . . ." He sat forward in the chair beside the bed. "I don't know what I'da done—"

"No worry. God don't want me," I said.

"Ma, Auntie Reece called my cell. She surprised me, because she never calls my phone. Said she's been trying to call you since you were supposed to go there this past weekend. She sounded off the hook."

"You tell her about the accident?"

"I didn't know about the accident then. She hung up on me."

"I'll call," I said, to ease his anxiety. "New York?" All I could think was how Nareece must be crazed by now. In twenty years, a day had not passed without us talking. Now it had been five. And there was still the envelope to contend with. I squeezed my eyes closed, then opened them again and refocused on Travis.

Travis bounced around the room with big gestures and expressions, talking about the grandness of his New York trip. I must have dozed during the telling, because at one point when I peeped at him he smiled, flicked on the television, and settled back in a chair. Dulcey slouched in the chair on the opposite side of the bed from Travis. A peaceful, painless sleep found me.

CHAPTER 8

Travis fumbled with the house keys. I held my breath, waiting for the shock of my house turned upside down. Instead, the faint smell of Clorox Clean Up and Pledge hit me before the familiar smell of home filtered through. A stack of mail on the couch end table was the only blemish in an otherwise spotless setting. Dulcey and Travis steered me to the couch, one on either side of me, and made me sit. Resistance was not an option. I sat back and eyed the spiderweb in the corner above my head.

Travis settled me on the couch. He put a pillow under my head and covered me with the navy afghan Nareece had crocheted for a Christmas gift one year, four, maybe five years ago. Times does get away.

I tried to relax and closed my eyes against the vision of Calvin still unconscious in the hospital. In all my years on the force, gunshot wounds, broken bones, cuts, nothing ever touched me. The cliché, "I always thought I'd die on the job," came to mind. I never imagined it might be on a date.

A week after I arrived home, Nareece was still missing. Calvin was still in a coma, though in stable condition. And I was still stumbling around, too well to stay in bed and too unsteady to go outside. Periodically my brain dislodged, floated around, and knocked against my temple, making me hurl.

John had graduated from irritated with Nareece for putting him and the twins through another disappearing act to hysterical with thoughts of her dead in a ditch, a driveway, or a Dumpster. Her cell phone went right to voice mail.

Nareece had disappeared on several occasions before, causing John and me needless worry. For the first few incidents, I drove to Boston on search-and-rescue missions. She returned home fine, just after I arrived, unwilling to discuss her whereabouts. I returned to Philly both times angry that I'd made the trip. Now I hesitated to call homicide detective Gerard Bates of the Boston Police Department, but I'd promised John I would. I held some concern, too, since this was Reece's longest escapade ever. And there was the letter to consider.

Detective Bates and I had gone through the Philadelphia police academy together. We stayed friends through the years since his wife, Vicky, was a high school girlfriend of mine. I solicited his help the first time Nareece disappeared. Thing was, I didn't share with him Nareece's real identity. He thought she was just a good friend. Nobody knew Nareece's true identity but me and her, Dulcey, and Cap. That was the whole premise behind protective custody, even if it was not official—and that was also me rationalizing my actions.

"Muriel Mabley, I'll be daggone," he said. "How are you doing, Ms. Mabley? You're still Ms., I presume."

"Hey, Bates. Life is good," I answered. "Time passes too fast, and yes, I'm still Ms."

"Nineteen years, forty-one days, twenty-six hours, and, let's see, thirty minutes and twenty seconds to be exact, since I've been graced with your mesmerizing beauty."

"You're pathetic, Bates. How are Vicky and the family?"

"Vicky left. She couldn't handle the job. The boys are young men."

"Time does get away."

"How about you and yours? Travis, right?"

"Travis is a young man now, too, first year in college. I'm still working forensics, firearms. Right now I'm recovering from a car accident."

"On or off the job?"

"Off."

"Damn. You're supposed to get hurt on the job so you can take a sweet retirement, and get out while you're still breathing." We laughed.

"Tell me, why am I being blessed with your call?" he asked.

I hesitated. I decided Bates should remain outside the loop of people knowing Nareece's true identity—for now.

"I need another favor, Bates. My girlfriend disappeared again. This time it's been more than a week. She's never been gone this long. Her husband, you remember John, he filed a missing person's report and I hoped you could check into it a bit, see what's getting done, if anything, and maybe do some digging."

"No need to be hoping, I got you." He asked several questions to reconfirm Nareece's information. "I'll call when something surfaces," he said.

"Thanks, Bates. As soon as I get on my feet good, I'll be up that way. I'll stop in."

The doorbell rang as I hung up. I hobbled across the room and barely got the door open when Laughton ducked inside as though hiding from somebody. I had not seen or heard from him since I'd returned home from the hospital. Cap called, Parker called, even Cap's assistant, Connie, had called to check on me, but not Laughton.

"How you doin'?" he asked. "About time you got dressed and hit the streets, don't you think?" He chuckled.

I rolled my eyes and moved past him to resume my position on the couch. A silent prayer kept a guard over my mouth.

He stopped halfway across the floor and stood there like he was waiting for directions.

"Got a beer?"

"Don't I always keep a beer here for you?"

He went into the kitchen and returned with a Heineken, working the opener. The bottle top popped off to the floor. He stumbled forward, kicking the cap out of reach, lunged for it and missed, then grabbed the cap and flipped it onto the coffee table.

"Been sippin' something already, huh?"

He took a swig of beer, swished the suds around in his mouth, and finished with an "Ah." I suppressed a laugh. Laughton took another swig, then sat on the coffee table facing me, knee-distance away.

"Look, M. I don't think your accident was an accident," he said abruptly, ignoring my question about drinking.

"What do you mean? Why would you say that?"

"Trust me on this."

"Now I have a problem, Laughton. You've been dodging me, working on things by yourself, holding back information—and that was all before my accident. Besides, the car came from Calvin's side. If someone wanted to hurt me, they would have struck my side or head-on." He did not respond. "Maybe someone was trying to kill Calvin," I thought out loud.

"Nothing is the way you think. What's happening behind the scenes is stuff you don't know about, that you don't need to get involved in."

"I don't need to know? I'm your partner, for chrissakes. You're telling me the accident was not an accident at all, but that someone tried to kill me or Calvin or both of us, and I don't need to be involved?"

"I want you to watch your back until I figure this out." He took another long swig of beer and set the bottle on the coffee table, then moved to the couch, next to me. "Calvin's still in a coma. Go to Boston like you planned. I promise when you get back, things will be straight." He raised his hand and moved a strand of hair from my face to behind my ear.

I couldn't believe a tingle surged through me.

"*Hm, hm, hm.* You are a beautiful woman."

A moment of silence, Laughton's arms around me, his hand on my leg, old ass embers trying to burn my butt. My leg twitched. This was not happening. No way.

I broke his hold, cleared my throat, and said, "What's happening in the Taylor case?" I regained my upright composure, grabbed the closest thing to me, his bottle of beer, and drank. The beer went down wrong and came up through my nose, choking me. Laughton bolted to the kitchen and returned with a towel. Repositioned and wiping spilled beer from my lap, I continued, "I mean, Cap confirmed Marcy Taylor was murdered. He also said Wade's execution pointed to a drug deal gone bad. Any leads there?"

"Not yet. The gun found at the scene didn't kill him."

Travis and Kenyetta came in as Laughton finished his sentence. He jumped up and hunkered over to Travis like a sumo wrestler going for the kill. I braced myself as Kenyetta bounded over to me like a puppy excited to see her master. This time she gracefully swooped down on me and kissed my cheek. I had no idea why the child thought she had to kiss me every time she came in the house.

"What's going on with you, young man?" Laughton said, jabbing Travis in his gut. Travis countered with an uppercut to Laughton's jaw.

"Doin' good, Unc," Travis said.

Unc, short for "uncle," was what Travis had always called Laughton.

Laughton grabbed Travis's head and pushed down to connect it with his uplifted knee.

"Gettin' ready to bounce, headin' to the Big Apple for the weekend." Travis grabbed Laughton around the knees and lifted him off the ground.

"Damn, boy." Travis set him down and Laughton swatted his head. Laughter filled the room. "I guess you're grown enough to make the Big Apple."

Travis came to the couch and kissed me, cuing Kenyetta to make a move downstairs.

"Better keep this lovely young lady close," Laughton said, then crouched and made a move toward Kenyetta. She giggled and slid in behind Travis, who pulled her to his side and blocked Laughton's access.

"Not to worry, babe. I won't let this dirty ol' man near you," he said and punched Laughton in the shoulder. Laughton followed Travis and Kenyetta to the basement stairs and closed the door after them.

"Muriel," Laughton said, returning to the living room.

Muriel. Laughton hadn't called me Muriel since the day we met. M and M; M; Partner; Knuckles (don't ask) . . . but never Muriel. I tensed and started to get up from the couch. Laughton blocked my effort. He stood over me, arms crossed. I settled back down.

"As long as we've been partners, we've shared everything, or so I thought," he said.

I felt like he was my husband about to leave me for someone or something else.

"But, Muriel, I need to work this out and I need to do it alone."

"I can't make you tell me what's going on. I can't make you

let me help. What do you want me to say? What do you want me to do?"

He uncrossed his arms and stretched them out toward me in a helpless gesture. "Stay home. Take some time off," Laughton pleaded, still standing over me. He switched to a hard tone. "The captain gave you clearance for a few weeks of sick time. Take it," he said, then he stormed to the door and out of the house.

Like I said before, I have never been married, never even been in a more serious relationship than with Laughton and now three months into things with Calvin, so I wasn't real clear about how a breakup could crush you. I imagine Laughton's leaving was as close as I wanted to get. I suppose Laughton *was* my husband in every way except sexually. That connection had ended almost from the sweet beginning.

I would have left the force to be with Laughton. But he said he didn't want the backlash of being blamed if I ever regretted leaving the force or if our passions ever cooled.

Now my body burned and sweat poured from every pore.

The house was quiet and dark when the phone woke me. I searched for it with one arm, not wanting to move from my position of facedown on the couch. The ringing stopped before I found the phone between the cushions of the couch. I checked the caller ID. The number was unfamiliar. It rang again. The same number showed.

"Muriel Mabley."

No answer.

"Hello, who's calling, please?"

No answer.

I could hear rustling on the other end, like cellophane being crinkled. I sat up at attention.

"Nareece?"

The rustling noise gave way to soft, steady breathing.

"Nareece, if this is you, please answer me."

Silence.

"Tell me you're all right. Think about the girls, and John."

More rustling.

"Please, Reece. Talk to me." The line disconnected. A few minutes later, the phone rang again.

"Enough of this. Reece, answer me."

"Reece called? Is she okay?" Dulcey screeched through the phone.

I sank back down into the couch. "I was about to go through the phone. There would have been no way, no how, no place for that girl to escape my reach." I told Dulcey about the phone call and Laughton's visit. "Dulcey, I need to go to Boston. I'm losing my ever-lovin' mind between Nareece and Laughton and Calvin . . . and these damn hot flashes." I jumped up and pulled off my robe, as sweat dripped from the tip of my nose. I paced the length of the living room, struggling against losing control and wanting to hit something or someone.

Dulcey jabbered away, "Breathe, girl, deep breaths. Go with the flow, M. Take deep breaths."

I threw the phone. It hit the wall and landed on the couch in several pieces—the phone, battery, and battery cover. Just as quick as my body had fired up, the cool registered and a chill caught me. I put my robe back on, retrieved the phone, put the pieces back together, then called Dulcey back.

"Are you there?" I said when the ringing stopped but there was no "hello."

"And you've only just begun, girl. I'm saying you need to learn how to flow with them flashes and feel the power in them," she said. "I'll make you a recording so you can push Re-play whenever you're needin'—"

"Dulcey, shut up. Please. Just shut up."

"Listen to me, M. When you think you're going to lose your mind and the temperature can't go any higher and you want to just melt and be done, get pissed, girl. Punch something, scream. You'll cool right down and your sense, what little you have"—she cackled, then continued—"will come right back, better than before you lost it."

"Yeah, except the hotter I get, the more out of control I feel, and Lord only knows what might happen."

CHAPTER 9

Another week passed before I regained enough strength to travel and Dulcey could clear her client schedule. I called Bates to let him know I was coming. He had called once since I'd asked him to look into Nareece's disappearance, only to say there were no new developments.

On the way out of town, we stopped at the hospital to see Calvin. The nurse at the station said his condition remained unchanged, now three weeks in a coma. Three weeks since someone had tried to kill us.

I stood outside the door unable to move farther until a nurse came and pushed it open. She was on a mission to take his vitals. I stood in the doorway for a bit, then stumbled in behind her and waited for her to finish and leave before I inched up to his bedside. He looked as though he was just sleeping. I mean, there were two jagged lines on his forehead, and a scrape across the bridge of his nose, but his expression was uninhibited. I rubbed my fingers over his forehead and down his cheek. His skin was as smooth and shiny as a sandstone. My heart beat hard and fast. I kissed his stilled lips and his cheek.

Driving through New York took two hours, a drive that really should have taken half that time. Another three hours passed before patches of green with splashes of yellow, pink, and purple streaked by, the backdrop on both sides of the Massachusetts Turnpike. A long winter riddled with record snowstorms had finally given way to spring peeking through. Spring had bloomed all the way twenty years ago when Cap and I had moved Nareece to Boston. The tepid breeze and vibrant colors were even more inviting then, until I almost decided to move with her. Nareece shunned the idea. She said she needed to stand on her own two feet, which was a major contradiction where she was concerned. I thought her being in Boston would give me relief from wondering and having to deal with whatever insanity she managed to find on any given day. Really, her move became a twenty-year, long-distance upbringing, with no vacation from worry for me, until she met John, ten years ago.

"Hmm, not even then," I said out loud without realizing it, but for Dulcey coming back at me.

"Girl, what you talkin'? I thought you were asleep."

"No, just thinking. Nareece and her crazy self. Twenty years and still she acts crazy more than she acts sane, and even then you have to wonder if she really does manage to exhibit a lucid moment in her madness. John *has* to love the ground she prances on to put up with her stuff. What is she thinking, leaving those babies?"

"She's not. You and John haven't let her. Every time the child burps, one of you wipes any spittle from her cheeks and then you want to wash her up while you're at it, and dress her up in bows and frills and put her in a bubble lined with cushiony stuff so she won't bump anything or get bruised anywhere."

Blah, blah, blah. Sweat beads popped out on her forehead.

I appreciated Dulcey being the devil at my back most times, but sometimes she pushed so hard I could hardly resist the urge to snatch her face off. I was watching her mouth moving fast, spit spraying out every other word, head bobbing up and down, and I was wondering how she was driving with so much other action going on. "You know I'm talkin' true," she was saying. "You and Reecey need to fix this so everybody can move on." She looked sideways at me. I glared *"enough"* to her—one eye brow up, the other furrowed, lips sucked to one side.

After about a half hour I entered the Nareece conversation arena once again. Dulcey could be hard to take sometimes, but she was my other half and I needed her mouth to be running, feeding me and helping me find a halfway straight path to follow through this situation.

"I'm really worried about her this time, Dulce. It's been three weeks since I was supposed to go there so we could open the letter."

"Wait one minute. You mean she still hasn't opened the letter?" Dulcey shook her head in wonder, then went on before I could say anything. "Yeah, I guess not since you been out of commission."

"She wouldn't open it until I got there and I never got there, and now I don't know where she is or whether or not she has opened it yet. It's been two weeks since I talked to John. He's not answering his phone. Bates says one of the neighbors saw John and the girls a few days ago, so no missing persons there. I don't know what the hell's going on."

An hour later we checked in to the Crown Plaza at Exit 17. The hotel hangs like a bridge over the Massachusetts Turnpike in Newton. Newton is about fifteen miles west of Boston and twenty minutes from Milton, where John and Nareece live.

When we got to the room, I called John. No answer. We went to the hotel restaurant, Applebee's, and ate, then drove over to the house anyway. The time was 9 p.m. when we left the hotel. Surely they would be home by the time we got there.

I did not know my way around the area well, but I knew my way between the hotel and Nareece's house. I had made the trip at least fifty times in twenty years: Massachusetts Turnpike east to Exit 14, I-95/Route 128, to Route 38N toward Milton, to Canton Avenue, right to Indian Spring Road. On most visits, I stayed with Nareece and John, but some situations warranted separate space.

The neighborhood consisted of a mixture of sprawling homes and medium-sized sprawling homes set on a minimum of three acres each, a pumped-up version of a Stepford Wives community. Yards showcased perfectly shaped trees, manicured lawns, and vibrant flower gardens, despite spring not having sprung to its full potential yet. Nareece and John's house was a medium-sized sprawling colonial set back a ways from the street, the front partly hidden by foliage. John had done well, though I still did not understand exactly what he did. Dulcey pulled into the half-circle driveway and stopped just past the front door. A faint light shone through the large picture window, giving off an eerie aura.

"Spooky," Dulcey whispered.

"Oh girl, get your scary ass out of the car." I chuckled with tentative sincerity.

Dulcey got out and came around to my side. "Now this is what I'm talking about," she said, looking up and down the street and perusing the houses. "Reecey done good for herself. Maybe I'll move here when I retire."

"Shut up. You've only been out of Philly twice, once on your honeymoon and now. You are never leaving Philly and that's a fact." We laughed until Dulcey choked. It took a few minutes for her to stop coughing and catch her breath.

"There's a time for everything," she said, stealing her way up the driveway to the front door. I got to the door first. It stood ajar. I pulled my gun from its holster at my waist and waved Dulcey to get behind me. I pushed the door all the way open and stepped inside, flicking the light switch on in the same movement.

To the left, the cushions of the Italian leather couch and chair, Nareece's prized possessions, were strewn across the floor, along with lamps, papers, and tchotchkes.

I whispered, "Stay put, Dulcey," which was a waste of breath. Dulcey followed me step for step as I searched each room, then went upstairs.

At the top of the stairs to the right, John and Nareece's bedroom door creaked open with a light touch. Everything seemed to be in its place. I tiptoed down the hall to the twins' room.

He charged out the door at us like a bull, knocking me back and causing my gun to fire. Dulcey swung and landed a punch, knocking the man against the wall. He pushed her back and ran for the stairs, as Dulcey flipped sideways over the railing. I reached out and caught her arm, holding on for about three seconds before my grip slipped, and she fell to the stairs below, barely missing falling on the man, who fled through the open front door to the outside. She tumbled down the stairs like a rag doll, flipped head over body once, and landed at the bottom spread-eagle.

I almost fell down the stairs on top of her, trying to reach her. She waved me away to the chase. I ran outside, but he was gone. I returned to Dulcey, who was struggling to get up.

"I'm going to feel this for the rest of my natural life," she moaned. She was bent over, massaging her lower spine with one hand, while I held the other and guided her to the couch.

She twisted her neck around until it cracked. I shuddered at the bone-breaking sound.

She held my arm to brace herself and eased back to lie down on the couch. I picked up a lamp from the floor and placed it on the end table for light. The *creak* of the front door made me spin around and draw my gun toward the intruder.

"Freeze! Police!" an officer yelled.

Dulcey popped up and hollered from the pain the sudden movement caused. I lowered my gun, set it on the floor, and raised my arms, slowly, against the fear of an edgy trigger finger. Bates marched in behind several police officers.

"Well, well. Police come running to gunfire in this neighborhood," I said, lowering my arms.

Bates signaled the officers to lower their weapons. "I was heading home and heard the ten-eleven for this address," he said. He did a one-eighty and ordered the four officers with him to check the house for more intruders. "Anybody else home?"

"No. The door was open when we arrived. Caught one of them in the act, but didn't get a good look at him. He was black, bald, about six-one, two-twenty, dark blue hoodie, black sneakers, gloves, nothing specific."

"For this neighborhood, that's specific."

An officer came into the room, holstering his weapon. "Place is clear, sir. Should I get a bus for the lady?" he said, gesturing toward Dulcey.

From a reclined position, Dulcey waved the offer away. "I know I'm gonna have a mother of a bruise and be sore as heck, but no, thank you. Nothing's broken."

"I'll take over from here," Bates said. The officers cleared the house, and the army of police cars left the neighborhood as fast as they had come. I was closing the door when Mrs. Crowley stuck her hand in to stop me. Mrs. Crowley was a munchkin, about four and a half feet tall, a female black version of Mr. Kim. I smiled at the thought. Mrs. Bourgeoisie with a capital *B*.

"Is everything all right? I heard gunshots and called the police," she squeaked, ducking under my extended arm to gain entry. "Another break-in, huh? I haven't seen John and the girls around for a bit. The good Lord only knows what would have happened if they had been home." She marched up to Bates and extended her arm for a handshake. "Carolyn Crowley."

"Detective Bates. You said 'another break-in.' Have there been other break-ins in the neighborhood?"

"No, no, only here. I saw two men looking around outside the house about three days ago. I called, but no police came. They were two black men. They didn't get in, however."

"How do you know?"

Giving Bates a twisted look, she snarled, "I watched until they left. I had hoped the police would come before then." Bourgeoisie got ghetto.

"Mrs. Crowley, do you know John's whereabouts?" I asked.

"Where John and the girls are? Oh, my dear, they've been gone for a week or more, I would say. John came back Wednesday late afternoon and left again on Thursday about the same time, three o'clock. I don't stay in people's business, so I couldn't tell you where they went." She stretched her neck to take in more of the house, then she began flitting around like a stray bullet bouncing off surfaces until it finds a penetration point. "That poor man, he can't handle this mess and the girls, too," she said, picking up a lamp and setting it on the other end table.

"But do you know where they went?"

"No. But they might be at John's mother's house in Watertown, no Newton, she lives in Newton. Yes. Lovely lady. Ama, I think her name is. The girls call her Ba, or something like that. It means 'grandmother' in Vietnamese. I met Ama when she came to visit a few months ago, I think it was."

"Thanks for your help, Mrs. Crowley, I'll check that out." I captured her arm and escorted her out with her pulling against my hold all the way.

"Now, you be sure to tell John he can call me to help clean this mess up. I have some oatmeal-raisin cookies for those little darlings, too. And tell Nareece she can count on me for the girls' school bake sale. You know, I bake my cookies and red velvet cake every year for them. They always tell me my baked goods are the first to sell every year." She chuckled, then shook her head and ranted on in a different direction with a darker expression.

I ushered her down the driveway and released. She muttered the entire distance to her door, snatches about how the devil had the neighborhood in his grip, and now the children needed protection from the devil's fiery breath.

Bates was sitting at John's desk in the corner of the room when I returned. "Is there anything missing? Because they were definitely looking for something." Papers covered the top of the desk and the floor around it. He sifted through some of them. "I don't think they found what they wanted, though. You must've interrupted the search."

I went to the couch to check on Dulcey, who had dozed off. She slept with a pained expression, which gave me pause about her decision to forgo the hospital. I threw a blanket from the back of the couch over her and headed to the kitchen. Bates followed.

"Want something to drink?" I offered, busying myself at the sink to keep my back to him. "Water, maybe." He ignored me.

"You might want to know that we have a lead on your friend's location. She used a credit card at a motel two days ago, the

Doubletree in Cambridge. The clerk said she was alone. At least she checked in alone and stayed two nights. That's it. Still nothing on her car, so it must be off the street. Her husband never filed a missing person's. If she's okay and doesn't want to be found, well, the odds change."

I stayed silent.

"Look, Muriel. If you want this to go further, you're going to have to file a missing person's report yourself. I can't authorize any more man-hours on this, officially, anyway."

When I turned around, Bates was in my face—nose-hair close. A dry mouth made me swallow hard. Cornered with the sink behind me, I leaned back, not sure if he was hitting on me, which I did not want, or if I felt guilty about lying to him. Technically, Reecey was still in the witness protection program and I wasn't sure sharing that information with Bates was best for her safety. A glass of water seemed an appropriate distraction. I turned around to the sink. When I turned back, glass in hand, Bates was still staring.

"I'll keep checking and write this incident up so it will remain open. It might lead to something useful. I don't think we're going to find any unusual fingerprints." He didn't move his body or his eyes. I gulped water, pretending I didn't notice. When I finished, I sidestepped his position and moved toward the front door, hoping he would follow my lead.

When I reached the door, a straight shot from the kitchen sink, Bates was still in the kitchen, turned around and staring after me. A twitch took over my right eye. I held his stare until he gave in and made the move toward me, to leave, I hoped.

"Thanks, Bates. I owe you. If you ever have issues in the Philly area, I got you."

He pecked my cheek and left.

I closed the door and went back to the kitchen to find something to eat. The refrigerator contained a bottle of soda, two sticks of butter, a half dozen eggs, and a half gallon of milk. The end date stamped on the milk carton was two weeks ago. Some canned goods, Smartfood popcorn, a box of Honey Nut Cheerios, and Cinnamon Toast Crunch were all that filled the pantry cabinet. The kitchen was clean with everything in place—even the dishwasher was empty. It seemed like there hadn't been any cooking going on or planned for some time. I tore into a bag of popcorn.

After a few handfuls, I went upstairs to John and Nareece's bedroom. A borderless king-sized bed set against a redbrick wall. The bed was covered with a beige down comforter that puffed up as though being fed by a blower. Large earth-tone pillows made up the headboard, and a reddish-orange throw adorned one bottom corner. At the opposite end of the room, a large redbrick fireplace extended up to the ceiling and the width of the wall. A light oak mantelpiece held several photographs of the girls, and John and Nareece. Mom's old Windsor rocker sat in front of the fireplace. It was the one keepsake Nareece took with her when she moved. I went into the master bath and opened the medicine cabinet. The three shelves were empty, except for a few cosmetics and some Q-tips. What nagged at me was that the house was too clean, almost unlived in.

I went back downstairs to John's desk. It was John's when he needed to work, and the twins' desk when the Twofer Detective Agency was on a case. The phone, which sat on the right corner of the desk, showed there were messages, but I couldn't access them without a password. I went through the papers spread across the desktop and rifled through the drawers, which contained mostly papers with drawings the girls had made. A picture envelope, pencils, pens, and paper clips filled the middle drawer of the desk. I accidentally pulled the picture envelope out by the wrong end, emptying photos on the desk. Travis and

Kenyetta stared up at me. I was stunned. The photos showed them going in and out of my house, at school, and in an unfamiliar location, the twins playing in the backyard here, and my mother and father leaving out the front door of our family house. Though no dates or other distinguishing marks on the pictures provided any clues, my parents' clothing was the same as the night they died. I was positive about that. Tears stung my eyes.

I flipped the envelope over, looking for markings or Carmella's name. Nothing, just a plain white envelope. I rifled through the drawer again, looking for a note or something to indicate who had taken the photos, or where they'd come from. The only thing I came up with was a photo of me and Nareece when she was about seven or eight. I would not have remembered when or where it was taken except that I had my cap and gown on, so I knew it was at my high school graduation. Still, I don't remember the picture being taken, or rather I had a mental block about it. About Nareece back then.

Now losing Nareece was not an option.

As close as I thought Nareece and I were, there was a canyon between us. Yes, we talked on the phone every day, or we used to anyway. Yes, we said we were each other's best friends, that we would always be there for each other, and that we'd always love each other—no matter what. And I knew we would. But we never talked about our parents, we never talked about their death, or the attack. We never talked about our feelings or changes we'd gone through after they died. We never talked about Travis, really *talked* about Travis. Five years ago, she'd started making inquiries, more like that of an acquaintance being polite. Now, suddenly, she wanted to know everything about him and she wanted him to know everything about her.

Dulcey stirred. "I guess the excitement wore my butt out," she said, peeking over the back of the couch at me. "What's up?"

I got up and brought the photos to her. On my way across the room, the front doorknob jiggled. I dashed to the door, gun in hand, and hid behind the entryway retaining wall with a visual of the doorway. Dulcey dropped to the floor behind the couch.

"Muriel," John called as he entered.

I exhaled and stepped out of hiding. "I'm here." He turned and faced me.

"I saw your car in the driveway and wondered what the hell you were doing here at this time of night. You should have called—" He stopped short, focused on the mess in the living room. "What the hell happened?"

"You had visitors."

John stepped farther into the room and perused the damage, then picked up a couple of tchotchkes and put them back in their place. He looked around with a blank expression, then stumbled over to his desk, fell into the chair, and began opening and closing drawers and shuffling around papers.

"Why haven't you been returning my calls? First you ask me to check into Nareece's disappearance, then you and the girls disappear."

"I haven't received any calls from you."

"John, I've called you at least five times."

He continued looking through his desk drawers and ignored me.

"Is something missing?"

"What? No, nothing's missing, I mean, uhhh. I think maybe some important papers I had gathered for a job I'm doing is all."

"Are they there?"

"Ahh, no, I don't see them." He shuffled through the piles of papers on the desk and then through the drawers. After a time, when he had straightened the piles and closed all the drawers, he sat straight up and forward in the chair. "I just remembered I left them at my office," he said as if he'd just experienced an aha moment.

I wanted to choke the life from him, but I felt a little tender physically, so I reeled in my emotions and backed off my aggressive intentions.

Calmly, I asked, "What's going on, John? I came down here to check on you and the girls and look into Nareece's disappearance. When I got here, the house was like this and someone was hiding in the twins' room. Almost killed Dulcey."

His eyes got big and darted around the room until they landed on Dulcey.

"Hey, John," Dulcey said, waving her hand from her perch on the back of the couch. He just stared at her like he didn't know her.

"Did you call the police?" he asked, still staring her down.

"No, Mrs. Crowley did when she heard gunshots," I told him. He looked big-eyed, then got up and headed to the staircase. I stayed at his back. "Whoever was hiding in the twins' room caught me by surprise and caused my gun to go off." I followed him up the stairs and into the master bedroom. He ignored me as he searched through dresser drawers and the night table drawers. I walked across the room and pulled his arm so he would face me. "Where are the girls?"

"They're at my mother's in Newton. She's taking care of them while I'm trying to work and deal with Nareece." He pulled his arm away, releasing my hold, and hastened out the door and down the stairs. I caught up with him again in the kitchen, all control lost.

"What do you mean, 'deal with Nareece'? You've talked to her? You know where she is? Tell me that's why you didn't report her missing, even though you told me you did?" The heat welled up inside me, this time anger feeding it.

John opened and closed cabinet doors, keeping his back to

me. "I lied because I didn't want you to insist on telling the police. No sense getting them involved. She's not missing, just off on another one of her mental escapades, I'm sure."

"That's not how you felt a few days ago. A few days ago, you were hysterical about whether she was alive or dead. What changed your mind?"

"Muriel, if we get the police involved, they are going to ask a lot of questions and get in our business."

"*What* business?"

He turned around so he faced me. "I'm sorry you made the trip. You should have called me first," he said and stormed away.

"I did call. You didn't answer!" I was yelling by this time.

"You are welcome to stay the night in the guest room. I'll call the housekeeper in the morning." I followed him to the stairs and stared at his back until he disappeared into the bedroom again and closed the door.

"What the hell?" Unable to swallow his last words, I hauled ass up the stairs and banged on the bedroom door. "John, we're not finished." I banged harder and kept banging until he opened the door and almost lost his face to my fist.

He grimaced at me. A snap later his eyes softened and welled up with tears. For the first time, I noticed how whipped he looked. He wore a rumpled suit, like he had worn it for a week nonstop, sported scraggly chin growth, and blinked through crusty eyes. John was an attractive Vietnamese man with a dark complexion, long straight black hair that he wears pulled back in a ponytail, and a scanty beard. His puffy eyelids covered dark, seemingly black eyes, and added a mystique that I imagined was what had caught Nareece's fancy. That and his sleek muscular build and dignified stature, which right now looked unsteady and ready to collapse. He backed up to the bed and sat down, tears streaming down his cheeks.

"Talk to me, John. I haven't heard from you in weeks. Then I come here and Dulcey and I are almost killed by some guy. What the hell is going on?"

He wiped his tears with his forearm, got up and went over and into the bathroom, then closed and locked the door. A few minutes later he returned, his composure regained and with a determined expression on his brow.

"Muriel, I have this under control and I don't need your help."

A Mike Tyson punch to my gut.

"Nareece is fine and will soon be coming home. Please don't hound me with any more of your questions. This is our business. We don't need your interference."

A Mike Tyson punch to my chin.

I tried to speak, but my tongue was dead in my mouth. I wanted to karate chop his big head, or better yet, shoot him. A little extreme, maybe, I thought. Perhaps just one kick to the head to crack his brain, so he could start talking sense.

He walked up on me, overcrowding my space and pushing me back, stepping to the doorway. My voice kicked in.

"Now I'm interfering? You blow up my phone for weeks, and now you don't need my help? Whatever's going on with you two, I don't have a clue, but I'm going to respect your wishes and leave you and Nareece to work it out." I turned to leave, then had a second thought and spun back around. "Before I leave, I want to talk to my nieces."

He reached in his inside jacket pocket and pulled out his cell phone. One push of a button, a few words in Vietnamese to whomever answered, and he handed me the phone.

Not knowing which twin was on the other end, I picked a name. "Hi, Rose. It's Auntie M. How are you and Helen doing?" It was a lucky guess. The twins took turns talking on the phone, telling me the latest about their detective agency and how they wanted to make me a partner and could they stay with me in the summer and had their mommy come home. I kept the conversation light, as though I'd just called to say hello. Throughout the conversation, I drilled a hole in John's face with my eyes. After about ten minutes, I gave him back the phone.

"You'll be coming home soon," he cooed into the receiver. "Mommy is excited about seeing you, too. I love you, too." Then he clicked off. To me, he snarled, "Satisfied?"

I stopped at the door and turned to him again. "I found some pictures of Travis in your desk. Who took them?"

He showed a flash of surprise. He walked toward me and started closing the door as I backed out. "Nareece had them taken. She's always kept an eye on Travis one way or another."

Now I flashed surprise, as he closed the door between us.

CHAPTER 10

As soon as we got in the car, Dulcey started in on me while I drove.

"Muriel, I love you, but you have got to wake up where Reece is concerned. All these years, you think she's been angsting over Travis. She's hidin' something. Girl, open your eyes. Or is it that you're afraid of losing Travis?"

"My eyes *are* wide open, and no, I'm not afraid of *losing* Travis. This is about Reecey."

"That's the M put on God's beautiful earth to kick butt. Can't nobody put nothin' over on my girl."

"Yeah, right," I said. We laughed uneasily, still shaken by the day's events.

"I *am* concerned that Travis won't understand. What if he can't forgive either one of us?"

"Travis is the most sensitive, gentle young man I know. He definitely picked up on the best parts of you. He'll be all right. As a matter of fact, he'll be just fine."

We decided leaving in the morning was best. Dulcey's fall had stomped her. Anytime she'd let me drive when we were in a car together, I knew something bad was up. Before we reached the hotel, I stopped for some ibuprofen and a bottle of Macon-Villages. Dulcey limped into the room with my help and sat down gingerly on the bed. I pulled off her shoes and socks, propped up some pillows and settled her, then got a glass of water and two of the ibuprofen pills. She had dozed off by the time I got back to her. I hated waking her, but she needed the pills. She attempted lifting an arm and groaned in protest. I sat on the bed and fed her the pills with water, then waited until she fell asleep again, or so I thought, before I eased off the bed.

"Don't be tiptoeing around like I'm a sick patient. I'll be fine in the morning," she said.

"Sleep, girl."

I opened the wine and sat at the table that was squished between the end of the beds and the wall. I clicked on the television, which hung on the wall directly over the table. It didn't take more than five minutes for Dulcey to get her snore on, the clashing of her nose and mouth drowning out any hope of hearing the television even at such close range.

I went into the bathroom and called Travis. Music and laughter from the other end of the line filled my ear.

"Shut up, y'all," Travis commanded, his voice muffled from covering the phone, I assumed. Then, clearly, "Hello?"

I took a sip of wine and a deep breath.

"Hello?" he said again.

"Having a party, are we?"

"Hey, Moms. I invited a few of my boys over to watch the game."

"No drinking or drugs."

"Ma, I'm not stupid. I got this."

"I know you got this. It's what you got that worries me."

"Damn, Ma. You talk like I'm a problem child of some sort. Chill. We're just having a few beers."

"Watch your mouth."

"Sorry."

A few moments of reconciliation passed. Cheers went up and the announcer's voice, describing the scene, trailed through the receiver.

"Oh yeah, Ma, I found an envelope addressed to you under the table by the front door."

"Under the table?"

"Yeah, Sam dropped a glass and I was cleaning it up . . ."

"Who's the sender?"

"No name, just yours printed on the front."

I wanted him to open the envelope, but my gut said no. I instructed him to put it away. Travis reassured me there was no weed or hard alcohol, before singing "I will always love you" and clicking off.

The envelope made me think about all that was happening. It had been three weeks since Nareece had called me, all panicked about the envelope she'd received addressed to Carmella Ann Mabley. Since then, my front door had flown open by mysterious means, Laughton had acted like a total fool, Calvin and I had almost been killed, someone had broken into Nareece's house, and John had followed Laughton's example and acted like a total fool.

A glance in the mirror made me do a double take. My eyes were puffy and bloodshot and my hair stuck out in every direction. I looked whipped. I sat on the side of the tub and filled it with hot water and hotel-issued bubble bath.

A quick check of my cell phone showed it was 12:17 a.m., too late to call the hospital to check about Calvin. My heart fluttered, my breaths came in short bursts, and chills shook my

body at the thought that Calvin might never regain consciousness. I undressed, slipped into the tub, and let the tears flow.

Calvin was the first man in twenty years I'd felt anything for
other than . . . Laughton. "Oh God." All these years, falling
in love, caring, wanting, needing any man was not my game.
Singlehood worked for me. *Who am I kidding?* Calvin—three
months and I was hooked, flat-out in love. Crazy. Especially
since Laughton still held major landscape in my heart. I tried
to imagine life with Calvin, the rest of my life. I let the visions
move through the darkness behind my eyelids. My breathing
slowed, the tears dried.

I dozed off and didn't know how much time had passed
when my cell phone rang, causing me to flail around helplessly
in the cooled water until I had my wits about me. I cracked my
neck and back and leaned forward, trying to get to an upright
position. My phone was a little more than an arm's length away
on the bathroom sink. I got to it too late. When I did, Nareece's name showed as the missed caller. I hurriedly dried off
and wrapped a towel around me against the chill of the cold
water and the rude awakening. Then I picked up the phone
and pressed Call Back just as it rang again.

"Reece?"

"Hi, M," she said.

"Hi, M? That's all you can say? Where the hell are you?"

She made a sucking noise and squeaked out, "I want to tell
you. So much . . . I . . . I need some time . . . I'm okay, though,
so don't worry."

I had heard those exact words from Laughton. What the
hell?

A few moments of silence followed before the transformation to a harsh tone came, as though an alter ego took over, a
remake of John's episode. She said, "I'll call you when I can,

when we take care of things. Don't worry, John and I are having some problems, but we're good. Go home, M."

"Reece, tell me what's going on. I'm sure there's something I can do to help you guys get through whatever it is you're having problems with. Just tell me."

"I love you," she said and clicked off.

One minute, I wished she would kick me to the curb, and the next she was kicking me and I was squirming around like roadkill. "Reecey, Reecey, what are you doing?"

We left the hotel at 6:30 a.m. since both of us had been awake since five. And when I told Dulcey that Reece had called, she popped up ready to go. She was feeling better; at least she was not so bad as to let me drive. Like I said, she thought I was the worst driver in existence.

"Don't you even think about driving, girl. You better get over to the other side of this veeehicle," she squawked as she motioned me to the passenger side and got in the driver's side.

I welcomed the direction, since the night had allowed me only pieces of sleep. I called Travis to check on the aftermath. I woke him, which meant the conversation would be one-sided and he wouldn't remember anything I said. I did get him to tell me he'd put the envelope he found in my nightstand.

When I clicked off, Laughton rang in.

"Muriel Mabley," I said, attempting a nonchalant manner.

"Ms. M and M. What's goin' on?" Laughton slurred.

"You tell me."

"The real question is, where are you?"

"I told you I was going to Boston for a few days." I waited for a response, but got only heavy breathing. "Are you loaded this early?"

"Miss M, you are . . . were, the best partner a guy good . . . could have. I wouldn't want to work the force with any other." He chuckled. I heard him drag on a cigarette and exhale before speaking more. "We've been somethin' together, M. Things weren't supposed to end up like this. I didn't know."

"Know what? End up like how? Laughton, you're talking trash. You're drunk or damn near." He stayed silent. "I'm on my way back now. I'll call you when I'm close. Get some coffee."

I clicked off. "I think everyone's losing their ever-lovin' minds. Nareece is talking trash, Laughton's talking trash. I've never experienced this side of him before. We've spent practically every day of our lives together for the past seventeen years, and I don't have a clue who he is right now."

"Wait a minute, back up. What letter were you askin' Travis about?"

"When I talked to him last night, he said he'd found a letter under that little table right inside the door. It had just my name written on the front . . . I'm thinking it's like what Nareece got."

"Well, what did it say?"

"I wasn't gonna tell him to open it!" I screeched like she must be losing her mind if she thought I would ask Travis to open the letter with Lord only knew what its contents were. I settled a bit. "I told him to put it away, so I was asking him where it was in case he isn't home when we get there." Seemed like Dulcey was speechless since she didn't respond, just stared straight ahead like she was fixed on driving. *Speechless* has never been a descriptor for Dulcey, so I knew her concern ran deep.

"I wanted to tell Laughton all that's going on, but he's acting like a crazy man. All of a sudden I don't have a clue who he is. I feel like I've lost my other half, for chrissakes."

"I know, girl, you think you know them, and then *bam*, they're somebody totally different. Stab you all up in the heart," Dulcey said.

"This isn't about anybody's heart." *It goes way deeper*, I thought.

Dulcey grunted for emphasis. "Y'all might not be doing the nasty anymore, but the nasty is definitely doing y'all."

I ignored her innuendo. Dulcey was like a hound dog—once a scent filled her nostrils, there was no holding it back from finding its mark.

"Seems like there's a place and a time for you and Mr. Laughton. Might not be right now, but time . . ." She trailed off. I changed the subject.

"I should have gotten Reecey some real help when it happened."

"She probably wouldn't have done what she was supposed to anyway. That just wasn't, *isn't* her way."

"I know. She always wants things her way. Doesn't listen to a word I say. It might have been different if I'd moved to Boston with her. But nooo, I had my career."

"Shoulda, woulda, coulda, girl, stop. Besides, she didn't want you up under her. You did the best you could, now stop talking nonsense and start thinking about what to do now. What's done is done. Besides, like I keep telling you, ain't nothing wrong that some growing up can't fix. It's good for a change she's not running to you to get her outta trouble, or crying about . . ." Dulcey stopped talking and checked the rearview mirror. "I think someone's tailing us. Hold on."

She made a sudden right turn across three lanes to exit the Massachusetts Turnpike, Exit 12, slamming me against the door. She checked the rearview mirror again and sped down the ramp through the toll booth. The Fast Lane light flickered green. At the end of the ramp, Dulcey cut off a pickup truck veering from the left to the right lane. She banged a right turn, sped down three blocks, and turned right into a Super Stop & Shop parking lot, stopping between a minivan and a pickup truck, blocking the sight of us and them.

Dulcey's chest heaved. "Black SUV. A Range, I think," she said, taking a deep breath, trying to slow her breathing so she could talk. "That *vee*hicle has been behind us since we got on the turnpike. Just didn't seem right. Made every lane change I made." Dulcey put her head back against the headrest and closed her eyes.

"Did you see who it was?"

"No." She lifted her head, gathering her pocketbook and keys in the same motion. "I don't know, girl, probably nothing. All this craziness is making me crazy."

"Good work, Ms. Dulcey," I kidded halfheartedly. "I think you lost them . . . whoever them was. But your driving can scare the crap outta a body." What had really scared me was the sudden recollection that Jesse Boone had driven off from the courthouse in a black Range.

"Let's get some coffee," Dulcey said, ignoring me. We were out of the car and about to step away from the protection of the minivan and pickup truck when Dulcey blocked my steps.

"There's the car," she said, nodding in the direction of a black SUV that had pulled to the corner and signaled for a left turn. It was quick—I mean, I turned to look at the car when it was almost at the corner, almost past my point of vision, before Dulcey pulled me back into the shadows. Then it replayed in my head in slow motion—that same crooked smirk that had chilled me to the bone in the courthouse. I could have sworn . . . no . . . yes, Jesse Boone in the passenger seat, his beady eyes flitting around, looking for something or someone. Us, maybe?

Dulcey motioned me forward. "C'mon, they're gone." I froze, not ready to step from behind our wall of protection. If I thought for a moment that I had not been a victim, that somehow I had stepped over that emotional stain, the moment ended right then.

"You saw him, didn't you?" I said, almost whining. I straightened up, cleared my throat, and repeated, "You saw him?!"

"That's who I thought I saw, too. But what would Jesse Boone be doing in Boston? That's just nonsense. We're definitely losing it." Dulcey took my arm and guided me into the Stop & Shop to the Dunkin' Donuts. She ordered a regular for her and a black coffee for me.

Back at the entrance, we scoped the area for a few minutes before venturing out.

My cell phone rang as Dulcey made the turn to get on the Massachusetts Turnpike heading home again. It was the hospital. Calvin had woken up.

CHAPTER 11

A lighter air fell over me with the news about Calvin. I tried calling his room, but I got no answer. First stop back in Philly, after I cleaned myself up, the hospital.

"We were definitely being followed," Dulcey said. "Not to worry, though. I got your back, girl." She cackled and started again. "Like that time I got shot saving your behind. Man thought he had you until I smacked him down. God stepped in when he pulled a gun and it jammed."

My girl should have been a cop. She could sniff out a bad situation, size it up, make a plan, and carry it out in one swoop. Did I mention she was fearless?

"If you had stayed in the car like I told you to, everything would have worked out just fine," I said.

Dulcey came back with a vengeance. "If I had stayed in the car like you told me to, you'd be dead. Things happen for a reason, M. Besides, if that no-good husband of mine had taken care of his own mess . . . but you know, drugs do you like that. You mess with the drug man's money, you pay the price. I'm not saying he deserved to be half beat to death, but you reap what you sow, and Hamp is so hardheaded."

The only time Dulcey got teary-eyed or quiet for any length of time was when she was talking about her husband, Hampton. She'd gone through hell with him after he lost his job and got hooked up on crack, but nothing and nobody could squash her love for him, including him. Hamp was one of those guys drowning in good intentions, always trying to do the right thing and ending up in the wrong place, at the wrong time, with the wrong people for whom he was trying to do the right thing. That said, the man was truly a sweetheart.

After a while she said, "I'ma ask you again, you think Reecey is somehow involved with drugs?"

"Mmm." For once she didn't push. I turned my attention to the outside and got lost in the abstractedness of the passing scenery. I hardly paid attention to Reecey until Ma and Dad died. Then Mount Everest loomed between us, Reecey on one side, me on the other. She was *the* drama queen: sixteen going on forty, drinking, smoking weed and whatever else, looking like a hoochie mama. She needed more time than I gave her. She needed a parent.

Hell, I had just started in the Unit, a last chance to get my act together after two years spent undercover for a special task force to infiltrate the Black Mafia that damn near killed me. I was recruited when I first joined the force, not because of any special talent I possessed; rather, my youth, gender, and color matched their need. I was stupid enough, or ambitious enough or insecure enough—no, stupid enough—to accept the assignment.

For two years I siphoned information to the task force that helped them slam the Mafia and work toward putting key figures away. Then my cover was blown. Those key figures I was working to put away made me an example. They filled my veins with heroin for weeks and then left me for dead in some garbage-filled driveway surrounded by the Richard Allen Hole—what

folks called the Richard Allen Homes public housing project—
in North Philly. But by the grace of God I stand.

Anyway, keeping up with Nareece's life then when I was
struggling to save my own, did not register on my agenda.
Even with Dulcey's help, Nareece was out of control. Our conversations always escalated to screaming contests about her non-
performance in school: drinking, smoking, not eating, coming
home at all hours or not at all. Always, in the end, she stormed
up the stairs and threw out the last words, "I hate you!"

*I reached out to hug Nareece, but she turned her back
to me. "I hate you!" she screamed. Her head turned
three-sixty. "I wish you were dead. I wish I was dead."
Red spit flew from her mouth to my cheek.*

*Mini-waterfalls flowed from Mom's eyes. She reached
out to me. "Your sister needs you," she said.*

I awoke in a start, sweaty, unsure of my surroundings.

"Dream workin' you, girl," Dulcey said.

I sat up, rolled down the window, and stuck my head out a
bit to suck in the cool air. A half hour later, Dulcey pulled up in
front of the house. She threw the car in Park, reached back and
grabbed her purse from the back floor, and said, "C'mon, girl,
let's go see bout that . . ."

I was out of the car and closing my door on her last words.
The letter was in a hidden pocket at the back of my night-
stand. I tore the envelope as Dulcey sat on the bed next to me.
Inside a folded piece of paper were photos of Nareece, John,
and the twins. On the piece of paper was a typed note from
Nareece.

    M, I know there is so much I never
    told you, so much I'm sorry for. Mom

```
and Dad. I don't know what I would
have done all these years without
you. I'm so grateful for all you
did. For Travis. That he is even
here. All grown up. I wish we could
all just go away together.
Disappear and never look back. I
know you'd just tell me I'm crazy,
always living in a fantasy world.
And I guess you're right. Except
now reality is setting in. I guess
I always knew this day would come,
sooner or later. So much time has
passed, until I was beginning to
believe that everything was going
to be all right. That everything is
the way it is and the past is the
past, long gone, done. But it's not
done, Muriel. And I know that I'm
the only one who can fix it now. I
love you.
     Reecey
```

Dulcey gave me her nonsense look—eyebrows lifted, causing ripples in her forehead, lips pursed.

"Don't even ask, girl. I don't have a clue what she's talking about. What she did. Only two things I know that will make a body hunt your behind down no matter how much time passes are money and more money."

After Dulcey left, I took my jacket off and checked the messages on the house phone.

"Hi, Auntie, please call us. We're worried about Mommy and Daddy and we want to go home or come to your house. We'll be good, we promise." They spoke in unison like they were rehearsing a script. Two other messages consisted of a hang-up and a message from the hospital.

I called the hospital and learned Calvin was in stable condition, but sleeping. I held off calling the twins back. They needed answers I did not have. The prospect of them staying with me required more thought than I was capable of at present.

First, Calvin. I showered, blow-dried and curled my hair, put my face on, then slipped into black slacks, a light green sweater, and black heels.

When I entered the hospital, the smell of disinfectant mixed with butt and sick made me gag. I held my breath until I entered the elevator, then again until I entered his room. Flowers filled the room, the fragrance weighing down the breathable air. I sat in the chair next to his bed and watched him sleep. He looked peaceful, despite the white lines that peppered his face, healed scratches, and the pink scar that went from the top of his head, cut his forehead in half, and ended above the bridge of his nose. Otherwise, his brittle brown skin was smooth and wrinkle-free, despite his fifty-eight years. He looked handsome in a rugged kind of way, with a few weeks of beard growth. I squeezed my legs together to maximize the tingle and shifted back in the chair. "*Hmph, hmph, hmph.*" I planned to be there when he woke.

My phone vibrated. It was Cap. I moved out into the hallway.

"Mabley, I hope you're better and back on your feet good. I need you here. We need to talk. Now."

I told Cap I would be at the lab within an hour.

Calvin was still sleeping when I peeked back in the room. I stopped at the nurses' station to leave a message for him on the way out, in case he woke before I returned. One of the nurses said it would be at least another hour or two before the medication they'd given him wore off.

While I waited for the elevator, I said a short prayer thanking God, whom I seldom visited with words, for Calvin's life. An amen and the elevator doors opened. A stately looking black woman stepped off and brushed past me. My brain grabbed hold of a mental uneasiness that stopped my steps. I looked sideways and watched her walk down the hallway, then shook off my foolishness and got in the elevator.

I reached the lobby and called Laughton's cell. The squawk pierced my eardrums: "The number you have reached is no longer in service . . ."

I clicked off. Another call came in, unknown number. I don't usually answer unknown numbers, but with all the unknowns that were registering around me, this time I did.

"Auntie M, please come get us, please!" Rose, or maybe it was Helen, screamed.

"Honey, don't cry. What's wrong?"

"Grandma's yelling and being mean. She won't let us do nothin'. We can't go outside, we can't play in the house. All she lets us do is sit around and do nothin'. Everything we do is wrong."

"*Mrl*," John's mother, Ama, said. She had taken the phone from the twin. She had her own way of saying my name, but I couldn't understand anything else she said. She ranted for what seemed forever in Vietnamese without taking a breath.

"Ama, I can't understand you."

"They are upset. No Nareece. No John. Come to get them. They should not be here. I cannot . . ." And she took off again in unintelligible garble.

"Ama, stop!" I yelled. It took her a few more sentences to quiet so I could talk. "I'll get the girls as soon as I can. I'll call you back to let you know when. You have to handle it for a little while longer. Maybe a few days." She stayed silent. "Ama?"

"Yes, okay. I wait."

"Let me speak to one of the girls, please."

"Hi, Auntie, it's Rose again."

"Listen, you girls need to calm down and behave. I'll come in a few days, on the weekend. You're not hurt, are you?"

Rose sniffled. "No, Auntie. We'll be good until you come."

I heard Helen crying in the background. "I-i-i-iss she coming?" she said with a bubbling sound.

Rose said, "Where's Mommy and Daddy? We're scared because they haven't called and they're not answering their phones."

"Don't worry, baby. Everything's going to be all right. Put Helen on."

Helen was snorting like she had been crying long and hard. "Auntie . . . please . . . come . . ." she begged.

"I'm going to come and get you. But you're going to have to be good for a few more days until I can get there, okay?"

"We . . . love . . . you." She snorted after each word.

I could hear Rose in the background trying to reassure and comfort her sister. "Don't worry, Hel," she said. "Auntie'll fix everything."

Then the line went dead.

"I love you, too," I mumbled to dead space.

My head spun. I fell into a seat in the lobby of the hospital. My stomach flip-flopped and I gagged. A passing nurse stopped and asked if I needed help. I couldn't answer. She left for a few minutes, then returned with an ice pack, slapped it against her hand, and set it on the back of my neck.

I managed a smile. "Flashing," I huffed.

Seemed I spent my days on edge, waiting for the next one to happen, hoping and praying it wouldn't be in the captain's office or while out on assignment, or in a crowded elevator or a store or a movie theater . . . The only two places that worked were in my car or at home alone, where I could scream, shout, dump cold water on myself or ice down my shirt, or jump out of my clothes. I smiled and shook my head at the thought of my aunt Moo, yes, Aunt Moo was her name, jumping around and shouting, talking about the Lord having put the heat in her and how He would lead her to the cool waters of salvation, her version of the true meaning and purpose of "the Change."

"Hot flashes? I got them, too," the nurse said and laughed with me. "You might want to see your doctor and get some medication to help get you through."

"I'm okay now. Thanks again." When I got up, I stumbled forward a bit like a drunk, then pulled it together and sauntered out. I heard my nana's squeaking voice saying, "*Getting old is not for sissies.*" Hell, I was only forty-nine. What was old? More like being a woman was not for sissies. We are the grand, awesome, wonderful, beautiful gender, but our calling was definitely not for sissies. No, it was definitely the "old" part that was freaking me out, making me feel like I was past my prime, done, with no brilliance left to attract, never mind keep, a man. Oh, but wait, I had never been able to do that up till now anyway—keep a man. I shook off the negative thoughts and went for the exit.

Outside, the cool breeze revived me.

⚜

The lab was empty and dark except for a few desk lamps left on and the lights in Cap's office at the far end of the room. There were no windows in the lab since we were in the basement. The only light was artificial. I allowed the desk lamps to light my way, not wanting to bear the harshness of the overhead fluorescents. I set my bag on my desk and started toward Cap's office, then I noticed that Laughton's desk was cleaned off—none of the usual mounds of bullets, gun parts, and guns decorating it. Never before in seventeen years.

The top half of Cap's office door was glass, so I could see him hunched over his desk in intense concentration as I approached. When I knocked and went in, he quickly closed the file he was examining and shoved it into his side drawer.

"Sit down."

I obeyed.

"You know, your partner quit this morning."

I popped back up. "What do you mean, quit?"

"He handed in his badge and gun."

I squeaked out, "Laughton?" I paced and circled the room.

"You have another partner? Yes, Laughton!"

"Okay, so you're telling me that Laughton just walked in and gave you his gun and badge without any explanation."

"That's what I'm telling you. Sit down, damn it, you're making me dizzy. He said he had some other business and it was time to call it quits here."

"Yeah, right. I just talked to him, and he didn't happen to mention that he had quit. He was . . ." I hesitated. I didn't want to tell Cap that Laughton was drunk when I last talked to him.

"I'll hold off from putting in his papers for a few days, until you have a chance to talk to him. And you're going to have to check in with Parker to get back on schedule. We got too many cases pending. The commissioner has his fist rammed up my ass."

"Okay, okay, I got it. But listen, Cap, Reecey is in some kind of trouble. She's disappeared, her and John." I pulled the note she wrote me from my pocket and handed it to him. "She sent this to me, but it doesn't make a helluva lot of sense."

I told him about the trip to Boston—the run-in with an unknown assailant, John's dismissive attitude, and the black SUV that had tailed us. I ended with the phone call I'd received from the twins. When I finished talking, Cap looked like he was having a hot flash himself, sweat dripping down the sides of his flushed face.

"If you weren't like my own daughter . . . You got a week, Mabley. Find Nareece and take care of your nieces. I'll get Parker to partner up with Johnson and Huy. Now get outta here."

"Thanks, Cap." Before I closed the door, Cap squawked, "And keep me posted."

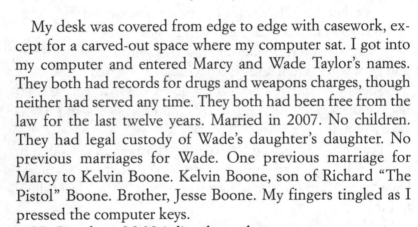

My desk was covered from edge to edge with casework, except for a carved-out space where my computer sat. I got into my computer and entered Marcy and Wade Taylor's names. They both had records for drugs and weapons charges, though neither had served any time. They both had been free from the law for the last twelve years. Married in 2007. No children. They had legal custody of Wade's daughter's daughter. No previous marriages for Wade. One previous marriage for Marcy to Kelvin Boone. Kelvin Boone, son of Richard "The Pistol" Boone. Brother, Jesse Boone. My fingers tingled as I pressed the computer keys.

No Laughton McNair listed anywhere.

I sat in front of Laughton's apartment without any memory of driving there—always a scary thought to have been on the road driving for miles and not realize the journey had happened until after the fact. The bell went unanswered, so I tried the doorknob. The door pushed open, the lock broken. I pulled my gun and went inside. The place was empty except for trash strewn across the floor. A rancid odor of funk mixed with a hint of ammonia permeated the air and made me gag. I moved through, room by room, the same smell in each room. The closets and cabinets were cleared out.

Laughton's next-door neighbor said Laughton had moved out a week ago. Said three men came the night before and kicked the door in, which explained the broken lock. She called the police, but the men left before they arrived. She had no information about a forwarding address, but she pointed me to the landlord's unit around the corner. The landlord did not answer the door.

I sat in the car, numbed by all I thought I knew, or rather all I did not know, about Laughton. We had a permanent link, at least I thought we did, no matter what, when, where. It went that deep. "I just talked to him and he doesn't happen to mention he quit, never mind he moved," I said out loud. I scanned my memory trying to recall something that would have led down this path to move Laughton off the reservation.

Then there was Marcy Taylor, whom he said he was once married to, but there was no record of that in the files. Ever since she committed suicide or got murdered, whichever, Laughton had been acting weird. I tried his cell again—no answer. I needed to find Laughton, but with no known next of kin or friends outside of the department and me that I knew of, I supposed I would have to wait for him to contact me. I returned to the hospital, so I would be there when Calvin woke up.

When I walked into Calvin's hospital room, he was engaged in a fit of laughter that had him coughing and choking and brought a nurse running to his bedside. His coconspirator was a beautiful young woman who shared his fine features and dusty brown curly hair. Her haircut, short to her head, intensified her gray-blue eyes.

"You must be Muriel," she said, regaining control, but not quite. The expression on my face must have told her I did not appreciate being the butt of their laughter. "Oh no, please." She came toward me with an outstretched hand. "I'm Shea, Calvin's little sister." She gestured for me to take her place at Calvin's bedside. "Believe me, the good news is that you didn't arrive a few minutes earlier. You were definitely saved from the disgusting outputs that escaped my not-so-classy big brother. Reminds me of when we were kids—"

Calvin interrupted. "TMI. Put all my business out in the street, why don't you?" he scolded, but not really.

"I'm happy you're back," I said. I leaned down to kiss him. He captured my arm and held me in place for a much longer kiss than I intended, especially with Little Sis at my back.

She cleared her throat and said, "Well, time for me to exit right."

I gently pulled away.

"Don't stop on my account," she said. "I'm leaving anyway. Unfortunately I didn't get away in time, before being assaulted, that is." She laughed. "I have to get back to work. It is a pleasure to meet you." She blew Calvin a kiss and left.

"I thought I'd lost you—" I said. He pulled me down and kissed me again, cutting off my words.

He let go and said, "I thought so, too. I decided to hang around because I had you to discover." He kissed my hand.

"I am so sorry about this."

"You don't have anything to be sorry about. It certainly wasn't your fault. I was driving. When I first woke up, I thought *you* were dead. I fell all out of the bed trying to get to someone to find out what happened to you. Almost killed myself for real," he said, laughing lightly.

"So, when can you get outta here?"

"They don't keep you in the hospital for long anymore. Your eyes are open, you're out. I'm going home on Tuesday."

We sat in silence for a good while, holding hands, letting the television fill in the spaces. For the first time in weeks, my shoulders released.

A nurse came in and gave Calvin more pills. Not long after, he went to sleep, but not before confirming I would return Tuesday to take him home.

Travis arrived home the same time I did. "Hey, Moms."

When we walked in the entryway, I could smell the greenery. I looked closer—glassy eyes, simple smile. Visions of my perfect child disintegrated. And so they should have long ago. Silly mother. He started upstairs.

"Travis, are you high? No, let me rephrase. You're high."

Still walking upstairs, he said, "I smoked a little weed, what's the big deal?"

"Boy, you must be losing your mind."

He stopped halfway up the stairs and spun around to face me, looking down.

"What are you getting all bent out of shape about? It's not like I'm a drug addict or something." He rolled his eyes and said, "God forbid."

My whole body shook. "I'm a cop, for chrissakes. You're a cop's son." The words made sense before they came out of my mouth. Then they sounded dumb, self-righteously dumb.

"Mom, please, give it a rest. I know all about being your son, and how I'm supposed to act. Cut me some slack, will ya?"

I knew if I started up those steps, I would lose total control and probably regret whatever actions resulted. Instead, I sucked in all the air I could hold into my lungs, let go, and said, "We need to talk. Now is not the best time, but before the night is done, once you sober up."

He made an about-face and continued up the stairs.

Then Dulcey was at my door. How she did it always amazed me, but she always showed up at the right time with just what I needed. This time it was Caribbean food and Gewurztraminer wine. The wine was flowery. The perfume bouquet offset the jerk-seasoned food perfectly.

While we ate, I filled Dulcey in on my visit with Calvin and meeting his sister. "First time I let myself even consider growing old with someone."

"Oh, please. You know you always wanted someone to grow old with. Don't know anyone who'd want to go there alone." She sipped her wine. "Why you think I put up with Hamp's mess?"

"You love Hampton's dirty drawers, that's why." We laughed to the depths that make you gasp for air and drive tears down your cheeks. I laughed; Dulcey cackled, her whole body shaking like she was having an epileptic fit. The commotion brought Travis downstairs, so he said. I knew he needed to satisfy the munchies. He and Dulcey hugged, then Travis made a plate and went back upstairs.

"Travis good?"

"Travis is high, in case you didn't notice." Dulcey signaled for me to keep my voice down. I spoke louder. "I'm going to go upside the boy's head if he doesn't straighten up."

"Oh Lord. Boy been straight as an arrow for nineteen years, give him a little room, Muriel. He'll be fine. He's practically on his own now at college, and believe you me, he doesn't want to disappoint Mama M."

"I guess I never thought he'd get into drugs. I'm a cop, for chrissakes."

"All the more reason you need to lighten up and talk to him. And he's not into drugs, he's just smoking a little weed. What's the harm? Boy's grown now, out on his own."

"Oh, for crying out loud, you sound just like him. Sure, he's out on his own nine months out of the year when he's at school, and all the way on my dime."

"Best way. I'm sure there's a lot you don't know. Ain't nobody as good as that boy makes out to be. It's because he's a cop's son that he got sense enough to keep his stuff under wraps. Give him a little space, girl. He's all right. He's no worse than his mother or his auntie was at his age, I'm sure."

"I know that's right, and that's exactly what worries me."

A moment of silence fell after Dulcey's words, each of us in our own heads. We looked at each other and busted out laughing while Dulcey refilled our glasses.

My laughter turned to anxiety again.

"Dulcey, what am I going to do? I can't stay in the department without Laughton. He quit, don't you know. Forty-nine and I have to start over, and Laughton, who is he anyway? Not the man I've known and worked with for seventeen years, and where the hell is he? What the hell is going on with him? What the hell's going on with Travis? What the hell's going on with Nareece? What the hell's going on, period?"

"Slow down, girl. Take a breath. What do you mean, Laughton quit?"

"Just what I said, he quit. And Travis, and his high self, trying to put something over on me. He knows better. And the twins. John's mother talking like I'm supposed to understand a word she said. And Nareece and John, where the hell are they, and what the hell are they into that they can abandon their own children? What am I going to do with two little girls playing detective and shooting up the place? They're babies, Dulcey. I can't believe Nareece would leave them, like she doesn't care. Like you said, always only thinking about her."

"Ahhh. At last, the truth spews from your lips." She sipped more wine. "Look, girl, you got a lot on your plate to deal with, and deal with fast. And you don't have a choice. You have to take care of those babies. They can stay with me until this is all put to rest."

"You're right. I do need to take care of them. I'm the only auntie."

"And your life ain't dependin' on Laughton, so scratch that thought right now."

By the fourth glass of wine, we were stumbling up the stairs to my bedroom, glasses and wine in hand. I pulled out some silk pajamas for Dulcey.

"Girl, give me some old T-shirt or something. I can't sleep in these, won't fit anyway."

"I don't own any old T-shirts. I spend enough time in man clothes with that damn uniform," I said, pulling out a night-gown for me. "They'll fit, I bought them for you. Now, put them on."

The fifth glass of wine sealed the night for both of us.

CHAPTER 12

No Dulcey when I woke the next morning in a pool of sweat, my nightgown slicked to my body. I rolled over, my head dancing with the unpleasant aftereffects of overindulgence. A pink Post-it on her pillow had "*I got your back!*" scribbled out with a smiley face at the bottom.

I reached for my cell phone on the nightstand and checked the time. Nine o'clock, and no kiss good-bye from Travis. I jumped up, staggered forward, and fell back on the bed, my head still unwilling, my body unbalanced.

"Travis." No answer.

This time I got up slowly and shuffled to his bedroom door. I called again louder. No answer. Agitated, I did something I never do, knocked and went in without waiting for his invite. His bed was made and everything in its place, but no Travis. He was avoiding me, no doubt. Getting through the day without a good-bye kiss would be difficult, especially having had harsh words as our last. It was our rule to never leave the house without kissing each other good-bye. My mom had made the rule, and I had not kissed her when I left the house the night she and Dad died. Instead, we had argued about Nareece. I quickly shook off the memory and went for the shower, hoping to minimize the pain that skirted the edges of my temple.

I emerged with a clearer head but an unforgiving body and slipped into jeans, a sweatshirt, and boots, and limped across the hall to my office. First on the agenda was retrieving the twins. Just thinking about driving to Boston again made my head ache worse. So I decided to fly. I flicked on the computer, then grabbed the bottle of Excedrin from the shelf above. I swallowed two, then a third.

John's mother, Ama, was clearly overwhelmed with the twins. She had kept them many times before without incident, so I gathered this time the twins were anxious about their parents and unleashing that anxiety on her. I also figured Nareece wouldn't be happy with the idea of the twins staying with me. Too many times we had planned a summer or winter vacation stay, only for Nareece to cancel at the last minute with a clear message that the girls didn't need any more of my unsavory ideas about crime fighting lodged in their pretty little heads. How I wished she was here to protest now.

"Where are you?" I said out loud.

I went to the JetBlue website and made reservations for Saturday; they could survive two more days. When I opened the top drawer for notepaper to write down the confirmation number, the Mabley case folder sat on top of everything.

I took out paper and a pencil and closed the drawer, then pulled it open again and took the folder out. I still didn't know why Laughton had the folder or how he'd even known it existed. I flipped it open and began reading from where I'd left off earlier.

Nareece was alleged to have been involved in local drug activity with named members of the Boone family.

My head spun. I had closed my eyes all these years, in complete denial.

I continued reading.

The last sentence on the fifth page caught my attention. It read: *The victim said one man smelled like a "funky dead person" that made her throw up while he was raping her. When the man finished, he pulled out a knife* . . . I stopped reading.

I called Nareece's cell and left another message, then called John and did the same. Laughton's phone still registered disconnected. A call to Cap got me another number for Laughton. One ring and it went to voice mail. While I was leaving a message, Laughton called.

"What's up?" For a moment he sounded like the old Laughton, taunting me.

"You quit?"

"M, I can't explain now. I told you, I need some time."

"You sound like a recording. Time for what? You're not making any sense." I struggled to keep my voice at a reasonable octave. When he didn't respond, I thought he had hung up. In a softer tone I pleaded a little, "Laughton? Laughton, where are you? Let's meet and talk. I'm going to get the twins, but let's talk first."

"Just get Rose and Helen, Muriel, and keep them with you until this is over. I'll call you." Then he hung up.

I quickly redialed and got voice mail. I redialed again with the same result, which agitated my fury. My hands were trembling when I set my cell on the desk and fell back in the chair. Laughton sounded almost vicious. Not like he wanted to brutalize someone, but more like he was fighting for his life or someone else's and losing. Fear.

What I did know about Laughton was that he would not give empty warnings. I needed to go to Boston and get the twins. I called Dulcey. She didn't answer, which made me freak out a little. That was when Travis came home and went to his room without a word—no kiss, no "Hi, Moms." I banged on his door. When he didn't open it fast enough, I rushed in. He was sitting on the bed, bent over, his head resting in his hands. He looked up with tear-filled eyes. My anger immediately dissipated, as I swooped in with motherly concern.

"What happened? Are you all right?" I wrapped my arms around him. "Are you hurt?" I pulled back to check him out.

"I broke up with Kenyetta."

I stopped short. "Okay. So, what's the problem? *You* broke up with her."

"She messed around on me, with one of my boys."

"You know that for a fact?" He didn't answer. "Well, do you?"

"I didn't see with my own eyes, no. But everyone in my crew—"

"How many times have I told you, don't fall into those holes, believing what other folks put on you?"

"A thousand."

"Good, you understand. Now, let me fill you in on something else. I don't go for you coming home high and having parties, serving liquor. I will slap you silly, boy. I don't give a damn how grown you think you are."

"Yeah, I got you."

"You got me?" I rose up, about to explode.

He slumped on the bed. "I mean, I'm sorry. I'll clean up my act. I'm just trying to fit in."

I tucked in my feathers and settled back down.

"I understand, but being somebody you're not isn't the way."

He straightened up and turned to me. "So, what's up with you, Moms? I hear what's happening even when you think I don't."

I might have been caught off guard, except it was good we were talking about things that really mattered between us. Maybe this was the time. Then again, maybe not.

I started in with, "I'm worried about your aunt and uncle."

He groaned. I gave him my *Don't go there* look and continued. "I made reservations to fly up on Saturday. John's mother can't handle the twins, and your aunt and uncle have gone off the reservation. The flight costs a small fortune, so I'm going to rent a car to get back." I decided not to fill him in on any details or tell him about Laughton's warning, my real reason for going sooner. What I told him was that Nareece and John were in some kind of mess they'd chosen not to share and had left the girls at John's mother's house, where they were very unhappy and calling every day for me to come get them. So, I would go to the house and get some more clothes for them, swing around and pick them up at John's mother's house, and bring them home.

Travis hugged me and said, "No problem. Cancel the flight. I'll ride up with you, save some bucks."

I called Dulcey to ride with us, too.

I spent most of the next two days at the hospital with Calvin. That is, after I made several calls to Laughton that went unanswered, and several calls to Nareece that went unanswered. The sleepless nights had me sleeping away most of my visits, while Calvin watched television.

"Tell me why you're driving up to Boston again?" Calvin asked during one of my awake moments.

"My sister and her husband have taken off, to put it mildly. Their kids' grandmother is having a hard time caring for them, so I'm going to get them and let them stay with me for a while."

"Where have their parents taken off to?"

"That is the question of the decade."

"You may need some muscle with you," Calvin joked lightly.

"And who might you be referring to?"

"Seriously, Muriel, be careful. I'm not sure about any of this and I don't even know what any of this is, really, but it sounds like more than you're saying. I feel so friggin' helpless, laid up in this damn hospital."

"I'll be fine. Travis and Dulcey are traveling with me for the company. We'll slip in to the house, get some things, and slip out, no problem. My detective friend in Boston said no one has even been seen at the house in weeks, so I'm not concerned. We should be home Sunday with plenty of time to break you out on Tuesday."

"Not to worry, I got family."

When we picked up Dulcey Friday evening, she shuffled to the car, makeup running, hairdo lopsided, shirt stained, and wearing dilapidated espadrilles. Girl was tapped. From the window I could see customers three deep in the waiting area. Dulcey had reduced her workload, taking customers by appointment only, since the shop had grown to ten chairs and a full spa that offered services from marine seaweed body wraps to ultrasonic facials, and she'd hired a manager. Still, she worked day and night, far more than she'd planned.

She didn't even protest about me driving. Two hours into the six-hour ride, Dulcey's chatter stopped and she and Travis both fell asleep.

I had visions of Nareece on the bed, naked and bloodied, Mom at the stove stirring and pleading with me to talk to Nareece. A horn startled me and made the road a priority again before more visions moved in, this time of a more nostalgic nature: Dad on the phone, police at the door, Travis in the nursery, Nareece waving good-bye, Laughton, Calvin.

"Welcome to Massachusetts," Dulcey read out loud, rescuing me from my thoughts. "Dang, girl, seems like we just left."

Travis stirred but stayed asleep, stretched across the back-

seat. It was four in the morning, so we planned to stop at Nareece's house and rest up before going for the twins. I also
needed to gather more clothes for them.

"Have you tried Reecey's cell lately?" Dulcey asked.

"At least one hundred times a day." I turned to make sure
Travis was still sleeping. "Bates hasn't had any developments,
either. It's like she and John have disappeared off the face of
the earth. The only saving grace is that she's called so I know
she's alive." My stomach rumbled, but not from hunger.

When we arrived, I drove into the driveway up to the front
door. The house was dark. I surmised it was supposed to be
dark since John and Nareece were not home. I reached back
and shook Travis's leg to wake him. "C'mon, baby, we're going
to stay here for a few hours."

"Looks like a scene from a horror movie, girl. I'm shaking,
especially after last time," Dulcey said, straining her neck to
view the whole house.

"Don't worry, Auntie, I'll protect you," Travis said, sitting
up and pounding his chest with both fists. "Man of steel, right
here." He opened the car door and leaned out. "Stay behind
me," he demanded in his macho-man tone, scratchy from
sleep. We chuckled just a little.

"Travis, wait a minute," I said, scrambling to get out and
keep him from going to the door alone. Dulcey jumped out,
ran around to the driver's side, and fell in step behind me, all
up on my back and carrying on.

"Both of you just stop," I said, shaking her loose and straightening up. I walked up to the front door, inserted the key, and
pushed. Immediately a rank smell took my breath and caused a
yelp to escape my lips. "Please, God," I whispered, rushing in
and flicking the light switch to the right of the door. Travis followed on my heels, but the smell forced him back outside,
where he puked. I tugged on my ankle holster and tossed the .22

to Dulcey. She pulled her outer blouse up to cover her nose and moved toward the living room while I started up the stairs. I hit the doorway of the master bedroom and immediately caught sight of John, sprawled out on the floor at the end of the bed. I gagged and worked through the tears that glazed my eyes. I stepped over his body and went to check the bathroom and closets, moved back into the hall to the twins' room, the two guest rooms, and two more bathrooms, whipping back shower curtains—point, rush, clear, point, rush, clear.

"Clear!" Dulcey yelled up.

I holstered my weapon, ran to the bathroom, and puked.

Dulcey and Travis were up the stairs and in the bedroom doorway before I could stop them. The sight forced both of them back, almost causing them to topple down the stairs.

In the bedroom, a dark maroon stain outlined John's upper body. His face was turned toward me, bloodied and bloated from decomposition. He was barefoot and shirtless. There were dark ligature marks around his neck, wrists, and ankles. I bent over his body and noticed a tube of ChapStick wedged between his thigh and the floor. I figured fists had pounded his face and driven into his blackened chest and stomach; a stranglehold cut off his breath. I could only pray that John had kept his secret to the end.

CHAPTER 13

"So far we've got nothing on this killing. No one in the neighborhood saw or heard a thing. This guy is squeaky clean."

"John. His name is John," I said. I was sitting on the couch. Bates loomed over me.

"Muriel," he said, "I'm sorry about your friend's husband. But what happened to the trust, to the loyalty, to helping each other out on the up and up?"

He went to John's desk and got the desk chair, half-dragging and half-carrying the ugly monstrosity over to me and straddled it, then rested his arms crisscrossed on the chair back. I could smell his breath, minty from the gum he snapped every few chews.

The sweats attacked, but I did not flinch.

"You need to tell me what the deal is, Muriel." His voice was low and gurgly.

A moment passed and he leaned back a bit.

"Look, I don't mean to be an asshole. I'm not an insensitive guy. But you got me running around with my dick in my hands and spraying cold water on me with a fucking fire hose. What happened to you stroke mine and I'll stroke yours?"

"Nice talk, Bates. No need to be such a pig."

He sighed with an air of disgust.

I turned to face Dulcey and Travis. Dulcey locked eyes with me and nodded. She sat next to Travis at the dining room table with her arm around his shoulders. Travis sat with his back straight, his attention taken by an officer standing over him writing something on a notepad.

"I'm in the dark, too," I said.

His heavy breathing subsided. "Well then, at least tell me what you've got."

"I came to get some clothes for the girls because they are going to spend some time with me. The house was dark. I used my key. I came in and found John."

"Where are the girls?"

"They're staying at John's mother's house in Newton."

"And your girlfriend?" He glimpsed the picture of Nareece he held. "Or is she your sister?" He tapped the picture against his free hand.

I relented. "Okay, Bates, she's my sister. And I don't know where she is."

"You certainly don't look alike."

"Different fathers," I snarled.

An officer beckoned him to the side. I watched as the officer spoke to him in a low tone. Bates's unruly bush hair contradicted the neatly trimmed full beard. His mustache curled over his top lip and showed gray speckles. He wore a crisp, long-sleeved white shirt open at the collar with a loosened black and red tie, embroidered initials on the cuffs. A shoulder holster hugged his left side and held a standard-issue 9 mm Glock. He looked ten years younger than his fifty, easy, I thought.

"Where were we?" Bates resumed his position straddling the chair. "Why the masquerade?"

"It's just remnants from an old story, nothing to do with any of this. Or at least I don't think it does. My sister was attacked twenty years ago and left for dead. Her attackers were never caught, so I moved her to Boston, gave her a new identity. Nobody knows who she is . . . was." Suddenly I was unsure I believed what I was saying. Bates read my thoughts.

"You don't sound convinced that this has nothing to do with that old business. You're going to get someone else hurt if you're not careful." He got up, pushing the chair sideways and gestured toward the living room, where Dulcey and Travis sat. "If that's all you have, get your son, your friend, and your nieces and go home. Back to Philly. This is way out of your jurisdiction, and if you ask me, I'd say you're too close."

I pounced like a lioness gone wild. "You can't shut me out, Bates!"

His bloodshot eyes laid into me like fireballs, but I held his stare.

"She's my sister." He kept his stance and did not react. I crumbled and pleaded, "I need to be in on this, please, Bates."

He walked away for a few steps and came back. "Stay in touch."

Another officer approached him and reported preliminary findings. No forced entry. No fingerprints in the bedroom, but maybe some on a tube of ChapStick found near the body. A lot of fingerprints throughout the house—might find one that doesn't belong. Been dead at least five days. Cause of death, most likely internal bleeding, more after autopsy. Neighbor did not see anyone enter or exit in the last week except for the victim last Saturday and the ladies who came in tonight. Neighbor said a dark-colored SUV came and left a few days ago, no plate number or vehicle type.

I whipped around to give Bates my back. The sound of my breathing filled my head like I was deep-sea diving. Jesse Boone?

Traffic was light on Route 128 as we approached the Massachusetts Turnpike to get to the Crown Plaza Hotel that hung over the highway. It was three o'clock in the afternoon when we arrived. Travis took a seat in the lobby and had fallen asleep by the time the clerk gave us the room keys. I woke him and guided him to his room, where he fell into bed fully clothed. I pulled the covers over him and went to an adjourning room.

My phone rang as I closed the connecting door. I didn't recognize the number, so I figured it was Bates calling with more information or a new development.

"Muriel Mabley."

A long silence filled in before Nareece said, "It's me." My heart raced.

"Reece, are you all right?" She did not answer.

Dulcey quickly moved from the table to the bed and sat close enough to share the receiver with me.

"Where are you?"

"Somewhere they can't find me, for now anyway."

"Reece, what's going on? Who's 'they'?"

"I went to the house and the police were there. I went home to meet John." More silence. "John's dead, isn't he?"

"Yes."

"M, I'm so sorry. I never thought anyone would get hurt. I never thought anyone would care after all these years. It's been so long, and I guess I thought it was over with. I wish I was never even born."

"Reecey, is this about the letter? Did you open it? Tell me where you are so I can come get you."

"The girls, oh Muriel, my babies." She cried, "Oh God, if something happens to them, I'll kill myself. I won't want to live. I don't want to live without John, without my babies."

"Reece, tell me where you are. We'll figure this out together, like we always do."

"They killed John, and they want to kill me. They said they would if I didn't give them what they wanted. That's what the letter said. If they find out where the girls are, they'll hurt them, too."

"Who killed John? Who was the letter from?"

"Muriel, you can't let them find the girls."

"Nareece, calm down. I'll take care of the girls."

Dulcey moved back to the table and scribbled something on a notepad and showed me.

"Reecey, Rose and Helen deserve better. They've already lost their father, they need you. They need you to take care of them, Reece. Now, tell me where you are so I can help you."

"They don't need me. I'm no good for them. They would be much better off with you, M. Like Travis. Muriel, I should never have taken it."

"Taken what, Reece?"

No response.

"Look, Reecey, whatever it is, we'll fix it."

"I don't want anyone else to get hurt because of me. It's all so stupid. Now John's gone, and for what? It's all for nothing, M, absolutely nothing. I should've died that night. You should've let me die."

"Well, you didn't die. You got married and you had two children, two beautiful little girls who love you. They want *you*, Reecey. Do you understand that? They want to grow up with their mother."

"Dulcey with you?"

"Yes."

"Can I talk to her?"

Dulcey took the phone.

"Hey, baby. You listen to Muriel and tell us where you are."

"I just want you to know that I love you."

"I love you, too, and I want you to be all right."

"I gotta go. I'll call back."

"Reecey, don't hang up." But she did.

"You know where she is." It was a statement, not a question from Dulcey.

"Yeah."

"What are you going to do?"

"I'm going to go get her, but . . ." I started and Dulcey finished my sentence.

"First we're going to get the twins."

"We'll go early and try to beat the police if they haven't already notified Ama. You take the girls and Travis back to Philly. I'll rent a car and get Nareece."

"Sounds like a plan, though I should be with you."

"You're the only one I can depend on, Dulcey. The only one I trust. You have to take care of the kids."

CHAPTER 14

The next morning we were on the road by seven o'clock, on the way to John's mother's house.

As I drove down Curve Street in Newton, an ambulance parked in front of Ama's house pulled away from the curb, followed by a police car.

The one-way street was lined on both sides with older colonials, capes, and ranch homes of various sizes and colors squashed together for a neighborly effect. His mother's house was a gray colonial with red shutters and shared a common need for paint with the other houses. A young woman and the twins ran from the porch to the street, as the vehicles were driven away.

The twins jumped up and down, crying, screaming, and waving. Their heads full of braids bounced in every direction, making them look spastic. As we got closer, I recognized the young woman as John's baby sister, Debbie. She struggled to catch the twins' flailing arms and avoid having her face slapped in the doing. She had barely gained control of them when they caught sight of our car and ran into the street to greet us.

One twin ran around to my window. The only way to tell the

two apart was a tiny scar Rose had under her left eye, a battle scar from defending Helen against a playground bully in preschool. Helen was at the window. I told her to back away until I parked. I pulled into the driveway and could barely open the car door and get out for their crowding and jockeying for position.

Rose won forward space. "They took Ba to the hospital, but she's gonna git better," she said.

Debbie caught my eye, making shapes with her mouth to communicate they did not know about their father. The twins bounced up and down in front of me, trying to wrap their arms around my neck. They were almost as big as me, so there was no picking them up. Instead they wrapped their arms around me, one on either side, and we two-stepped our way to the porch and up the stairs.

The wide porch, encased by windows, led into a darkened hallway. To the right was the living room. Farther down on the left, a stairway went halfway up and turned the corner to the second floor. The hallway emptied into a small kitchen with counters on three sides and a round table set in the middle, leaving little room to move between the sink and stove. The twins released me once we were in the kitchen, and I plopped down in a kitchen chair, spent and sweaty. Dulcey gained Debbie's permission through sign language of sorts, then opened and closed cabinet doors until she found glasses and brought me a glass of cold water.

"Auntie, are you sick?" they said in unison, which on a good day worked on my sanity and sometimes made me want to put the little darlings out of their misery—in unison. This was anything but a good day.

Travis gained their attention. "We finally meet. You guys are a lot smaller than I thought."

"You're Travis?" they said in unison, scrunching up their noses while backing away to get a better stance for sizing him up. They had only met Travis through phone conversations.

"Yeah, I'm Travis. And Auntie's fine, so let's go outside." He ushered them toward the back door off the kitchen to the backyard. I got up and followed them.

"We're going to be detectives," Rose squealed, commandeering Travis's arm and taking the lead to the outdoors.

"Yeah, we're going to be detectives, like Auntie," Helen echoed.

"So you wanna catch bad guys?" Travis said, letting Rose lead him to a swing set in the far corner of the yard.

Rose said, "Yep. We're gonna be the baddest detectives in Philly."

"In Philly? You're going to move to Philly?"

I closed the door and watched from the window. Each twin got on a swing, and Travis pushed them. Their giggles filled my ears. They fit with Travis as though they had always been together.

"Ma said you, you, you were co . . . coming," Debbie said, gasping for air and snorting through tears. I went back to the table and sat down. Debbie was a tiny young woman—five feet, ninety-five pounds on a heavy day. At eight, the twins matched her stature. I met her once ten years ago at John and Reece's wedding. Now she was twenty-one, and studied economics at Suffolk University in Boston.

Dulcey gave her a tissue and she honked like a 1920s car horn.

"Ma collapsed when the police called and told her about John. I think she had a heart attack. If Jerry hadn't been here . . ." She whimpered and blew snot again, mostly missing the tissue. Dulcey passed her more. "He'll call from the hospital." She hung her head and twisted her fingers. "I couldn't bring myself to tell them about John. They're already upset because they haven't seen their parents in weeks." She looked up at me and reached across the table. "You will tell them?"

"Yes. Not now, though. They won't be doing anything with John's body until after an autopsy."

Debbie's face puckered.

I reached across the table and covered her hands with mine. "I'm sorry. I didn't mean to . . ." I squeezed her hands and let silence finish my sentence.

After a short pause, I said, "Debbie, your mother called me a few days ago really upset. She said she was concerned because of the twins' behavior, but I think other matters were pressing. I didn't understand most of what she said because she spoke in Vietnamese. Do you have any idea what was going on?"

"Mom said she got a phone call from somebody who threatened to hurt the girls if she did not tell them where John and Nareece were. I told her to call the police. She wouldn't. That's the only other thing I can think of that made her upset." She hesitated, then continued, "Sometimes Rose and Helen are hard to handle."

"Did she know where John and Nareece were?"

"No, I don't think so. She hadn't heard a word from them since they dropped off the girls, except when you and John called that day."

"Do you know if she has received any more threatening calls?"

"I don't think so. She didn't say anything about any others." She reached in the pocket of her sweater and pulled out a letter-sized manila envelope. "I almost forgot. I found this stuck under the door this morning." She handed me the envelope.

The envelope contained photos of John and Nareece holding hands and walking along the Charles River in Cambridge near Harvard Square. Other photos included the twins playing in their backyard in Milton, and John and Nareece getting out of their Lexus here, with the twins. The last picture showed

John, sprawled out on the bedroom floor. I put the pictures back in the envelope and handed them to Dulcey, who had been quiet. Unusual for her.

"I didn't show them to Ma, only Jerry," Debbie said. "Then the police called and she collapsed. Jerry said not to show them to anyone, especially not the police." She gave me a wide-eyed look, like she'd just realized I was the police. As quick as the look came, it disappeared and Debbie's tears flowed again. "Who . . . who . . . who would want to hurt John anyway? And what about Nareece? What if . . ." Her chest heaved as she wound up for another round of sputtering. "Wha . . . wha . . . what if they find her and then come . . . come after the twins?"

"I'm going to find Nareece." I got up and headed toward the door to call the twins in. "Right now we're going to get the girls ready to go."

The twins took turns sitting in the clutches of Dulcey's thighs getting their hair rebraided. While Dulcey worked on Helen's hair, I went upstairs and helped Rose pack their belongings, including a laptop and briefcase filled with papers. Rose said the briefcase was the Twofer Detective Agency's portable office.

I put the last pair of blue jeans in one suitcase and snapped the top closed, then focused on the second.

"Auntie, bad men want to hurt Mom and Dad," Rose said as though she'd misbehaved. I sat on the bed and gathered her in my arms. She continued, "We heard them talking the day before they brought us here. Daddy said they had to go away for a little while."

"Did he say why?"

"No, but Mommy was crying. She said she made them get in trouble. A time before two scary men came to the house, and Mommy made us go to our room and close the door."

"Did you recognize the men?"

"No." She moved away and put more clothes in her bag. "Ba's worried, that's why she got sick."

"I think you're right. But I'm going to be with your mom soon, and we'll straighten everything out. You'll be home again in no time. And so will your grandmother." I got up and helped her snap the second suitcase closed. We rolled both to the stairwell. Rose went in front and backed down the stairs holding the ends of each while I steadied the tops. Halfway down Travis hoisted both bags in one swoop and brought them downstairs.

An hour later, we began our good-byes. Debbie gathered Rose and Helen in her arms and spoke to them in Vietnamese. They responded in kind. I was surprised at their ease in speaking and understanding Vietnamese. They gave her a picture of a flower they had drawn and asked Debbie to give it to Ba. Debbie and the twins bawled. Dulcey stepped in and maneuvered the twins to the car.

Ten minutes into the drive, the twins settled. Travis sat up front with Dulcey. I sat in the back between the twins. "Listen, girls. Auntie's going to get your mother, and you're going to Philly with Travis and Auntie Dulcey."

"But, Auntie, what if something happens to you? What if the bad guys hurt you?"

Travis turned around, the twins' words echoing the ones he used to say to me all the time: "What if the bad guys hurt you and then you don't come home again?" little boy face full of worry. Now he smiled and nodded.

"Nothing is going to happen to me. I'm going to get your mom and bring her home, and I want you two to be good and pay attention to Travis and Auntie Dulcey."

Dulcey dropped me at an Enterprise Car Rental about a mile from the hotel where we stayed, on Washington Street in the center of Allston, an abutting town to Newton. Travis got out of the car and hugged me hard. "Bad guys better chill."

He chuckled, then got serious. "Be careful, find Auntie, catch whoever killed Uncle, and come home," he said. "I should be going with you." I ran my hand through his hair. *Boy always needs a haircut*, I thought. But I kept my mouth shut about it.

"Done, done, and done," I said, kissing his cheek and opening the car door for him. It was two o'clock, so I figured they would make Philly shortly after dark. My heart ached watching the twins, teary-eyed and looking worn, peer out the back window. I waved to them until the car turned the corner to the entrance of the Massachusetts Turnpike heading west.

I secured the only available car at the Enterprise Car Rental, a flaming red Kia Soul. The only saving grace, it had Sirius Radio. On second thought, there was no saving grace.

When I got back to the hotel room, I called Calvin. He had left a message on the hotel room phone and on my cell.

"Lady, you need to be checking in."

I think it was the way he posed it. Calvin's words sliced through a thin layer of tolerance I had for people who imposed their will on me. You might say I had been single too long. I should say Calvin and I had not been together long enough.

"Thanks for your concern."

"Oh, that's how it is, huh? You sounding all formal like, 'Hey, brother, don't put yo'self out for me.'" He fell silent, an uncomfortable silence, which usually signaled to me I'd made a mistake and it was time to cut this man loose. But somewhere in the back of my mind, a little voice said, *This one's worth it.* Or maybe it was the sexual fantasies that Calvin had reignited. A tingle surged through my body.

"I'm sorry. I didn't mean it like that, Calvin. There's just a lot going on."

"I'm always here if you want to talk, or if you need to talk." His voice washed over me like silk.

"We got here last night and found my brother-in-law, John, dead. Murdered, in their house. My sister is still missing, and her mother-in-law had a heart attack after hearing about John's death. My nieces don't know their father is dead yet, and I don't have a clue what the hell is going on."

"You ain't told me nothin' yet. What else you got?"

His play at a country-gangsta accent caused a laugh to escape my lips. It allowed me the second I needed to reel in my emotions.

"You know I can be there in a minute," he said.

His tone indicated he was talking serious support and not throwing out some flirtatious suggestion for a sexual encounter.

"You need to finish healing."

"I'm well enough. Protecting your back will do wonders for my health."

"Tomorrow I'm going to find Nareece and bring her home to Philly. I'll call you after that if things get difficult. A friend in the Boston PD is keeping me posted about John's death. I'm on my way to his station now."

"This is definitely police business. You take good care."

"I will. Thanks, Calvin."

I walked down the narrow path made by the detective's desks to Bates's office at the rear of the squad room.

"Well, well, well, what have we here," Bates said in a playful manner, pushing back in his chair.

I pulled up a chair to the front of his desk.

"Talk to me, Bates. Please tell me you have something."

He hesitated, then got serious. He closed the file that was open in front of him and pushed it toward me.

"We haven't found a match yet for the partial fingerprint from a tube of ChapStick found near the body. Footprints around the outside suggest someone tried to gain entry through the patio doors on the side of the house and through the windows in the back, but no forced entry, suggesting John let them in."

"Them?"

"One to hold him, one to beat him, one to give the orders and taunt him. I'd say three, anyway." He opened his desk drawer and pulled out another folder, then got up and came around to the front of the desk and sat on the edge. "John is clean, though he had some trouble in his younger days. We're still checking into that. From where we are now, I can't see any reason anyone would want to kill him . . . unless your sister is into something. She is your sister, right?"

I slid him a sideways glance, turning my mouth and eyes up in a semi-disgusted nature, just for messing with me, still.

"Your sister has had a few problems, but you're privy to this stuff, being on the PPD and all. As you noted before, it's old stuff and probably has nothing to do with this," he said, handing me the other folder. "Drug-related. She was picked up during a raid on a drug dealer's place in Philly, about twenty years ago, got off with a fine and probation."

My stomach gurgled.

"I did some digging, deep digging I might add, and learned that your sister's real name is Carmella Ann Mabley. No news to you." He smiled down at me. "Your sister hung around some pretty bad characters in her youth. Then she disappeared. Want to tell me about that?"

I flipped open the file and ran my hand over the arrest picture of Nareece. "Twenty years ago, some guys broke into our house, raped and beat her. How'd you get this? It should be sealed, she was underage." I looked up from the file and he gave me a "*duh*" expression.

"They were never caught. The police had nothing to go on,

and she wasn't any help. She was so scared, so damaged. The things they did to her . . . We changed her identity and moved her to Boston."

"Who's 'we'? How deep is the new identity?"

"As deep as the witness protection program, but unofficial. Only between Cap and me."

"Your captain went along on this?"

"Cap was my father's best friend. After my parents died, he watched out for us. He got me into the firearms division. I wanted off the force after an undercover experience went bad. He convinced me to stay. I never . . ."

"Where's your sister?"

I shrugged ignorance, still unsure whether I could trust Bates. He was a straight shooter and might not bend the rules for Nareece, if necessary. I needed to find her and learn what she had gotten into, what twenty years had uncovered, before I said too much.

"Mabley, if you're holding back something after everything we've talked about, I'll kill you and your whole family ta boot."

"That's all I got, Bates, really."

He looked at me with raised eyebrows, his head tipped to one side.

I refused to squirm.

"Your sister was recently seen with this man." He pointed to a mug shot in the file. "Name is Jesse Boone. We linked him to two killings here a year ago, a man and a woman, we think drug-related. Linked him but not enough evidence, no witnesses, you know the story. You have to know this guy. Back in the day, his father was a major player in the Black Mafia of your fair city, aka Richard 'The Pistol' Boone." I nodded in slow motion, numbed by his words. "He was a scary dude, a hit man for one Bobby Martin, the head nigger in charge. Your sister was seen with him and this woman, Linda Shields." He

pointed to another picture. It was of Linda Shields and Nareece in front of Nareece's house. "This was taken a month
ago, a few days before Shields was killed."

He stopped and let me digest this before continuing. "This
guy was also with them, Frank Mann Johnson, aka 'Big Daddy'."

My brain burned with thoughts of the Post-it in Nareece's
file with *FMJ* and a phone number scribbled on it. A picture
behind the one he pointed to fueled the burn to raging flames.
It showed Nareece letting a man into her house in Milton. I
couldn't tell the man's identity from the first picture, as his face
was blocked by a shadow. But when I flipped to the next one,
the black eyes and crooked grin of Jesse Boone pierced my
soul.

"Hey, you with me, Miss M?"

I fingered the photo of Nareece and Jesse and pushed it toward Bates. "All this time I'm thinking that whatever is going
on is a Nareece and John problem. But Jesse Boone at her house?
What if all this is about my testifying in the Hodges case?" I hesitated.
"I don't remember Boone from working undercover. I only know
Boone as a suspect in four murders in the past few years, none of
which we could get him on because of scared or dead witnesses." I looked up at him. "You know the story . . . Still, it
doesn't make any sense. Jesse Boone at Nareece's house?" I
shook my head in disbelief. "No, there's definitely something
missing."

CHAPTER 15

I was about over the edge when I returned to the hotel room. How was Nareece connected to Jesse Boone? The big question that Bates kept asking me, and the answer to which I had not a clue.

I poured a glass of Four Sisters Sauvignon Blanc wine I'd picked up on the way back and gulped it. The citrus and vanilla flavors cooled my throat and warmed my insides. I collapsed into the chair next to the bed, poured another glass, and downed that one, too. My neck muscles loosened enough to allow some sideways movement, a few cracks, and my shoulders settled with a little more distance from my ears, allowing me room for clarity of thought.

Buzzed from the wine, I tried to piece together the disjointed thoughts pounding in my brain. Jesse Boone, Big Daddy Mann, and Nareece? Mann supposedly died in prison ten years ago. I put him there with the information I'd gathered when I was undercover. He was my specific charge. Then my cover got blown and I almost died. I remembered being in the presence of Richard "The Pistol" Boone on two occasions: at a party at Big Daddy's house, and when he came to Big Daddy's house unannounced and I—that is, Lakisha Butler—was ordered to get out. I had never met Jesse then. At least I had no recollection of him. Lakisha, my undercover identity, had short hair, green eyes, a much darker complexion from makeup and tanning, and was skinny—a far cry from who I was now. But if Jesse Boone knew who I was, or if it was about me testifying in the Hodges murder, he certainly had plenty of opportunities to kill me.

I shuddered at the thought.

I couldn't make sense of it. I poured more wine and sipped this time. None of it made sense, right down to Laughton and his dead, supposed ex-wife. I did not believe in coincidences. No way. I had buried my head in the sand long enough; there was no denying a connection between twenty years ago and the events of the past three weeks. What I still could not figure was Nareece's place in it.

The sweats came on with a fury and sucked the air from my lungs. I jumped up and paced, trying to keep my brain from exploding. My thoughts jumped from one dark hole to another. Paranoia gained ground. I stripped down to my bra and panties and moved forward, sidestepped, punched forward, down for a low block, jump-kicked, back kicked, high-blocked, low blocked, moving through the self-defense forms of tae kwon do. Forty minutes later, dizzy and dripping, this time from conscious exertion, I fell on the bed. I fanned myself with the card that listed the cable television channels and fought back the urge to scream at the top of my lungs. I grappled with the reality of being old and out of control at forty-nine. Damn my doctor's diagnosis of "premenopausal." What the hell kind of word was *premenopausal* anyway? I threw myself forward on the bed, screamed at the top of my lungs, face in the pillow, and punched the bed with both fists. Unable to hold my breath any longer, I stopped and flipped over onto my back, where I remained until the room darkened and my mind cleared. The whirring sound from the air-conditioning and faint voices from the next room eased me back from the dreamy mellowness I had settled into. The cool air had dried the sweat from my body and now made me shiver. I got up, showered, and got in the bed.

I tossed for an hour before surrendering to insomnia, watched television, read the newspaper shoved under the door, meditated, and prayed to put thoughts of Nareece and Jesse at bay, and finally found sleep about twenty minutes before my 4:30 a.m. wake-up call. If Boston was anything like Philly, leaving after 6:00 a.m. would put me in rush-hour traffic, so I allotted extra time. If I left by 5:30, I hoped to be out in front and make the hour-and-twenty-minute drive to Woods Hole on Cape Cod and my seven-thirty ferry reservation with ease.

I took the Massachusetts Turnpike to I-495 to the Bourne Bridge, then followed I-28 south. The allure of Cape Cod rushed back, especially with spring offering all of God's vegetation born-again status.

Tiny buds capped the bare limbs of some trees, and green leaves sprouted on others. Defiant splashes of color had pushed through the moist soil along the banks of I-28, the first footholds of spring showing through on Cape Cod, as well.

In another four miles, I reached Falmouth Center. Shop owners and contractors were painting, planting, and pruning, making ready for the invasion of tourists. It seemed like I had entered a time warp. Little had changed in the twenty-plus years since my last trip to the Cape. I marveled at the spray of plantings adorning the yards of many houses. Every year I told myself I would do the same to my house, but it never happened. I hated digging in the dirt, and I certainly didn't understand the science of planting at a certain time of year to ensure the beauty in another season.

I took a left and a slight right on Cowdry Road. The densely populated area went for about three miles before opening up to Cape Cod Bay on the left and the ferry dock straight ahead and to the right. I stopped at the small hut before the dock and got my ticket, made a sharp right, and drove around to Lane 8 to wait for boarding instructions. Only a few cars were lined up in the lot as the ferry pulled in—a much larger and newer ferry than the one I remembered named *The Island Home*. I got out of the car to stretch and soak up the soft breeze and the tangy smell of the ocean. I leaned against the car and closed my eyes, ready and wanting to sink into oblivion, except for what lay ahead—and my cell phone ringing.

"Hey, girl, where are you? Did you find Reecey yet?"

"Let us talk, Auntie Dulcey. Let me and Helen talk, please, please," the twins whined before I could respond.

Dulcey shushed them. "You girls go play now until I finish talking to your auntie. Go on now, go play detective." Their protests grew softer as they moved away. "They are something, those girls. Reecey's wrong for causing them to worry like they are. Children shouldn't have this kind of trouble on them."

"I'm at Woods Hole waiting for the boat. I'll call you when I'm over and find her."

"You okay, M?"

"I will be."

"I'm sure this is dredgin' up a lot of stuff for you, memories you been sittin' on for a long time. Sometimes things get in your face, though, so you're forced to deal and can get rid of them for good."

"Dulcey, what the hell are you talking about? Stay out of my head," I yelled, enough to gain people's attention.

"*Hmph*. Somebody needs to be in it. You never dealt with your parents' death and Nareece's hurt or your own. Never dealt with what happened to you."

"I gotta go, Dulcey. They're loading. Tell the twins I'll call them later . . . tomorrow." I clicked off. I had enough to think about without her digging in my brain. This wasn't about me. It was about Nareece and helping her for a change, instead of always thinking about myself.

I got back in the car and drove up to the ramp and onto the ferry as directed by the handler, pulling to the far right and forward. I considered getting out and going topside to air my thoughts, then decided against the move. A full boat meant lots of activity and nowhere else to be alone.

When the boat sailed, I called Calvin.

"I was just thinking about you. But then, I'm always thinking about you. How are you doing, my lady?"

"I'm good, on my way to the Vineyard."

"I should be on this journey with you."

"This is one I need to make alone."

"The mystery of Muriel. One of these days I'll be privy to everything about you."

"One of these days for sure, I'll tell you all mine, and you can tell me all yours. No secrets."

"Ouch, woman, you're asking a lot from a brother. But I can hang with it." We were silent for a moment, this time in comfortable space.

Forty-five minutes later, the ferry docked at Vineyard Haven. The Oak Bluffs dock did not open until Memorial Day, still a few weeks away. I was the third car to exit into a throng of people awaiting the arrival of friends and family. I inched along, then slammed on my brakes to keep from squashing a little mousy-looking dog that jumped from the window of the car in front of me. It caused a flurry of horns and cursing from drivers behind me. Such crude behavior exhibited on the other side was expected, but not here, on the white sandy shores washed with soft ocean breezes, enhanced with exotic shopping and eateries. Life was carefree and easy here—especially since nothing of everyday deeds could be done until the next boat out and a forty-five-minute ride. I supposed folks exiting the ferry had not breathed enough of the Martha's Vineyard formula air yet.

Dad used to say it was like arriving on another planet.

The same traffic policewoman who had directed cars on Water Street and waved our Volvo station wagon into traffic when I was a kid waved me out now. My eyes were playing tricks, or she looked exactly the same. I drove a few hundred feet, inched my way out at Five Corners, where five streets merged into one intersection. No lights, no police officer directing traffic. I would say you took your life in your hands, but this was the Vineyard, which translated to polite drivers. I sped across the intersection, then slowed and cruised down Beach Road, bound by water on both sides. The island's peaceful ambience and scenic grandeur evoked buried memories.

The last family vacation on the Island, the vacation from hell, was right after I graduated from the police academy. I remembered Nareece fought Mom not to go, because she didn't want to leave her friends. The night before, in the heat of an argument, the girl raised her hand ready to slap Mom. I got up from the kitchen table to intervene, but Dad hustled in and caught her in the downstroke. He slapped her so hard her head spun around like a demon's, the first and only time he ever struck either of us.

When we got to the Vineyard, Reece continued her hell-raising mission: She pouted, argued, kept a scowl on, stayed out past curfew, snuck out after everyone was in bed, and came home loaded. "I should have intervened," I said out loud. Guilt crept up my spine. "But noooo, too busy doing the cop thing."

I drove past Martha's Vineyard Hospital and veered to the left instead of going straight, which would have brought me to the house. Instead I drove down New York Avenue toward Oak Bluffs' center. I passed Oak Bluffs Harbor on the left, Circuit Avenue on the right, and drove straight to the Oak Bluffs dock and Ocean Park, then turned right on Seaview Avenue, drove down a few blocks, and pulled to the curb at Waban Park. Waban Park was a large square lot that faced Inkwell Beach and was surrounded on the other three sides by houses.

A lone swimmer crawled between the two jetties the length of the Inkwell. A sick person. The winter storms had recaptured much of the sandy shore and deposited remnants of seashells, seaweed, and other ocean junk.

My own junk had caused an oceanic gap between Nareece and me. I supposed it was jealousy.

"Now, there's a thought," I said aloud. "I was jealous, and then Mom and Dad died and all we had, correction, all we *have* is each other."

I rolled down the windows and opened the sunroof to abate the heat welling up inside of me, whipped the wheel around, and headed toward the house.

Chapter 16

A right off West Tisbury Road put me on State Road headed to Chilmark. Twenty minutes later, a hundred feet past a row of seventeen mailboxes, I turned left on Quenames Road. Forty-five years ago, during the planning stages of the housing development, it was decided there would be no street signs, house numbers, or family names posted so that residents could be assured of privacy. So Quenames Road was known only to the inner circle. It was a one-lane dirt road you would never find or know the name of if you were not privy to the secret directions.

Granted, the secret directions did often leave visitors who could not identify the third telephone stump, second "big rock," or third pullout, lost in the maze. And, after dark, the prospect of finding a destination was nothing short of a miracle, should one succeed.

A few hundred trees in, I swerved into a pullout to allow an oncoming car to pass. The unspoken rule, the person on the way out has the right of way. Another unspoken rule, you must wave to passersby. I pulled back out to the road and continued to the next landmark—the first telephone stump.

I bit my tongue hard enough to draw tears, having miscalculated the circumference of a rut in the road that scraped the undercarriage of the car. Depending on the season, the road was hard and dusty or wet and muddy and rutted enough to force a ten-mile-per-hour speed limit. I bumped along to the second telephone stump, veered right, drove past four houses, turned left, and drove five hundred feet down a pebbled driveway. The trees gave way to a large clearing, where our family summer house, a two-level, three-bedroom cape, was set, center field.

I pulled in short of the front yard and parked beside an unfamiliar blue Toyota Camry parked off to the side of the graveled driveway.

With all the windows and curtains closed, the house looked abandoned. Tree branches and other debris were strewn across the dead grass that made up the front yard, along with several empty soda and beer cans and other trash.

The grass crunched underfoot as I made my way to the front porch, which ran the length of the house. The wooden steps groaned under my weight. Sneaking around the house was not happening. I knocked, called Nareece's name, and tried the doorknob. Another shout out also settled on a deafening silence. I backtracked down the stairs and walked around to the side of the house. In the flowerless flower bed a lockbox was attached to the foundation with a spare key. The combination, 8926, Dad's old registration number, popped the lock and the key dropped out. When I stood up, I noticed the curtain moved in the window above my head. Nareece was watching me. At least I hoped it was Nareece.

The door creaked when I pushed it open. When I stepped inside, a cool, stuffy air, dense with particles of mold, attacked my nostrils and threw me into a sneezing fit. The door slammed shut behind me. I spun around to Nareece hunched in attack stance, wielding a two-by-four. She dropped the piece of wood and plowed into me.

"You came. You found me."

Sneezes jerked me forward and broke her hold. She ran

down the hall and came back with a wad of toilet paper, ran out again and brought a glass of water and a wet facecloth. All the while, sneezes hammered me. Through teary eyes, I saw Nareece's freaked-out expression. Her arms captured her body like a straitjacket as she swayed back and forth from one foot to the other. I thought, *God, don't fail me now and leave this child to her own.*

I finally had the sense of mind to go outside. The fresh air eased my sneezing, but lack of oxygen from the attack made me woozy and weak. I sat on the bench built along the circumference of the porch. Nareece followed me out and joined me on the bench. Neither of us said a word for what seemed a long time. I noticed Nareece looked pale and puffy-faced, puffy-bodied, too, way more than I had ever seen her. I decided not to comment.

With my breathing normalized and my senses regained, I opened the conversation. "What's wrong with you? Coming at me with a two-by-four? Don't you know your own sister?"

"I guess I was too scared. I tried to peek out the window, but I didn't want you or whoever was out there to see me. I wasn't really scared. I mean, nobody knows about this place but us." She sounded more like she was trying to convince herself rather than making a firm statement. "How'd you know to come here?"

I got up and walked the length of the porch. "Where else? Like you said, nobody else knows about this place, although I'm not so sure about that anymore. I really think we need to get off the Island and go back to Philly as soon as possible. *The Island Queen* is the only boat operating right now, so I couldn't get a reservation until tomorrow morning, first boat, so we're stuck here for the night."

"He's dead, M. He's dead and I killed him," she said just above a whisper. Nareece hung her head and wept. I slid in beside her and draped my arm across her shoulders. She snotted, then said, "They'll try to kill the girls, too."

"The girls are safe." I held her shoulders, one side in each hand, and twisted her around so we were face-to-face. I hesitated, because Reecey can act the fool one minute and seem like she's brain-dead the next and shut down. "Reecey, what's your connection to Jesse Boone?"

She closed her eyes and shook her head. "I don't want to talk about all that right now. I'm hungry. Let's go get something to eat." She pulled away.

I grabbed her shoulders again. "Reece, this is not a game. John is dead. I need to know why someone would want to kill him. Why Jesse Boone would want to kill him, because that's who I think did it. I saw a picture of you with him and a guy named Frank Mann at your house, for chrissakes! We're talking Mafia shit, Reecey. Drugs, money, the whole nine."

"Muriel, I can't talk about this right now!" She pulled away again and went and got into the car.

It was going to be a long night. During the drive to Linda Jean's in Oak Bluffs, one of the few eateries on the Island open year-round, Nareece jabbered about store closings, new store openings, Mad Martha's ice cream, Harbor Festival, and how we should vacation together this summer with the twins and Travis. I listened for something in her voice that even leaned toward fear or sadness about John. We parked in front of Mad Martha's ice cream place and walked the few hundred feet to Linda Jean's. Nareece babbled the whole time about how wonderful the Vineyard was. In the restaurant, she stopped talking only to order waffles, a cheese and broccoli omelet, and sausages. I ordered a cheeseburger and fries.

"I forgot how much I love this place," Nareece said. "It's so peaceful and different from anywhere else on earth. I'm really happy Mom and Dad never sold the house. The twins love the beach and everything else here, too. They love running around Ocean Park, chasing the birds, playing on the beach, and the carousel. Oh God, do they love the carousel. John . . ."

She stopped and looked at me, her eyes filled with tears. She sniffed and went on, diverting her gaze. "John loves coming here, too. He says it's like nowhere he's ever been. He did a lot of work on the house, painted the bedrooms, put new cabinets in the kitchen, and refinished the wood floors. He's planning to paint the living room this summer."

"Nareece, stop."

The waitress saved me, or rather, saved Nareece. For the next half hour we sat in silence wolfing down the food and slurping hot chocolate and Coke. The silence continued through the ride back. When we arrived back at the house, I stayed out on the deck while Nareece went in to open windows, cover the furniture with sheets, and start a fire.

An hour later we were nestled on the sofa watching the fire dwindle.

"I'm sorry for all this, M," Nareece said in her whiny voice. I had her cradled in my arms like she was a little girl. The room darkened except for the firelight that made the graying living room wall paint look new again.

"I really did hate coming here with Ma and Dad. I should've been grateful they wanted to give us a good life, get me away from all the stuff I was into."

"I know that's right. You made everyone miserable."

"I did my own thing."

"And exactly what was your own thing?"

She twisted around to face me. "What do you care? You never paid any attention to me. You didn't care." She turned back around and pouted. "Not until . . . Ma and Dad . . . died." She picked at her fingers. I noticed her nail beds were scabbed over from biting them, even worse than mine.

"I'm sorry, Nareece. You dropped into the world, and all of a sudden everything revolved around you. Before your dad and you, it was just me and her."

"Dad loved you."

"I know that, and I loved him. But before they got married, me and Mom talked a lot and did things together. All that just about stopped when they got married and it completely stopped when you came along. Hell, I was an impressionable and very needy thirteen-year-old, and my whole life changed because of you, this cute little baby. I guess they couldn't help themselves." I chuckled lightly. I shifted my position so she faced me.

"Nareece, we need to stop dancing around this whole thing. You need to tell me what's going on and why you're here. You haven't even asked about the twins." She tried to turn away, but I held her shoulders.

"M, I've been trying to tell you . . . I thought everything was done, ya know?" She started sniveling, which grated on my already-frazzled nerves.

I silently prayed for patience before speaking. "What was done?"

She snapped around. "Will you listen, M? For once, listen to me. Don't say anything until I'm done talking." She got up and went to the fireplace. She stood to the side, staring into the flames. "Remember the night . . . when . . . after Mom and Dad . . . I was the reason they died. They didn't die in an accident. They were murdered. Killed because of something I did."

I started to speak, but cleared my throat instead, minding her request.

Nareece walked back to the couch and sat beside me. "Dad was trying to save me. He . . . he . . ." She whimpered and snorted. "Men came to the house and threatened Mom and Dad because of something I did. Dad told them to go to hell, said he'd go to the police." She hesitated, more whimpering and snorting. "He asked me about it and I lied. I lied, Muriel. Told him I didn't do anything, but I did. They killed Mom and Dad to shut Dad up. They wanted to punish me. They wanted me dead, too, but you came home." She took my hand and held it against her cheek. "You saved me."

I snatched my hand away and got up. "Who is 'they,' and what did you do that was so bad someone would kill Mom and Dad and come after you? Did it have something to do with drugs or money? Because those are the only two things I can think of that would make someone want to kill someone else. And I can't see you involved with either. I say that, but then I see a picture of you with Jesse Boone . . ." I immediately chastised myself for sounding judgmental.

She bent forward and covered her face with both hands. She talked through her fingers, which distorted her voice, giving it a mannish quality. "I wanted Jesse Boone to feel pain, like the pain he put on me and the other girls. I thought he really loved me. All he wanted me to do was be a whore, a prostitute for him. After he made me sleep with some old guy and beat me because the guy said I wasn't good enough, I took his stupid heroin and money."

"You were dating Jesse Boone?" It came out screechy. I was dumbfounded. Shocked. Wrecked. My mouth dried into desert quality.

Nareece stayed silent.

"You and Jesse Boone."

"Yes, Muriel, me and Jesse. I was sixteen, and to me he was God."

I relived snippets of Nareece at sixteen, going out and coming in, dressed like a hoochie mama, glamour makeup, arguing with me when I was home, cussing at me.

"How much, Nareece? How much heroin and money did you take from him?"

"A pound of heroin and two million dollars. I flushed the heroin and hid the money at the old house—behind the bins Daddy built for us."

"How did he find you?"

"I don't know, Muriel. He just said there was no place in the world I could've gone where he wouldn'ta found me."

"Why didn't you tell me? Why didn't you just give him the money back?"

"I wanted to, but when I told John about it, because I was worried that Jesse would hurt the girls if I didn't do what he said, John said not to. He said he would take care of Jesse so I would never have to be afraid of him again."

"So what did Jesse tell you he wanted you to do?"

She uncovered her face and stared at the wall. My frustration went haywire. I grabbed her chin and squeezed. "Nareece, John is dead, for crying out loud. Talk to me!"

She popped up like a jack-in-the-box and stumbled backward, her body zombied out, face drained. Her lips quivered, and a line of drool slipped from her open mouth. She made a gasping sound and collapsed. She would have whacked her head on the stone floor in front of the fireplace, or worse, fallen into the fire, but for my quick reflex. I dragged her to the couch, laid her out, and rubbed her cheeks and hands.

"Quit playing around, Nareece." She remained unresponsive.

I began to panic. "I'm sorry, Nareece. Don't do this. Wake up. Think about Rose and Helen. They need you."

Her eyes opened wide. She stared as though in a trance, no brain sparks, her pupils dilated.

"Nareece, you have to talk to me," I pleaded. I reached my arm under her shoulders and tried to make her sit up. She flopped like a dead person. I laid her back and checked her breathing and pulse, which was slightly elevated. I covered her with a throw and went on the hunt for medications. I checked the bathroom medicine cabinet, her purse and suitcase. An inside pocket of the suitcase held a small folded piece of paper containing colorful pills and an amber prescription bottle. I surmised she had been using whatever they were for days, or weeks even, to keep her going. The bottle was mostly full, so it didn't seem likely she had overdosed.

I went back to the living room, sat at the end of the couch, and stared at her, feeling quite helpless and willing her to wake up. Unsuccessful, I couldn't decide whether to shake her, slap her, or leave her be.

I went into what used to be my parents' bedroom and called Dulcey. I sat on the bed that was half made up with a sheet and blanket spread over the top of the plastic-covered mattress.

"Did you find her? Is she all right?" Dulcey squealed loud enough to damage my eardrums.

"Dulce, remember when my parents died and Nareece was acting the fool and I was never at home to keep a check on her, working my last chance to stay on the force? You remember, I had just started with the forensics unit? Well, Jesse Boone had his hooks in her back then."

"What do you mean, 'had his hooks in her'? She was just a baby then."

"Yes, she was. She was one pissed-off baby at some point, because she stole a lot of drugs and a lot of money from him. And I bet it was Jesse Boone who raped and beat her half to death all that time ago and now he wants his money. She says that's why John is dead. I'm sure he wouldn't give up her location, so they, Boone, killed him. I have to get Reece back to Philly to the FBI." I hesitated and took a deep breath. "Damn, I need Laughton right now."

"When you coming back?"

"Got a six a.m. reservation. So we'll be on the road and home by noon, one o'clock." There was a moment of meditation between us.

"Dulce, I think you should take the girls to your sister's house. Jesse Boone is a psychopath. There is no telling how far he'll go or how far his reach is. As comfortable as I am that he could never find this place, I'm not. He found Nareece."

"I got these babies covered. You just make sure you cover your behind."

A rustling noise under the window made me flinch. I threw the phone on the bed and grabbed my gun off the dresser. I flicked the light off and stood against the wall listening. I looked in the living room to check on Nareece. She had not budged. I peeked out the window. More rustling. Dulcey yelled my name in the phone. I tiptoed over to the bed and picked up the phone. "Shhhh, Dulcey. I think someone is sneaking around outside."

"Muriel, you're scaring the hell outta me."

"Shhh." I put the phone down and went to the living room, hugging the wall and peering out the windows into the thick blackness. I stopped and listened more. Silence. Nareece remained as still as a body in a casket.

I hastened back to the bedroom and picked up the phone. "Probably a skunk or a deer or some other forest creature. Black as black can be out there. Someone would have to be familiar with the area to find us in these woods."

"Who are you trying to convince?"

The nervousness in my stomach lingered long after Dulcey and I hung up. Over the years, I'd learned to heed the grumblings.

Nareece lay on her back with her arms crossed and resting on her stomach, her lips slightly pouted as though molded for viewing at her wake. I got the blanket off the bed and covered her, then I settled in an upright position at the opposite end of the couch. I made sure I had my purse and my gun was in its holster.

"Wake up, Muriel." I pretended I *didn't hear* Ma's *whisper in my ear.* "Get up now, Muriel!" *she yelled.*

I sat up, rubbing my eyes, and took in a deep breath that threw me into a coughing fit. I tried to open my eyes, but they burned and I couldn't see anything. The realization that smoke filled the room propelled me to action. "Nareece. Nareece!"

I reached forward and shook her, but she did not respond. I slid to the floor and pulled my purse and Nareece down with me. She hit with a *thud* but still did not respond. I crawled along the floor, dragging Nareece and my purse behind me. When I got to where I thought the door was, I reached up and rattled the doorknob until it opened, but there was no air, only more blackness. I inched farther along the floor, staying close to the outside wall, dragging Nareece behind me. Rest a minute. Need to get out before the smoke . . . I lay on the floor and closed my eyes from the burning.

Next thing I knew, a fireman was carrying me away from the house and handing me off to an EMT, who carried me to the back of an ambulance where they labored over Nareece. I knocked away an oxygen mask one of the EMTs tried to corner me with, as another EMT called, "Clear," and zapped Nareece. He rechecked her pulse and rubbed the paddles together. "Clear." He checked her pulse again. "I got a pulse," he announced and pulled an oxygen mask over her face.

"She's fine, right?"

"For a minute I thought we lost her, but . . ." He lifted the stethoscope from his neck and listened to Nareece's chest. "She'll live," he assured me.

An EMT helped me into the ambulance and sat me on the cot next to where Nareece lay. "Miss, you need to wear this for a while," he insisted, now on full attack with an oxygen mask.

I pushed it away, taken by the scene—red, orange, and yellow flames boogied skyward against a black easel, embers dancing like disco lights.

The EMT followed my gaze and came at me again. "Miss, please."

I fell back and surrendered.

The siren sounded off in the distance and sputtered to silence, as we pulled into the emergency entrance of Martha's Vineyard Hospital. An EMT rattled off stats to the attending nurse until we reached a treatment area.

"You two are lucky." He squeezed my hand and headed out.

"Thanks," I mumbled. "What about my car?"

"Call the fire station in the morning, they'll know."

I swung my legs over the side of the bed and reached for my purse. The attending nurse snatched it back. "Now, young lady, you lie down," she said, guiding me to a lying position, objection not an option. She took my blood pressure and pulse and said the doctor would be in shortly.

I was uncertain how much time had passed when the doctor woke me.

"Your sister is going to be fine, but we're going to admit her and watch her overnight. She's got quite a bump on the back of her head," he said.

"She banged her head when I pulled her off the couch trying to get out."

"Good thing you did. Better a bump on the head." He lifted my eyelid and flashed a light, then listened to my lungs and heart and checked my pulse. "I'm admitting you for the night, as well. You're clear but better to be safe."

The next morning, before I left the hospital, I checked on Nareece. She was resting peacefully. I thought about waking her, but decided more sleep would serve her better.

I took a taxi to the Edgartown Police Station. An officer drove me to the impound yard to pick up my car, then I drove out to the house. When I turned into the driveway, I gasped at the sight of charred objects strewn over the lawn. Only the foundation of the house remained. Its confines trapped a black hole.

I got out and walked the perimeter. A charred refrigerator and dishwasher and the scorched remains of an electric floor-sanding machine stuck up from inside the black hole. I remembered that Nareece had said John refinished the wood floors.

An unscathed soccer ball rolled along the property edge. I retrieved the ball, tossed it in the backseat of the car, and got in. While I was backing out, a car pulled in and blocked the way. My heart leaped before I recognized the man exiting the car as Mr. Galloway, our closest neighbor since we were kids. We were separated by a block of woods.

"Nareece, that you?"

"It's Muriel, Mr. Galloway."

"Muriel, girl, I haven't seen you in a coon's age. How are you, young lady? You're all grown-up, that's how you are." He didn't wait for me to answer before offering his condolences. "Sure is a sorry sight. Good thing no one was hurt, though, and they kept it from spreading"—he waved his arm in an arc to indicate the entire wooded area—"or we'd all been in trouble." He searched the scene with his eyes. "Nothing left. Not a thing. Shame."

"Nothing that can't be replaced," I offered with the conviction of an ant.

"Will you rebuild?"

"I guess." I struggled not to seem anxious to leave.

"How are those little ones doing? They are something else." He chuckled and bent down to rest his arms on the car, so he was on my level, head to head.

"They're fine. Growing up," I said, pulling back a bit to allow more breathing room between us, though his breath smelled of spearmint.

"There were two cars here early this morning. It wasn't Lambert's truck, though. Lambert's the fire chief. Bret Lambert. I think one was blue and the other gray. I was out for my morning walk. They were leaving as I approached from the right, so I didn't get a good look at who was inside. I did see that there were two men inside. What started it, anyway?"

"Actually I'm on my way to the fire station now."

"I won't keep you then," he said, straightening up and moving back from the car. "Don't mind if I nose around a bit, do you?"

"Not at all, but be careful."

"You take care. Tell Nareece and John—nice fella, that John—tell them I came by and asked after them," he said on his way back to move his car. He got in and pulled alongside my car. "Frances and I will support her and John any way we can if they decide to rebuild."

"Thanks, Mr. Galloway."

I did not tell him John was dead. More questions would arise that I did not have answers for. I drove away wondering about the two visitors.

When I arrived at the West Tisbury Fire Station 2, Chief Lambert ushered me into his office and offered me a seat. "Good thing your neighbor called. We would have arrived sooner, but it's hard getting down those roads." He leaned forward in his chair and rested his elbows on the desk, clasping his hands together in a prayerful fashion. "I'm glad you and your sister got out in time. We suspect arson, but we're still investigating. I'll know more in a few days."

I flashed back to the noise I'd heard outside the window while I was talking to Dulcey.

The chief sat back in his chair. "Ms. Mabley, you know anyone who'd want to hurt you and your sister?"

Chief, to be honest, I am investigating a suspected murderer named Jesse Boone. I came down here to get my sister, who is in fear of her life from Boone. Didn't think anyone would find us. But I did hear some rustling around the house last night. Brushed it off as some animals.

"Who knew you were coming?"

"That's just it, nobody. Neither of us told anyone we were coming here. It was an unexpected trip, and what's more, nobody even knows about the place down here."

"Might be that someone sure the hell does," he said.

I got up to leave. "I'm hopeful that when you finish your investigation, the findings will change."

"I hope our findings change, as well. We've never had a problem with arson before, not as long as I've been chief, which will be forty years this August."

I dug in my bag for a card and handed it to him. "Please let me know what you learn."

I drove to the Vineyard Haven dock, checked the boat schedule, and rescheduled our reservation for 5:00 p.m. that afternoon. When I returned to the hospital, the nurse stopped me on the way to Nareece's room.

"She's gone."

I gasped and stumbled forward. She caught my arm.

"Oh no, I'm sorry. Your sister checked out, as in left the building. She went with some fellas who said they were her cousins. She said she was meeting you and would check in with her primary physician on the other side."

CHAPTER 17

The nurse said she'd overheard one man say they could catch the 3:00 p.m. ferry. A quick look at the time on my cell phone showed I had ten minutes before the ferry left. I dashed out. My adrenaline surged at the slim likelihood of me catching the three o'clock.

A docker was waving the last few cars to the loading ramp when I pulled curbside under a FOR DROPOFF AND PICKUP ONLY sign. I got out and ran to the pier.

"Slow down, miss," he told me, then stepped in front of me and held out his hand. "Ticket?"

"No. I mean, I just want to make sure my sister got on. Did you notice a young woman with two men drive on?"

"What kind of car?" He took tickets from a woman with two young boys who were arguing and slapping at each other. The smaller boy cried and called the bigger boy a "dummy," "stupid," "crackhead," and my favorite, "bugga butt." The mother walked ahead of the two in denial, tuned out, or just plain fed up.

"I'm not sure," I said.

"Lady, over a hundred cars pulled onto this boat. If you

can't tell me the kind of car . . ." He rubbed his chin in thought. "You know, I vaguely remember a young woman who looked kind of sickly, a dark blue Ford Taurus. My brother-in-law has one. Nice car."

He held up a finger for me to wait and talked with another worker who approached. A driver who was insisting on passage despite not having a reservation leaned out of his car window. He talked with the driver and directed him back to the holding area, as the dockmaster pulled the pins and the ferry chugged back from the dock, the bay doors closing.

I regained his attention. "You said a young woman. I only remember because the car had a big dent in one side. The woman was lying across the backseat. I asked the driver if she was okay."

"Was she?"

"She didn't look so good, but the guy ignored me and drove on."

"Thanks for your help. Is there a ferry sooner than five o'clock?"

"Yeah, but I'd bet it's full. Best you keep your five o'clock reservation if you have one." He gestured to the cars lined up in the holding area. "End up in standby and not get off until tonight."

"Can you say what the men looked like?"

"They were black, dressed up in suits. Looked like hoodlums, no offense."

"None taken. Thanks again."

The realization of the situation bowled me over. I watched the boat back away from the dock and move along the shoreline toward Woods Hole. The waiting area was near empty now. Flustered, I sat on a bench under a canopy where people waited for arrivals and called Laughton—wishful thinking. No answer. Then I called Cap. His administrative assistant said he was gone for the day and his cell phone was off. Then I called Travis. He answered on the first ring.

"Ma, where are you? You got me worried to death not knowing whether you're okay or if something bad happened. Did you find Auntie?"

"I'm fine, Travis. Yeah, I found her. What's going on with you?"

"Lying low is all. I'm at the crib now, but I been hanging at Aunt Dulcey's every night with those crazy twins." There was a moment of silence. "What's wrong, Ma?"

"Everything's fine, son. I'll be home soon."

"Everything's not fine. Just please do what you gotta do and get back in one piece. I can't take another episode. You hearing me?"

"I'm hearing you. I can't take another episode, either. See you soon. I love you."

"Love you, too."

My next call was to Dulcey. She answered on the first ring, too. Women talking and laughing filled the background.

"Muriel, I've been calling you since early this morning."

"Muriel"—that was new. Girlfriend called me everything but never Muriel. I hadn't bothered to check my phone since that morning. I'd put the ring on silent while in the hospital and forgot to switch it back to a ringtone.

"How are the girls?"

"Are you all right?" she shot back.

"I'm hanging."

"The girls are worried but good. They're having a ball helping me in the shop and amusing my customers till they be falling outta the chair and switching their heads every which way. Can't hold me responsible for a lopsided perm or styling job." She let out a slight laugh, then quieted. The background noise faded. "I'm away from everybody now. What's really going on?"

"Someone tried to burn us up last night. I mean, I think someone set the house on fire. Coulda been electrical or something."

"Someone tried to kill you all!"

"We're good. Well, we were good until I left the hospital and Reecey to get the car. Dulcey, two men kidnapped Reecey from the hospital. She was sleeping this morning when I left the hospital to get my car and check out the damage to the house. When I got back to the hospital, the nurse said she left with two men who said they were cousins. I think they got on the boat that just left the dock. I know they're some of Boone's henchmen. And there isn't a damn thing I can do until I get off this island."

"I can't believe what you're telling me. Burn you out? Kidnap Reecey?" I heard her sigh. "You don't know who took her or where they're going to take her or whether she's even alive at this point."

"I'd guess they're heading to Philly. And she's alive. Whatever it is she did or has, they aren't going to do anything to her until they get it." My brain said Nareece would die before telling her captors where it was, whatever "it" was, but I didn't want to think too hard about that right now. "I'm going to see Bates first. I'll head back after. I'll call you when I leave Boston."

I hung up and checked my messages. Dulccy, Travis, and Calvin. I called Calvin, but he didn't answer. I clicked off without leaving a message.

It was 3:05. I had two hours before my reservation. The next boat was in an hour. I decided to get in the standby line in hope of getting off an hour early. Back at my car, a police officer stepped off the curb to check my license plate and write a ticket just as I arrived. She smiled and moved on to the next car.

I got in and drove around to the reservation booth. A man poked his head out of the door. "Lane two," he said and handed me a receipt and boarding pass. I rolled to a stop, the last car in line for a forty-five-minute wait. If I didn't make the next ferry, I still had a confirmed reservation for the one at five o'clock.

The quiet breeze was in direct contrast to my mood and the day's events. I got out of the car, walked to the water's edge, and sat on a bench facing the ocean. Waves of anxiety belabored my breathing. My emotions climbed to near hysterical and kept climbing. My phone dinged—a text from Travis. *Be safe. lol xxxxoooo.* My anxiety waned.

Travis had Nareece's high forehead and green eyes with a broad toothsome smile. He was soft-spoken like her, but unlike Nareece, if you pushed Travis to the wall, and even through it, he would keep control. That was the opposite from Nareece, who was quick to get enraged if denied her way. Tell that girl "no" and she would go ballistic, especially after Mom and Dad died and I inherited the parent role. She aimed my revolver at me once and pulled the trigger. The almost dying didn't haunt me, but the fact that she was the one who pulled the trigger would scrape my flesh from my bones if I thought about it too long. The gun misfired for no reason that I could find. No reason but God.

"And it's not her time now," I told myself out loud. I called Bates.

"What's going on, Mabley?" he said. "You lose your sister again?"

I ignored his sarcasm. "As a matter of fact, I did. I found her here on the Island, Martha's Vineyard, then someone tried to kill us by burning our house down, and then two guys kidnapped my sister from the hospital."

"Now tell me what really happened." Bates sounded unconvinced.

"I know it sounds crazy. And I'm sorry I wasn't completely

up front with you before, but I am being up front now. No bullshit, Bates." I told him the whole story about Nareece dating Jesse Boone and taking the drugs and the money. When I was done, Bates was quiet for a good while.

"I'm on the Island waiting for the ferry now."

"Then that seals it. It was Boone's fingerprints on the Chap-Stick and on the chair the guy, John, was in. We have a warrant out for him now."

"I'm pretty sure he's back in Philly by now and that's where they're taking Nareece." I stopped short of telling him the part about where Nareece hid the money. "Look, Bates, I gotta go, but I'll call you when I get back to Philly."

"Muriel, I know you think this is all about your sister, but I'm telling you to watch your back out there. I did some more deep digging and used up a few favors, top gun favors, and it seems like there is someone in the PPD, someone in the know, who might be feeding Jesse Boone information. We took a computer from your sister's house, and there was a picture of a chick named Lakisha Butler and you on it, in the same frame."

CHAPTER 18

A raucous noise assaulted me, snapping me back to consciousness. The car I was driving swerved over rumble strips along the breakdown lane. I jerked the steering wheel too far to the left, too far to the right, to the left again, to the right again, before finding balance and straightening the ride. Suddenly the decision to hit the road back to Philly at 10:00 p.m. seemed a stupid one.

I pulled into the next rest area on I-91. My knees buckled when I stepped out of the car. My saving grace was that I had hold of the door. I straightened and limped across the lot and into the building to the bathroom, where I splashed cold water on my face. I pulled a paper towel from the wall dispenser and held it to my face. When I took the towel away, my reflection in the mirror shoved me back a step. The devil's fury showed over my face—dark circles framing my eyes, hair standing on end, eyes bloodshot. I stepped forward again, daring the image to say something bad to me. "Emergency services definitely needed now, Dulcey girl." I wiped at my eyes, patted my hair down, straightened my posture, and moved on.

I stopped at the McDonald's counter and ordered a large coffee on the way out. Resettled in the car, I chugged down half a cup before my eyes opened and my nerves hardened a bit.

An old man, bent and unsteady, with a woman of the same stature on his arm, passed in front of my car. Next to me, a beat-up Chevy Bel Air had four children in the back, slumped right, each one's head anchored on the other's shoulder except for the last kid, whose head hung back, mouth gaping. A woman driver leaned forward, her head resting on the steering wheel. Three cars down to the left and across the lane a dark SUV was parked. The burn of a cigarette signaled an occupant.

My full attention on the SUV, I sipped more coffee and attempted to set the cup in the holder between the driver and passenger seats, but missed and dumped the contents in my lap. I pushed the car door open. It banged back and caught my foot. "Shit!" The coffee cup whipped from my hand and washed coffee over the passenger seat, door, and dashboard, then settled on the floor on the passenger side.

I leaned forward, removed my shoe, and jammed my shoulder on the steering wheel on the way up. "Shit! Shit! Shit!" I kneaded the pained spot in my shoulder with one hand and coddled my injured foot with the other. A second attempt to get out succeeded. I got a roll of paper towels from the backseat, dabbed at my lap, and wiped my hands, then moved around to the passenger side and did the same to the seat and carpet, though the paper towels were hardly the solution for the stains. I got back in the car and started the engine. I checked out the SUV again and did not notice anyone inside— at least no more smoking was going on.

My phone rang, but stopped before I clicked to answer. The lit screen showed 1:25 a.m. and Laughton as the missed caller. I pushed the button to call back, and after five rings was about to click off, when he answered.

"Why didn't you pick up?" Laughton shouted.

"You can't say, 'hi, how are you?' I've been driving." I pulled out of the rest stop and back onto the Jersey Turnpike. "What do you mean, why didn't I pick up? Why haven't *you* answered any of *my* calls?" I waited for a response. We challenged each other's silence, two minutes, three maybe.

He broke it. "Where are you?"

"I'm about two hours out."

"Meet me. Please."

"Laughton, Reece has been kidnapped, and I know it's Jesse Boone."

"Muriel, meet me," he demanded and spouted off an address.

"Laughton, did you hear me?"

He clicked off. I was rattled. What did he have to do with what was going on with Nareece? I hoped the answer would lead me to her.

I stayed wired for the rest of the two-hour ride. The car clock flashed 3:38 when I turned right down a dead-end street in the affluent residential neighborhood of Chestnut Hill in Northwest Philly. I pulled in the driveway of a sprawling white colonial nestled on a secluded property at the end of the street and double-checked the address, 740 Thomas Road. It was the right one.

Laughton answered the door dressed in tan slacks and a seafoam-green shirt topped with a tan and green jacket. I checked him out with an exaggerated look from head to toe. He had slick Italian leather loafers on and no socks. Laughton never wore socks, another of his quirks. I decided not to comment on his look, which I found alluring. Instead, I entered and turned my attention to the surroundings.

"Pretty ritzy," I said.

"Thanks," he answered.

I glanced at him sideways. "Yours?"

"A little pleasure I picked up along the way."

"You'll have to school me so I can pick one up, too."

"Not a problem." He closed the door and gestured toward the left. "Please, after you, Mademoiselle."

"I'll 'mademoiselle' you."

The entryway opened to a large living room with a bar at the far end and a manteled fireplace at the halfway point. At the other end was a large taupe couch shaped into a half circle, with two cushy burgundy chairs set in the room's center.

Laughton rushed past me to the bar. "Drink?"

"At three thirty in the morning?" I said. He stood by the bar waiting for my answer. "No thanks." I plopped down and sank into the couch cushions, feigning a nonchalant attitude but singed with curiosity. He poured a Scotch, sipped, added ice, and stirred before gulping it to empty. He poured more, then set it down and slid out a long-stemmed wineglass from an overhead rack.

"I said no."

He continued what he'd started, then brought both drinks to the couch and sat down next to me, handing me the wine.

"Are you deaf? I said, 'No thank you.'" I set the drink on the coffee table and slid back so I could see him better. "Okay, I'm here. What's going on?"

He shook his head. "I should have figured you wouldn't listen to me. I told you to back off. I told you I'd handle everything. I just needed a few days." I held his glare even after he continued. His voice caused a prickly sensation up my arm. "Now John's dead and Jesse's got Carmella." He slugged back his drink and went for another.

"Carmella? Wha . . . What the hell do you know about Carmella?"

"I knew, know, Carmella when she was Carmella, not now,

not as Nareece or whatever the hell her name is now. I didn't know she was your sister until recently."

Now it was my turn. I gulped the wine.

"The situation is off the hook now."

"What 'situation', Laughton? I can't believe you've been running with this and didn't tell me what's been going on and the danger my sister was in. That you even know I have a sister and didn't tell me before now."

Laughton finished his drink and went for another.

"You might as well spill it, Laughton. I'm not going anywhere until you do. And nothing is going to happen from here on without me."

Laughton took his time making another drink. He dropped one, two, three ice cubes into the glass, a squeeze of lime, the Scotch: two fingers, no, three. I resisted the urge to voice my irritation with his drinking, compounded by the heat building deep inside me. He lifted his glass and strolled to the window. Then he just stood there, looking out. I was about done when he said, "Jesse Boone is my brother."

Only my eyes worked. They kept Laughton in range and watched him fall from grace, slamming his beautiful face into the pavement. *He's waiting for a response*, I thought. Then I saw my reflection splashed against the nighttime backdrop of the picture window. My mouth was gaped open, eyes wide, face frozen. Anger quickly blew the shock away, anger that carved a path from my heart to my brain, blowing through my nose, ringing in my ears, burning my eyes, drying my mouth to desert status, and ramming my stomach. I stayed anchored to the couch.

Laughton turned from the window to look at me. His face was drawn, accentuated by dark bags under his now-hollowed eyes. Silence perched on the now-stagnated air between us.

"What are you saying, Laughton? How can Jesse be your

brother? You can't be part of Jesse Boone. You're not . . ." I ditched his eyes, taking it in. I was reeling.

He came to the couch, sat down, and in the same motion grabbed my shoulders and twisted me around to look at him. I let him, still in disbelief.

"Muriel, I'm telling you because Jesse's crazy and he has Carmella or Nareece, whatever you call her, and we can't get her back alive if I don't square up."

"The only reason you're telling me this now is because you think Jesse will kill Reecey and you don't want that on your conscience?" It came out all screechy.

I pulled away from him and rested my head on the couch, willing my stomach to settle. Gold specks in the ceiling twinkled and danced from side to side depending on which eye I kept open.

"Listen to me. My father is . . . was . . . a big deal back in the days when the Black Mafia had Philly bagged. He was a real sick fuck. He killed people, made people beg for their lives and killed them anyway. Pistol-whipped them 'til their bones broke through flesh. He only cared about two things: power and money."

I jumped up off the couch and shouted, "Stop! I don't need a breakdown of your family history, Laughton. What I do need to know is where's Jesse holding Nareece?"

"You need to hear this now, M. You have to let me tell you."

"I don't have to let you tell me a damn thing."

Laughton snagged my arm and yanked me back down on the couch. "My father was third in command with the Black Mafia running with guys like Sam Christian and Ron Harvey, all deadly. For as far back as I can remember, guys with guns watched while people cried, begged, pleaded, and bowed down to my father like he was the Black Godfather. He'd be soft as a baby's butt one minute, and mess you up in the last five seconds before the minute was up, then he'd walk away settled and composed, going on with his day like nothing had happened, leaving the mess for his soldiers to sterilize." He hesitated, then leaned forward and rested his elbows on his knees, holding his glass with both hands. When he spoke again, his voice was light and easy in an insane way.

"But I loved him. He was my father. All I could see was how great I thought he was, how powerful, how people came to him with everything and he fixed everything." The light and easy tone faded quickly. "One night we were at the dinner table— Mom, Jesse, me, and Pop. Jesse and I were talking about something, I can't remember what now, and my father reached over and started choking Mom at the dinner table while Jesse and I watched, too fucked up to stop him. I was seventeen and Jesse was only twenty-one—we weren't about nothing. When he let her go, her head dropped like a brick onto her plate and broke it." Laughton deepened his voice. "C'mon, boys, it's your time to shine now.' On the way out, he said to his soldiers, 'Clean up in there.'" He gestured with his arms as though her body was nearby. "I thought I didn't care. She wasn't my real mother. Jesse and I have different mothers. But she was the mother I really remember, the mother who had raised me. He threw my real mother out when I was five, and I never saw her again until I found her seven years ago."

In a hushed tone, I said, "Where's your real mother now?"

"In a nursing home outside the city. She has Alzheimer's. Man, she has some fierce nightmares and talks really crazy about some scary shit. I'd bet it was some real shit, too.

"Anyway, I left. I disappeared a year later, after he killed Harriet, Jesse's mom. Jesse stayed and became much like my father. Got involved in the heroin and cocaine trade, prostitution, numbers, and whatever else made money and hurt good people.

"About a year and a half after I'd left, Jesse came looking.

He found me down in Baltimore and had some pros work me over good. He was there for the finale. They beat me, broke my legs, and bashed my teeth in. He kicked my face 'til there wasn't anything left: no face, just raw flesh. He left me for dead. I always wondered if my father gave the order." Laughton set his drink down, got shakily to his feet, and shuffled back to the window. "A lot of plastic surgery, a new identity, then a few tours overseas, special ops. When I got out, I joined the force."

"How'd you get in the department?"

"I got folks on the force who helped me. I'm nothing like Jesse or my father."

"You mean, you got people you bought? You hate what your father and Jesse stand for, but you like the benefits." I spread my arms and gestured to the surroundings.

He went back to the bar for another drink.

"So, where does all of this leave my sister? Will Jesse kill her?"

He stumbled on the trip back to the couch. "No. He won't kill her, but he'll mess her up. He's obsessed with her."

"Jesse isn't capable of love."

"I said he's obsessed. Hasn't got a damn thing to do with love."

"He already tried at the Vineyard," I said, unable to find a smooth place in my mind to settle.

Laughton's raised eyebrows registered a glint of surprise before he said, "M, please shut up and listen to me." He sat down again. His stare burned through to the backs of my eyeballs. "Carmella was Jesse's girl. She was everything to him. But Jesse's crazy and badass jealous. One day he accused Carmella of messin' around on him, and it got really ugly. She had enough on him to put him away, so he'd been shooting her up awhile with drugs to control her. I couldn't stand seeing her keep coming back for more of his drugs and abuse. But still, I didn't know she'd ripped Jesse off until the next day."

"... of a pound of heroin and two million dollars," I said, almost absentmindedly.

"You knew about it?"

"Not then. Reece just told me. What would Reecey do . . . How could she do anything with two million dollars without me knowing?" No sooner had the words escaped my mouth than my thoughts traveled to Nareece's expensive house in Milton, how I didn't really know John's occupation, the exclusive private school the girls attended . . . "Where was I? How'd all this get by me?"

I gagged on overlapping images flashing in front of me, spoiling Laughton's beautiful couch with vomit. Laughton rushed to the kitchen and returned with a wet cloth and a glass of water for me. He leaned over and tried to wipe my face. I slapped his hand away. He put the cloth and the water on the coffee table in front of me and sat down.

"This isn't easy, M. I didn't . . ."

"Didn't what? Think it was important to tell me you had a fake identity? That you're Jesse's brother? Or that Jesse might try to kill my sister? What, Laughton?"

"I didn't even know you were related to Carmella until a few weeks ago! Remember? Carmella was in *my* family back then. And she wanted to hurt Jesse because he treated her like shit and wouldn't let her go. So she took the two million, destroyed a stash of heroin and coke, and split." Laughton snatched his glass off the coffee table and went for another drink. "Her dumb move was going back home. She had to know he wasn't just going to let her get away."

"She was barely sixteen, Laughton. Did she even have a choice about anything? And the three men who almost killed her, were you one of them?"

He shot me a hard look that melted almost immediately. "I can't believe you would even ask me if I was involved."

"It was twenty years ago. You were someone else. You *are* someone else."

He hesitated, then said, "It was Jesse, Wade Taylor, and a cat named Billy Davis. Davis died in prison a while back."

"Did you know?"

"I found out my father ordered Jesse to get rid of her, so I went to Carmella's house, your house. When I drove up, I heard gunshots and Jesse, Wade, and Billy came running out. I drove off when I saw them run out."

"Why now? Why's Jesse coming at her now?"

"He's been in prison for the past fifteen years, serving out time for killing our father."

"All these years, the anguish, the guilt, and you said nothing?" I lashed out. "You bastard!"

"First off, I didn't know who *you* were, and I certainly didn't know about Nareece being your sister or that she was even still alive."

I picked up my glass and threw it at him, then rushed him, punching and clawing. Laughton got his arms around my arms, so I kicked and tried to head-butt him away. He released me and stumbled backward. I grabbed his shirt by both shoulders, flipped him over to the floor, and lodged my knee in his neck. My heart banged against my chest at breakthrough force. Laughton swung his arm up and knocked me away, flipped me over, and put his knee in my neck. After a few minutes he lowered his body on top of mine, his face inches away.

"I felt you, girl, the moment we met," he whispered.

My heart leaped, but my mouth spoke on its own accord. "Oh, please," I spat back with all the sarcasm I could muster.

He stayed put until my breathing slowed, and stayed longer, then kissed me. I struggled against his hold, but his lips stayed on mine no matter which way I turned, and the "*no*" I screamed in my head, stopped. I flopped like a fish out of water and turned my head away.

"Have you lost your mind?" I yelped.

He loosened his grip on my wrists and rested his head on my shoulder.

A wave of guilt swallowed my anger, mostly. I pushed at him to get him off of me. He responded and moved aside, lying on his back with his arms spread-eagle. I sat up and slid back to lean against the wall. I would never have imagined how anything could dampen my feelings for Laughton until now.

"Did you get Jesse off?"

"No. He doesn't even suspect I'm his brother," he said, sitting up. "He thinks I'm dead. Kelvin Boone *is* dead."

"A new face doesn't make a new person," I said, buttoning my blouse, which had come undone. I felt my face flush. "How'd he find out Nareece's name and where she lived?"

"Good question. I also think Jesse is controlling someone in the department."

"What about John? Do you think he knew about Jesse?"

"I'd bet John only learned about the whole mess a few weeks ago, after Jesse found out about Carmella and went to her house."

I thought about the note Nareece had told me about, the note I'd ignored because I figured she was exaggerating again and just being paranoid. I also reflected on the photograph John's sister and Bates had shown me of Jesse going into Nareece's house.

Laughton sat up on the floor in front of me and put his hand on my leg. I pushed it off. He stood up and moved away.

"Wade Taylor found out who I was and tried to blackmail me. I don't know how he knew. He was scared of Jesse and said I'd have to kill him before he'd tell me anything about what Jesse was into. I know Jesse has someone inside the department. Wade told me Jesse was looking for Nareece . . .

Carmella. He was scared Jesse would come after him. I think Jesse killed him just to tie up loose ends."

"And what about Marcy Taylor? When were you married to her? And why was she killed?"

"We were kids. She was sixteen. I was seventeen. She thought she was pregnant, but it turned out she wasn't. My father made me do the right thing, then when it wasn't happening, he made me divorce her. He beat the shit outta me for that. I think she really did commit suicide. That's what it's looking like anyway."

I got up and moved to the couch.

"I also think Jesse paid big bucks to get out on parole. The police ain't shit."

"Yeah, well, you're one of us, no wonder."

Laughton came and sat next to me. "Look, M, you could end up dead if you don't listen to me."

"Why would he target me? He's still ignorant about me being Reecey's sister." It was a statement more than a question. I didn't need Laughton to answer. I stood and straightened my clothing.

"It doesn't matter whether he knows you're Carmella's sister or not, you're testifying against him in a murder case. How do you think he's gotten away with murder 'til now? All except one—our father."

"So, where's he holding Nareece?"

He got up and stood over me. "I'm working on it. I'll call you when I know something."

"Are you kicking me out now? You'll call me. That's all you got? You'll call me. And what am I supposed to do with all of this until you call me?" I grabbed my purse and sweater and went to the door, anxious to breathe fresh air. Laughton followed.

He grabbed my elbow and spun me around. "M, I care

about you and Travis. I didn't know you and Carmella were sisters until I read the file, after Jesse got released from prison. I'll help you get Carmella back, put Jesse away for good, and then I'm gone."

"Seems like you're suited well for leaving." I backed away from him and stepped over the threshold. I turned back to him. "Why'd you come back?"

"Something about home, I guess," he said and cracked a half smile.

"So many lies told, Laughton. Just like that, it's all shit." I spun around and walked away, pissed because a tear blazed a trail down my cheek.

CHAPTER 19

At 5:00 a.m. on Monday, Dulcey's street was deserted except for a Bigfoot kind of guy who lumbered behind a shopping cart overflowing with trash bags stuffed with possessions. He stopped every few hundred yards to rummage through a trash barrel for treasures to add to his collection.

I pulled curbside in front of Dulcey's house and waited while he finished "shopping" in her neighbor's barrel. He wore a dirty hoodie under a dirtier beige raincoat with sleeves that capped at his elbows and lengthwise barely reached his thighs. Gobs of matted hair stretched the hood of the undergarment and hung over his face. He pulled soda cans from the barrel and stuffed them into a half-filled trash bag tied to the end of his cart. Then he pulled out a football trophy and rubbed it off with the sleeve of his hoodie, placed it atop his cart, and moved on with a straighter stature.

Dulcey lives in a twin row house at 4604 Locust Street in West Philly. While many of the neighborhood row houses were dilapidated, Dulcey's house was like an oasis, freshly painted, lawn manicured with seasonal plantings. That's what Dulcey did: make things beautiful even when hope was dimmed. "Lost causes are the only ones worth fighting for, child," she quipped at the mere mention of something being impossible to recover or the enormity of a failed prospect.

Though the house was dark, I knew Dulcey, and Hamp, if he was home, would be at the kitchen table sipping a hearty blended brewed coffee and reading the *Inquirer*, Philly's prime newspaper. I got out of my car and went around to the side of the house to the glass-enclosed porch. She answered my tap immediately. She pulled me inside and hugged me with enough force to crush a bear, pushed me back to arms' length, and gave me the once-over, making sure all my parts were in the right places.

"I been crazy worryin' about your behind," she whispered, reeling me in for another hug. "Travis hasn't moved from my side, and the twins are detectin' 'til I wanna lock them up for obstruction." She cackled.

The smell of bacon and cinnamon made my stomach squeak out a hungry verse. I could not remember the last time I ate.

"I hear you," Dulcey said, patting my belly. I swiped her hand away. "C'mon, girl, and sit yourself down." She ushered me into the kitchen and pulled out a chair where she wanted me to sit.

"Where's Hamp?"

Dulcey got a dish out of the cabinet and started filling it with bacon, cheese eggs, grits, and cinnamon biscuits, her specialty. She responded with her back to me. "He got him a little job delivering newspapers. Gets him outta my way early in the morning, keeps him outta trouble—some—and puts some money in his pocket." She sighed, then continued, on her way to bringing the mile-high plate to the table. "He's doing much better, and I thank God for that." She set the plate in front of me and plopped down in a chair.

I inhaled the first helping and devoured a second before I

sat back in my chair, a Buddha to behold. She stayed quiet while I pigged out. Now she sat straight in the chair with her lips pursed and hands folded, her thumbs circling each other at warp speed as though conducting a mini-orchestra, the sound of which came from her feet rubbing back and forth.

"Your belly's full, now talk to me."

"I just came from Laughton's." I hated that I teared up before I could get any more out.

Dulcey sat forward in her chair and hunched over the table with folded arms. "Girl, you just need to take a breath and let it flow."

"Laughton is Jesse Boone's brother—half brother."

She pushed back in her chair like I had socked her in the jaw. "I'll be a monkey's auntie."

"That's only the short of it. Jesse has Nareece, and someone in the department or in the FBI is on Jesse's dime. That's how he's been getting away with murder, how he found Reecey, and how he probably knows about me being her sister and being the one that helped shut down the organization. It's a friggin' mess."

"And Reecey took that maniac's money. Sounds like you gotta get the police . . ."

"Yeah, right, and get Reecey killed! No way. Laughton is going to find out where Jesse is holding Reecey, and we're going to get her back."

"Laughton and you."

"Laughton and me. I don't know what else Jesse knows. That's why I think you need to take the girls and Travis to your sister's place."

She got up and cleared my plate from the table. "Don't you worry about the kids. I told you I got them covered. You just do what you gotta to bring Reecey home without getting you or her killed in the doing."

Travis shuffled into the kitchen at Dulcey's last words.

He limped across the floor to me, kissed my cheek, and plopped down next to me. "Man, Moms, you need to be calling Laughton and get him on the case. You can't be jumping off by yourself. Can't leave you alone for a minute," he said with a slight laugh.

"Why are you limping?"

"I banged my knee messing with them crazy twins."

"They love you."

"Don't be trying to change the subject. And don't be trying to make like I'm too young to see what's happenin'. I'm not stupid," he said with a stern look and a fatherly tone.

"You think Laughton's the savior for everything." I rubbed his chin and sniffed him. "You need a shave and a shower, boy. A haircut wouldn't hurt, either," I said, running my hand through his hair.

"Yeah, yeah. You sound like a recording." He brushed my hand away. "Ma." His agitation was slight but sincere.

"Who's the cop here anyway?" I countered. "Not to worry, son. I got this." I gestured with my hands and raised one shoulder, giving back some of his mannerisms. His face lightened, and he playfully punched my shoulder.

Dulcey set a plate of food and a glass of milk in front of him. "Eat, boy. Your momma been doing police work way before your scrawny behind was even thought of, now eat. Put some meat on them bones."

"What? And I'm just supposed to sit around like a sissy while my moms gets picked off by some crazy guy who doesn't have a clue who he's dealing with? You sure do know how to make a man feel inept."

"Inept, huh?"

"Word."

"Eat, boy," I said, hoping that would be the end of that conversation. I was blessed when I heard the twins. They stormed down the stairs sounding like thunder and raced into the kitchen trying to squeeze in the doorway at the same time. When they finally burst through, they charged me, squealing in unison, "Auntie, Auntie!" and jumped in my lap, in unison. Helen landed on the floor. Travis saved the day from a catastrophe as my chair toppled backward.

When everyone was settled, Rose said, "Where's Mommy and Daddy?" She twisted around on my lap until she faced me.

Dulcey gave me a sideways glance, as she set the table for them.

"Mommy says hi and she'll be here soon," I said, stung anew by the reality of John's death and their ignorance of the fact. Now certainly was not the time to tell them. The time would come once Nareece was back in their presence. I quickly changed the subject. "So, Auntie Dulcey tells me you're working hard at the shop."

"Yeah, and Helen poured some color in a lady's hair and turned it green."

I looked at Dulcey in horror for confirmation.

"Child sure did. But we fixed her up. Ms. Greely. Turned out she liked the color Rose made better than the nasty red she'd been using for years, long as I been doing her hair." Dulcey cackled, shaking her head as she put plates of food down for the twins. "C'mon, you detectives sit up here and eat. We gotta leave in a bit."

"Auntie, can we go with you now?" Rose asked, her lips stuck out, eyes droopy, for effect.

"Soon, baby, soon. Auntie's got a few errands to do today to help your mom finish some business."

"Mommy and Daddy are still in trouble, huh?" Helen asked, taking a mouthful of food.

Getting up from the table at the vibration of my cell phone,

I said, "Nothing Auntie can't handle," and went into the living room.

"Muriel Mabley."

"Mabley. You need to get in here now!" Cap yelled. "You hear me? *Now!*"

"But—"

"Now, Mabley." And he hung up.

The twins choked up when I hugged them good-bye, jabbering at lightning speed. I hugged Travis and left him and the twins at the kitchen table to devour the breakfast Dulcey had made. Dulcey walked me outside to my car.

"You call me if things get outta hand and you need some blocking." She furrowed her brow and pointed her finger at me. "Be careful, M."

I nodded and got into the car. After Dulcey went back into the house, I made a U-turn and headed to the station, then decided I needed a shower and some clean clothes. I also wanted to retrieve the initials and phone number I had found in Nareece's file. Cap could wait a half hour longer.

When I got home, I found a note from Mr. Kim stuck to the door. It read, *Please come over to my house. I need to see you.* I dropped my purse and briefcase on the couch and went next door. Kim did not answer. I made a mental note to call him later.

I checked the house phone for messages. There was one from Cap yelling obscenities and two hang-ups. I went upstairs to my office and retrieved the Mabley file from under the blotter on my desk. The notepaper with the mysterious initials and phone number was stuck to the inside cover. I dialed the number. Someone picked up after the third ring but didn't say anything. They stayed silent for a few seconds before clicking off.

I showered and changed into street clothes, locked up the house, and went to the station.

"Hey, M," Parker called out, raising his hand above the top of his cubicle. "Get ready to rumble." He snickered. "You got some seedy folk laying for you. Call me if you need help."

I stepped inside his cubicle. "Do me one better, Parker. Get me a name and address for this phone number, please."

He looked at the paper and grinned back at me, the kind of grin that said, "*You owe me two now*," though at the moment, I could not remember what the first one was for.

"Take a seat," Cap ordered after I entered his office and closed the door. I sat in a chair in front of his desk. Two men sat off to the side facing me, one white with dark, squinty eyes and a pocked face. The other looked almost as scary, except for Dumbo ears. "This here is Agent Jakes and Agent Janey." He nodded in their direction, but kept his eyes on me. I coughed to mask my amusement of Jakes and Janey. "They want to ask you some questions."

"Mabley, we need your help," Agent Jakes—or was he Janey?—said as he got up and moved to the front of the desk and sat directly in front of me, his knee at my chest. "We're investigating several murders we suspect Jesse Boone is responsible for." Agent Janey—or was he Jakes?—whichever one Agent Dumbo Ears was, stayed put off to the side, perched on the corner of a file cabinet, and silent. He failed miserably at looking tough.

I pushed back in my chair and met the detective's stare.

"You're familiar with Boone," the detective said.

"Familiar? If you mean, did he *almost* rape and kill me, yes, I'm familiar with Boone."

"The only time you've encountered Boone was during that recent altercation?"

"Yes."

"What's Laughton's connection to Boone?"

"Why're you asking me these questions? What's this about?"

Dumbo Ears grunted, uncrossed and crossed his legs, and closed his hands together, capturing his raised knee. I met his stare briefly, then refocused on the agent who blocked my view of the captain.

"Please answer the question."

I shifted in my chair and sat forward. "I don't know that Laughton has a connection to Boone more than working with me on the case."

Both detectives got up and moved toward the door. My interrogator turned at the door and said, "Thanks, Captain. We'll be in touch again if necessary."

The captain and I stayed focused on the two strolling down the corridor until they passed through the exit door.

"Mabley, you're walking a thin line here. This can get bad."

"Cap, I found out Jesse Boone's the one who almost killed Reecey. I would bet the letter she got was from him, that's why she was scared. She's known all along it was Jesse. I think he's got her now."

Cap got up and moved to the front of his desk and sat in the same place where the FBI agent had sat. "Before you get yourself killed, let me fill you in on some things. I should have told you all this a long time ago, but you were so fragile, and then Elliot and Esther . . . Your father was the best friend any man could have . . . I'd hoped it was dead forever."

"Hoped what was dead forever?"

I got up and moved around the room, stopping at Cap's wall of fame—photos of him with politicians, the police commissioner, honored officers, my father, and his wife and two daughters. My stomach grumbled, letting me know no good was coming down the pike.

"You've been good for this department, Muriel."

Cap had not called me Muriel since I started working in his section.

"All right, Cap, you're starting to sound guilty of something." I turned and stumbled over to where he sat. "Why did you let those detectives interrogate me like I did something wrong?"

"Laughton—"

I spun around, swinging my arms up. "Laughton, Laughton, all anybody talks about is Laughton. I don't know the man anymore. How about that?"

"He's Jesse Boone's brother."

I acted surprised. My instincts told me to shut up and let him talk, though guilt swamped me again and singed the hairs on my arms.

"Look, M. Nobody knew who Laughton was, not even me. He's a war hero, for chrissakes. Started his life over . . . buried Kelvin Boone. Kelvin, that's his real name. He told me when he quit what the deal was, said he needed to finish some business before he moved on."

"What business?"

"He found out Jesse was the one who damn near killed Nareece. He's afraid Jesse will find out you're Nareece's sister and the one who helped bring his father down, and the whole Black Mafia operation. And just so you know, it gets even better. Jesse worked with the Feds after he got sent up for his father's murder. That's how they managed to cripple those sons a bitches. That's also how he got paroled."

"Yeah, but how did he get off from killing that young college girl after he got out?"

"I hate to think the Feds are that low, but I'd bet they made some kind of arrangement for some reason we'll probably never know. Boone's been locked up for a while, but don't underestimate his influence. He's been working from inside, and now he's out with a vengeance. He learned well from his father."

"How'd Laughton find out about me and Nareece?"

"He said someone in the department is dirty, somebody high up. He discovered your file during his own investigation."

"You don't just 'discover' a cold case file, Cap. You have to be digging for it, that specific file."

I felt like he was avoiding the subject when he got up and moved around to the front of his desk and pulled a file from his top drawer. "Boston Police contacted me, unofficially of course. You've been meddling in a murder case up there, John's murder. They found Boone's fingerprints at the scene."

"Boone's gotten away with three murders, maybe more, because he's pro–tec–ted," I spat, sarcastically. "I'm not about to let him make Nareece another statistic."

"I've got your back for as long as I can, but it could mean both our careers." He hesitated, then continued. "I owe your father, the best friend any man could have."

"You said that already. And it's a debt you've paid a thousand times over—you saved my ass, you helped me get Reecey away, watched over us always." I reached across the desk for his hand and squeezed.

"You would have been off the force if I hadn't stepped in. They should never have put you undercover so soon out of the academy. They wanted you because you were a fresh face. There was so much killing going on, so much corruption. The whole Black Mafia thing scared the crap outta everybody. Nobody was safe, and so many good cops died. Many turned, too."

I closed my eyes against crushed memories. Crushed, burned, buried, entombed.

Three years after I joined the force, I was scooped up for a special operation—going undercover to infiltrate the Black Mafia. The directive was simple: gather enough information to enable a successful prosecution of key figures. An intense week of instruction on how to identify drugs, contraband, terminology, and prices, and away I went. Muriel Mabley became Lakisha Butler. It was scary how well I succumbed to Lakisha. A key figure in the Black Mafia of the seventies and eighties, Big Daddy Mann latched on to me at first sight. The operation was all good until my cover got blown. In truth, it was all whack. I couldn't get past the nightmare that was resurfacing now.

I let my head fall back and felt a slight adrenaline rush, a skeleton of the real deal right after a hit of heroin. I inhaled and held it until my brain quieted, then opened my eyes and focused on Cap.

He eyed me. "It's still a part of you, isn't it?"

"Always. Doesn't mean it owns me. I sail through every day and thank God for blessing me."

"Keep it that way. Now go on, get outta here. Keep me abreast of your movements."

I stopped at Parker's cubicle on the way out. He handed me a piece of paper with "*4603 Bryn Mawr Avenue*" and "*Frank Mann Johnson*" printed on it.

CHAPTER 20

Like I said, Frank "Big Daddy" Mann Johnson was supposed to be dead. At least that's what the FBI had me believe all these years—killed in prison ten years ago while serving a life sentence for murder. Now here I was, chasing down an address that was listed as his.

It was dark by the time I veered right off Wynnefield Avenue to Bryn Mawr Avenue in West Philly. I pulled up a half block past the 4603 Bryn Mawr address and parked curbside. The street was lined with large half-timbered-style houses, art deco versions of English Regency constructed of dark red brick and stone trim. They were set back and screened by sycamore and magnolia trees and other shrubbery.

Sweat trickled down from my armpits as my breathing rhythm quickened. *Pull yourself together, Muriel. Don't freak out now.* I closed my eyes and focused on a tiny light spot in the darkness. After a few minutes, my breathing slowed. I tried Laughton. He didn't answer. I got out of the car frustrated, but determined.

A black Range Rover was parked in front of 4603 Bryn Mawr. It was probably the same vehicle that had picked Jesse Boone up from the courthouse, that followed Dulcey and me in Massachusetts, and that I'd seen in the parking lot at the rest stop on my last trip. Then it had been too dark to see the kind of car. But I did remember it was a SUV.

I did not have a plan. I'd never expected to see Mann again, so first I needed to know whether he was really alive. What was I going to do, just walk up to the front door and knock? Not a good idea, since Mann and everyone associated with him thought I was dead. And then there was that small detail that I wasn't equipped to take on Jesse Boone and his goons alone. There was no superwoman testosterone pumping through my system.

I decided on some reconnaissance.

Trees hugged the house, and vines streamed over the windows. Rhododendrons overarched the walkway, and dead petals covered the flat stones. The light of a full moon behind broken clouds cast ominous shadows over the lawn. I tiptoed up the walkway to the front door. Loud, muffled voices filtered through. I snuck around to the side of the house.

An icy exhilaration ran through my body when I peered inside the living room window and saw a much older, fatter, and uglier Big Daddy Mann sitting on the couch with his back angled to me. Jesse Boone stood over him, his face contorted, his finger jabbing the air around Big Daddy's face. Two other men stood on either side of the entryway. They were Jesse's bodyguards, I supposed. I nearly crumpled backward. The ground covering snapped under my weight and drew the attention of one bodyguard through the open window. I crouched down in the bushes and froze, my breath zapped. His shadow spread across the bushes as he looked out the window. He moved away, and I stepped out from the bushes just as the front door opened. I stepped back and plastered myself against the house, as the man stepped cautiously down the walkway in my direction.

He breathed like a bull, his finger readied on the trigger of a semiautomatic pistol, maybe a 9 mm. A glint of light bounced off the shine of his shoes. He peered into the darkness long enough to make me almost pee my pants, then spun around and went back into the house.

When the door closed, I sprinted down the sidewalk to my car, drove down the street with the lights off, turned a corner, and stopped. The shakes took over. Flashes of the lopsided sneer that contorted Jesse Boone's face and the wrinkled, bulging neck of Big Daddy Mann blocked my vision.

I shook my head, then shook my hands, making them flop back and forth, and sucked in a deep breath—ten deep breaths, trying to ease a familiar urge that raced through my body. I could not believe that seeing Mann had evoked such a reaction. Sixteen years, six months, twenty-four days—I checked my watch—twelve hours and thirteen minutes I had been off of heroin. My head whirled.

Call the police. Nareece may be in there. But what if she's not, and Boone has her held prisoner somewhere else? He'd never give her up, and the FBI doesn't give a damn about anything but getting Jesse.

I could not erase the image of Daddy Mann, his touch, his voice, his hot breath in my ear. *"You'll wish you were dead when I'm finished with your sweet little ass."*

My cell phone rang, ripping through my thoughts. Calvin's name showed on the screen.

I wanted to answer, but I felt like I'd lose it if I heard his voice. Instead, I waited until the *dong* sounded, indicating he'd left a message, then clicked on the bar to listen to it.

I put my head back and let Calvin's deep, silky voice calm me. "I'm just checking on you, baby. You didn't call, so I was worried. Call me when you get a moment. I'm here for you whenever and for whatever you need." I clicked off when it ended and stayed put, unable to move.

I shrieked at a knock on the passenger-side window.

"Unlock the door, M." It was Laughton.

I pressed the Unlock button, and he got in, talking way too loud even before he closed the door.

"What the hell are you doing?" he said. "I told you to wait for my call."

I didn't respond, trying to recover from near–heart failure. I leaned forward on the steering wheel, rested my forehead on my hands, and shut my eyes. Laughton finally tuned in and came at me from a softer place.

"Are you all right? I didn't mean to scare you, but what are you doing here?"

I sat up and faced him. "What am *I* doing here? What are *you* doing here? You said, '*I'll call you.*' Yeah, right."

"Move the car. Drive up and pull into the plaza."

I started the car, took a right to Larchwood, drove down a half mile and into Garden Court Plaza to the far southwest corner of the lot, and parked. The lot was empty except for about a dozen cars spread out.

Laughton waited a few minutes after we parked to speak. For the first time since I'd met him, I was uncomfortable in his presence.

"I'm sorry you're back in this, M. I tried to get this done without you."

"We've already been over this. And I'll say it again, evidently the only way it's getting done is *with* me."

"We can get Jesse and Mann this time, for good."

"What do you mean, 'this time'? Mann's supposed to be dead. Jesse's supposed to be in prison. Instead, Mann's sitting his fat ass in a pretty fancy house talking to Jesse, who, by the way, has kidnapped my sister and is probably torturing her with his sick ass."

"She's definitely not here. I got a tip that Jesse's got her at an old mill building that my father owned. He owned a few in the same block."

"By 'here,' do you mean the house down from where I was parked when you scared the hell out of me? And why the mill building? Who owns it now?"

"Yes, and it's the best place he can go where nobody would find him. There are some underground tunnels that go between them if he needs to escape. I'm guessing Jesse owns them now. I told you, he's out for payback. In the old days, Mann would've had Jesse killed for tripping over a woman. Mann's old and weak now."

"Sure, old and weak. He didn't look so old and weak to me. Fat and ugly, but not old and weak." I shook my hands out again.

"Mann's small-time now. He's nothing. The FBI used him, too, to shut down the whole Black Mafia thing in the day. It was all cool when they were killing each other, you know, blacks killing blacks. They used Mann and Jesse separately and without knowledge of each other to get to some of the lead guys, my father for one. Mann's been hold up for years until Jesse came back on the scene."

"Jesse. Who is Jesse to command anything?"

"He's a psychopath stepping into a door of opportunity. With most of the head guys gone, he thinks he can rebuild the organization and rule the streets again. This is a fantasy world with him where he's king of the mountain and anyone who tries to climb up is dead."

"This keeps getting better. And you're working with the FBI to stop him."

"Somehow they figured out I'm his brother. They're using the information against me. Someone inside the PPD is on Jesse's payroll, which is how he got off. I haven't been able to figure who it is and the FBI is clueless about a lot of things."

"You know where Jesse is now?"

"I told you, at the mill building."

"No, he's with Mann."

Laughton drew back.

"I just told you I saw him and Mann and—"

"We have to let Jesse lead us to Nareece before we get the FBI involved." Laughton covered my hand with his. I pulled away. "We need to go back to Mann's and wait," he said. He caught my arm, stopping me from starting the car. "How did you get this address?"

"I found a phone number with initials *FMJ* on a sticky note in Nareece's file. The one you were hiding in your desk drawer." I seethed. I had to stop and take a breath. I continued when I felt more in control. "I asked Parker to run the number. The note was in your handwriting."

"Frank Big Daddy Mann Johnson, *FMJ*. I didn't put a sticky note in the file."

"The writing looks just like yours." I reached back to retrieve the file from the rear seat pocket. The sticky note was on the inside cover.

He turned on the overhead light and examined the note.

I backed out of the parking lot and drove the block back to Bryn Mawr Avenue, then parked on the opposite side of the street from Big Daddy Mann's house. The black Range Rover was gone.

"Stay here," Laughton said.

"I'm in this all the way, so do not even try playing the knight in shining armor. It doesn't suit you."

The sound of our heels echoed off the silent air. We crept up the walkway. The door was ajar. Laughton pulled his gun from his back and pushed the door open. I followed with my weapon drawn. The only light came from the right in the living room, where I had seen Jesse and Big Daddy earlier. I moved toward it. Big Daddy Mann lay on the couch, his shirt soaked in blood from a gaping hole in his stomach, no doubt made by a shotgun. His eyes popped the moment he saw me. The next moment, a demonic smile split his face.

I stretched his arm above the wound and then let go. He groaned. I hawked up a good one and spit into his eye. "You got off easy, you son of a bitch," I told him.

It was the last thing he ever heard. I backed away and felt Laughton's arms around me. I held on to him and cried—I mean, sobbed. Hell, I hadn't really cried in fifteen years.

Finally Laughton nudged me back to a drier platform. "Let's do this," he said.

"Like I told you, I'm all in. These are tears of joy, my dearest, tears of joy." I wiped my nose with the back of my sleeve and regained my composure.

We moved around the room searching, then moved to the dining room and kitchen and searched some more. There were no signs of Nareece ever being there and no clues of her whereabouts.

"Talk to me," Laughton said.

"What do you want me to say? You're the one working with the FBI."

"I'm only privy to what they tell me," he said.

"Then you're definitely screwed."

He abandoned his approach to that conversation and changed direction. "You need to call this in and be here for the troops." He hesitated. "Agents Jakes and Janey will respond."

"I've already had the pleasure."

We looked at each other and laughed.

"Jakes and Janey. Sounds like a damn circus show," Laughton said. Then our laughter waned.

I took a seat at the kitchen table. Laughton sat across the table from me.

"What happened to me was like I was in a movie," I said. "I guess I thought when I'd done my job and put them all behind bars, I'd go back to my life and never look back. Or I'd look to the next starring role. Those bastards glamorized undercover work. I wanted to prove something, I guess. I mean, the FBI wanted *me* to join their team, to be their star player. I was good, too, did everything right, got all good info. Plucky girl.

"Mann was pretty good-looking back then. Still a pig, though. And I gave a stellar performance as Lakisha Butler, the pig's 'main squeeze,' as he called me. He trusted me with everything. It got so I knew enough to destroy his operation. It's still a mystery how my cover got blown, but when it did, Mann didn't even blink when he filled my veins with heroin, over and over." I faltered for a second, and the next second, calm surged through my body, making me weightless, hovering over the pictures that flashed before me. "All those pigs . . . every damn day . . . twenty-four/seven, climbing on me, leaving their stench. I prayed for death every one of those days and more when they found me."

"Report said you were missing for three months before they found you in a burned-out building in Bartram Village."

"I thought you only knew what they told you. Only reason I'm here is the cap. He stayed with me through rehab and took care of Reece. Then, when my lieutenant wanted me out of the Homicide Division, and I wanted out of the whole police thing, Cap convinced me to stay and join the firearms unit."

"And you didn't know about Carmella, I mean, Nareece and Jesse?"

"No, we moved her not long after I went undercover."

"Explains why Jesse didn't connect you. Wow, this shit's crazy . . . So Jesse and Wade go to your house to kill Nareece and get the money and drugs back, only Nareece never gave up

the money or the drugs. She couldn't give up the drugs because she had flushed them down the toilet."

"That means she still has the money?"

"Somewhere. She has to, and that's why Jesse went after her."

"Yeah, but he tried to kill her first. He wouldn't have gotten
anything if I hadn't gotten her out of the house before it
burned down."

"Yeah, I can't figure that. I'd bet he sent some of his goons
and they messed up. You saved their asses."

"Great. And now we have to save Nareece's ass."

We resumed our search and ended in Mann's office, which
was located in the back of the house. A massive, oval Victorian-
style desk was set at one end of the room. Laughton went straight
to the desk and began rifling through the drawers.

A brown vinyl-looking sofa, flanked by two matching chairs,
was at the opposite end of the room from the desk. Built-in
bookcases covered one wall. The back wall was made up of
windows above a stretch of cabinets. The other wall was plastered with photographs of Mann shaking hands with Frank
Rizzo, the mayor in 1975, and Black Mafia leaders Sam Christian and Eugene Baynes. I peered more closely at one photograph on the wall, where Mann sat at a table in a nightclub, a
woman hugged up in each arm and men crowded around him.
One face popped out. Calvin's.

CHAPTER 21

Calvin. It was a younger, thinner, Afro-ed Calvin, hidden behind dark shades standing guard next to another soldier in a power stance, arms folded across his chest.

The saliva I tried to swallow stuck in my throat, parched and narrowed, causing me to choke on it, the kind of choking when your breath fails and the end of life approaches. A grating, sucking sound escaped my mouth every few seconds until air finally got through my windpipes. Laughton was at my side trying to pat my back as I swatted his hand away. I stumbled to a chair next to the desk and fell into it.

"Yeah, seeing Mann on that wall with all those damn politicians definitely makes you choke." He feigned a laugh.

I wanted to ask about Calvin's photo, but I figured if Laughton knew Calvin back then, Calvin would not be in my life right now. And then I did not want it to be true. He would have at least pointed him out in the photograph.

"His tentacles reached far," Laughton said, moving from the front of the desk. "Okay, I'm out. Use this number to call me." He handed me a piece of paper he tore from a notepad on the desk and, I noticed, slid something from his other hand into his pocket. "FBI is tracking the other one," he said, turning away and moving toward the door. "You got this?"

"You know I got this."

After Laughton left, I took the picture off the wall and checked the back for identifying information—names. There were none. I stuffed it in my bag and went to the desk. Indentations of letters and numbers were visible on the notepad Laughton used. I got a pencil from the desk drawer and shaded lightly across the pad to reveal the last letters and numbers written. I tore off a few sheets and pocketed them as Agents Jakes and Janey entered, behind a storm of agents, weapons drawn.

Two hours later, I sat in an interrogation room at FBI Arch Street headquarters.

I figured Jakes and Janey stood behind the two-way mirror either arguing about what strategy to use to get information out of me or they were ogling me. I gave them the award for being the two least intimidating FBI agents I'd ever met. The thought tickled me, for a moment anyway.

A fire sparked in my bones. I waved my hands together in fan fashion, trying to conjure up some breeze. Failing that, I got up and paced, waved harder, faster, gagged, sat, and spread out on top of the table, face-first.

"Can't possibly understand unless you're going through or been through the same," a female agent said, entering with a glass of water. "You learn to cope."

I nodded appreciation with a weak smile. "That's what they tell me. You learn to cope. Right." I drank the water and rubbed an ice cube from the glass on the back of my neck. Cooled, I resumed my position.

The agent left with, "Knock if you need more."

I rose when I heard the door open again. My composure

somewhat regained, I pushed back in the chair and crossed my legs.

Janey sat down and opened a file folder. Jakes stood at the door and leaned against the wall.

"What's this about, Agent Janey?"

"I'm Jakes, he's Janey," he said, nodding toward Dumbo Ears. He pulled his chair in closer. "Mabley, this is serious. A man's dead, and you were seen along with someone else entering the premises. What was your purpose for being at the Bryn Mawr address?"

I mirrored his glare.

I thought as dark as it was that night, there was no way anyone could identify me specifically. I brushed away the threat.

"Following a lead," I said.

"Following a lead, huh? What are you working on?"

"Agent . . . Jakes, are you holding me on charges? If not, I'd like to go home."

"We can hold you as long as we choose without filing any charges. But I'm not telling you anything you don't already know." He pushed back in his chair. "You had a history with Mann. Did you kill him?"

"If you thought I killed Mann, you wouldn't be questioning me. You'd be arresting me. I went to Mann's to talk to him about Boone's whereabouts. When I got there, the front door was open. I went inside and found Mann dead on the couch. I called in. End of story."

"And the other person reported entering the premises?"

"Whoever killed him maybe, before I arrived, I guess."

It was almost noon by the time I left FBI headquarters. I drove north on Seventh Street and thought a dark sedan was following me as I turned onto Fairmont Avenue. The car I focused on kept moving straight when I turned on to Cecile B. Moore, or at least I think it kept moving straight. Headlights at night made all cars look the same. I drove around awhile to make sure before I went to Calvin's.

Calvin's Place, a four-story brick building, housed Calvin's living quarters on the third and fourth floors and a nightclub on the first two. It was the kind of club people waded into with their own sense of rhythm and opinions and walked away from with a semblance of sanity and satisfaction. A large oval bar, a stage area, some booths and tables, and a dance floor made up the first floor and a private party space, the second. Calvin also served the best crab legs and chicken wings in Philly.

I drove by the front on Hunting Park and made a left into the parking lot that led to the rear of the building. The night spot looked shabby compared to the happening, ritzy place presented under the veil of night. I pulled into a dirt parking lot where Calvin's white late-model Mercedes S430 was parked at the stairs to the rear entrance. An old Chevy Malibu and Ford Mustang were the only other cars in the lot.

I knocked on the armored door fastened under a CALVIN'S PLACE sign and rang the bell. It took a few minutes of leaning on the bell before Calvin opened the door.

"Frank Mann Johnson, sound familiar? Well, he's dead, and I want to know what your connection is to him. You smiled for a picture with him hanging on his wall, this one." I took the photograph out of my bag and held it up. "Okay, so maybe you weren't smiling. Remember this?" I shoved the picture at him and stormed into the club. Calvin stayed positioned at the door, seemingly stunned.

I sat bar-side. He closed and locked the door and followed.

"Drink?" He set the picture on the bar facedown.

"Coke, please."

He retrieved a Coke from a cooler below the counter, filled a glass with ice, and set it on the bar in front of me, then popped the tab top. While he poured he said, "First off, my darling, Mann died years ago, killed in prison if memory serves me."

"Yeah, says who?"

"You know I will do anything for you, Miss M." He smirked, setting the glass of Coke in front of me and tossing the can in a barrel at the far end of the bar. "So why don't you tell me what you're into and maybe I can help."

I gulped the Coke and savored the burn in the back of my throat. Calvin leaned forward, resting his forearms on the bar, and waited for me to finish.

"Where did you get that picture anyway?"

"Off the wall of the residence of Big Daddy Mann. Apparently the FBI lied. He didn't die in prison. He is—was—very much alive until earlier this evening. And there you were in that picture hanging on the wall alongside all his other trophies."

"And what, you thought I was a gangster?" He cupped my chin with his hand, forcing my attention. "Not even close, though some may think different. You are the last person I would want to think of me in that way."

I brushed his hand away.

He backed away from the bar. "You can be so sweet, open, and warm, and then"—he snapped his fingers—"in a heartbeat, closed and so, so hard."

My heart thumped. I resisted the urge to defend myself. "So, what's your connection?"

Calvin moved around to my side of the bar. He sat on a stool next to me and spun my stool around to face him.

"This isn't about Mann. So, why don't you tell me the real deal."

"Yes, it is. Mann didn't die in prison. He was killed last night. Please, Calvin, just tell me what your connection is. I need to know."

"Is this official? Am I a suspect?"

"I think Jesse Boone killed Mann. I also think Jesse Boone has my sister and will kill her, too."

"Frank Mann Johnson was once a pretty decent guy. We were homies before the Black Mafia. He was more like my mentor, a big brother even. I went in the service. Mann didn't. The Black Mafia was in full throttle when I got back from the war, killing anyone who breathed wrong, hooking children on heroin. They were supposed to help folks out of oppression. Like a neighborhood watch–type gig. Instead they became the oppressors."

"So, where did you fit in?"

"Frank and I started a community center–type gig with a mission to protect the neighborhood, stop the crime and police brutality that grew out of the violence instigated by the Mafia.

"The community center grew into the Black Coalition with an even bigger vision: promoting the socioeconomic conditions of black folks in Philly, educating the youth, providing cultural programs. Mafia served up death threats, scared the hell outta folks. A lot of young bloods looked up to the Mafia 'godfather,' Sam Christian, thought he was some kind of Shaft or Superfly or some shit.

"Frank got brainwashed by the glitz—the clothes, the cash, the cows. Only takes one time stepping over the line and they got your ass. Frank took a giant step and ended up all the way in with Christian, Baynes, Harvey, Farrington, all major players. Anyway, Frank did well for himself, if you call becoming a kingpin in the kill game good. He got bagged for murder and, well, the FBI does what they want, when they want, and to whom they want. They were all over him." He quieted and looked around the room as though sizing up its worth. "This place is what's left of the community center."

Mann was giving the Feds information when I was undercover, I thought. He didn't go to jail until after I was out of play.

"How do you rate? I mean, how did you manage to stay out of the game?"

"We parted ways when Mann got involved with Christian and them. I kept the community center going, then, when that phased out, I opened this club for the community. Always been kind of a dream of mine to own a club, perform in my own place. You know."

"What about Jesse Boone? You must have known him and his father if you were involved with Mann."

"Boone's a crazy bastard. He'd kill his own kid for a buck and not even blink. He's got some kind of terminal illness. He'd always been a sickly kid. Some kind of rare disorder makes the boy smell very unsavory. There's a name for it. Trim . . . ethyl . . . ami . . . nu . . . something. TMAU for short. I only know that because this cat who served with me in the military had it, too."

"Like funk, only worse," I whispered to myself. I remembered that smell in the house where Marcy Taylor died and where John was killed.

"He had a brother, Kelvin. Don't know what happened to him. He disappeared some years ago. It wouldn't surprise me if Jesse killed him, too."

I wanted to tell Calvin about Laughton being Kelvin Boone but decided against it right then. Trust between us was still a bit shaky. I could not believe I'd just happened to get involved with a man connected to my past. No, two men—Calvin *and* Laughton.

My phone rang. I rummaged through my bag, but it stopped long before I found it. The screen showed Travis as the missed caller. I clicked the Call Back button, but Travis did not answer.

"Why does Jesse Boone care about your sister?"

"I'm not sure, but I'm going to find out and find her." Another lie.

"It doesn't sound like you're working on this with the police force behind you."

Avoiding the questions, I said, "You look good, all healed up. How are you feeling?"

"Come here." Calvin guided me into his embrace. "Just be safe."

❧ • ☙

I left Calvin's and went home to shower and change. When I finished dressing, I checked my phone. Two more missed calls from Travis. I clicked the Call Back button again.

"Now, I wonder how obedient you can be," Jesse Boone said. "Don't say a word. Listen. You get my money—all of it. Don't play with me, bitch, or I'll make sure they both beg me to kill them—your son, oh, wait a minute, *our* son, and your baby's mama." His evil laugh gave me goose bumps. "Be talking to you real soon," he said, and hung up.

CHAPTER 22

I called Laughton, and for once he answered. Within ten minutes, he was pounding on my front door like a crazy person.

"You have the money?" he asked.

"I only found out about the money when you told me," I said. "Nareece never . . ."

"The money doesn't really matter. He'll kill them both anyway. I got a lead from my man where he is. He's not at the mill building."

"Laughton, call Cap. We might need backup."

"No way. Someone in the department is on Jesse's payroll."

"But we can trust Cap."

"No. I have reason to believe he may be the man on the inside."

"Cap can't be the man on the inside. He just can't be. Cap's been a good friend to me and Nareece. He was my father's best friend. He wouldn't do something like this, and besides, I'd know. Why would he turn Nareece over to Jesse Boone, or let someone like Boone go free to kill people? Not happening."

"Yeah, well, we'll revisit that after we get Travis and Nareece back."

We drove to Haverford Avenue in West Philly to an abandoned factory building that used to house the Philadelphia Traction Company. Laughton cruised by the front of the building, turned the corner, and parked half a block down from the rear entrance.

"Jesse will kill her before letting anyone else have her," he said. "And Travis . . ."

We sat in silence for at least an hour. Waiting. Watching. I flipped through everything that had happened in the past month, twenty years' worth of ugly crammed into four weeks.

"Laughton, do you know anything about my parents' death? Nareece said it was because of her involvement with Jesse."

He shifted in his seat away from me. "Dad remembered your father from the old days, before the Black Mafia got outrageous. Your dad and my father had a connection early on when folks were about making the neighborhood a safe place to live. Your dad was a good guy, always helping folks out. When things got funky with drugs and shit, your father walked. Funny thing, Pop always respected your father for his decision to walk away from that life. Your father had a fit over Jesse and Carmella hooking up. He asked my father to stop it, but Pop refused. Your father threatened to go to the police, since Carmella was a minor."

"So your father had him killed."

Laughton did not respond.

"Where were you in all of this?"

"I was around, going to school, learning the business. I met Marcy during those days. I loved that woman. We were married on July 17, 1971." He stayed quiet for a few minutes, remembering. He shifted in his seat again, this time facing front, sat straighter, and started talking again.

"Richard jumped up one side of Jesse and down the other to

leave Carmella alone, not because of your father's threats, but because of who he was and how much he respected him. Richard always got on Jesse about everything and nothing. Anyway, after Carmella destroyed the drugs and took off with the money, Richard did a one-eighty and told Jesse he'd kill him if he didn't take care of her."

"How come you didn't stop him?"

"Carmella called me, out of her mind with grief, and begged me to help her get away. Like I told you, I hid her in a hotel in Jersey, but she insisted on going back home. Said she couldn't leave without making things right with you."

"That's when she came home and Jesse tried to kill her. Thought he had killed her. She was waiting for me." I rested my head in my palms, trying to absorb the insanity. My brain started flashing pictures again. This time of the crash site where my parents were killed, Nareece's battered body, my mother's smile, the funny face Dad made when in his silly mode. The screen went black, and I took my hands away. Laughton sat motionless, staring down into his lap.

I growled and lunged across the console, punching and clawing at Laughton's face, wanting to make him bleed, to leave a scar so deep the world could see it. For the second time that day, I wished him dead and gone.

"Muriel, stop, don't do this shit again," Laughton shouted, struggling to grab my arms. When he finally captured them, he pushed me back in the seat. "Don't pretend you're innocent in all of this."

"What does that mean?"

"You could have told her to return the money."

"I told you, I didn't know about the money until now, or even about Jesse and Carmella. None of it."

"Look, it's all going to end here, and you and Carmella can go on living your lives and not have to worry. Jesse Boone is going to be gone. If I had just stepped up years ago, none of this would be happening." Laughton cocked his 9mm Glock and turned to me. "I'm sure it's pointless, but I'ma tell you anyway, stay in the car."

Twenty years as a weapons examiner and I'd never chased a bad guy, never even had a fight other than with Jesse Boone after he killed the college student. I could kick some butt now, but the opportunity had never presented itself. And I'd only fired my weapon once. I turned toward Laughton. His lips were moving, but I could not hear his words, only the ringing in my ears until he shouted my name.

"Don't even think about going alone," I said.

I stopped talking as the same black SUV that I had seen many times, along with a silver Mercedes, drove up to the rear of the building. Three men got out of the SUV, one of them Jesse. He helped Nareece out of the back. By "helping," I mean she seemed willing and at ease, letting him guide her by the elbow, but not in a dragging or threatening manner, what I would have expected. I sensed she was drugged.

Laughton pushed the door halfway open and moved to get out, then stopped and said, "We might as well finish it right here." He closed the door. "Is Travis Carmella's son?"

I could not answer.

"Carmella said she was pregnant the night she called. You never talked about going through pregnancy or childbirth. You never talk about the boy's father, whether you loved him, why you split from him, nothing. Seventeen years—seventeen years we're partners, together every damn day, and yeah, you're right, we don't have a clue about each other."

My throat tightened.

"You trusted me with your life every day, but never with your heart." Laughton took his cell phone from his pocket and made a call. "Come in guns blazing, man. I'll get them out front, then just do it," he said into the phone, then clicked off and threw the phone onto the dashboard. "Trust me now, M."

No more, I thought. "Let's go," I said, and we got out of the car.

Laughton led the way to the rear of the building, where a man stood guard. Laughton signaled to hold up behind a car parked across the driveway. He holstered his gun and walked up to the guy, then exchanged greetings and more mumblings before Laughton knocked him out with a single punch. He waved me forward. I stepped out and stumbled, twisting my ankle. Laughton rushed back to help me and held my arm. I pulled away and moved on, faking it through the pain from my ankle. It was not bad enough to be a sprain, but it still took a minute for me to adjust. There was no way I was not going in with Laughton.

We entered a darkened hallway. A hundred yards down was an entrance that led into an open area, empty with at least forty-foot ceilings. To the right, was a staircase—a long, steep staircase. Voices came from above. Laughton motioned me to stay behind him, as he approached the staircase, seemingly the only way up.

What if someone decides to come down as we're climbing up? What if a stair step creaks? I began to hyperventilate. "Please, God, not now," I whispered, my insides heating up. I readjusted my grasp on the gun. Laughton looked back at me and raised his finger to his lips.

My stomach bubbled.

At the top of the stairs, we turned left to a doorway that was three-quarters closed.

"Leave her alone, asshole."

I froze, stung by the recognition of Travis's voice.

The sound of footsteps made us move, one on each side of the door. I had a sliver view from my side. Nareece was slumped over on the couch, an arm resting across her back. Travis's arm. Boone passed back and forth like a panther preparing to pounce. I wanted to rush in shooting, but Travis and Nareece might be killed in the cross fire. I could not tell who else was in the room nor how many from the limited view. I motioned Laughton to my side. He motioned me back down the stairs. A silent argument ensued before we made our way back down the stairs and outside.

Laughton ran his hand over his head. "He's out of his mind."

"Laughton, I'm not leaving without Travis and Reece."

"C'mon," he said, moving back toward the car, I surmised to wait for the cavalry he'd called. Almost immediately after we got in the car, shots were fired.

I bolted out of the car ahead of Laughton and raced inside, up the stairs, and kicked the door open. Jesse walked backward toward another exit dragging Nareece along with one arm while, with the other, aiming his pistol at Travis, who was laid out on the floor. Jesse moved the gun away from Travis, back at Nareece's head. He then disappeared out the door, leaving three men with guns cocked. A fourth man lay on the floor with a gunshot to the head.

"Give me the boy and we all walk away alive," Laughton said. He kept his gun pointed on the lead man.

I stood in the center of the room, my gun aimed at another of the men. "C'mon, Travis, come over here," I said.

Travis got up from the floor and moved slowly toward me. When he got close, I stepped in front of him and walked us backward to the door. Once there, I grabbed his hand and pulled him out the door and down the stairs. I heard shots ring out, then the door slammed and Laughton was at my back.

We burst through the door and kept running.

Jesse's men came out the door behind us shooting. I fell,

smashing my face into the pavement, pushed down by a heavy weight, which pinned me down. I turned my face sideways and saw Travis duck behind a Dumpster at the side of the building. The whirring noise of bullets echoed above my head. An eerie silence followed. I felt the weight being lifted off of me, my body being turned over. Two blurred faces came into focus, Travis and Calvin. Laughton lay next to me. I struggled to sit up with Calvin's help. Travis moved to Laughton and lifted his upper body to his lap, sobbing and willing him to wake up.

CHAPTER 23

Sirens wailed in the distance, as Calvin pulled me up and steadied me, then reached his hand out for Travis. "Let's go, son," he said. He bent over and grasped Travis's elbow. Travis looked up at me. Tears cleared paths down his dirt-smudged cheeks, his right eye bulged black and blue, and his lower lip, cracked and swollen, dripped blood.

"They got my man, Laughton," Calvin said, nodding toward two men who had approached from behind us. "We need to go before the police get here."

Travis and I allowed Calvin to guide us to a dark sedan. He turned the car around and drove down the side street where Laughton and I had parked, turned right down a driveway, then blasted across a main street and through another driveway before he slowed.

I twisted around to Travis. His pants and shirt were stained with Laughton's blood. "Travis, baby, you're all right."

Travis nodded with deadened eyes.

I turned sideways to Calvin. "He's still got Nareece," I said to Calvin.

"Let's get you and Travis safe first."

Prickly fingers massaged my cheekbones. Blood dripped in

my lap. I gently touched my cheek and felt dirt and pebbles and torn flesh. I settled in the seat and dug deep for the strength to handle what would come next.

"You know the police are going to be all over this?" Calvin said.

"Yes."

"With you all and Laughton out of the way, they'll think it was a drug deal or something gone bad."

I looked sideways at Calvin and started to speak, then decided to keep my mouth shut.

When we got to Calvin's, I led Travis to the living room and helped him lie down on the couch. I knelt on the floor beside him and held his limp hand.

"Baby, I'm sorry about all this. I should've told you some things a long time ago." I placed his hand under the afghan and got up. "Everything's going to work out, you'll see."

When Travis appeared to be resting, I went on a search of Calvin. He was at the sink when I entered the kitchen.

"We don't have a fix yet on Jesse," he said. I sat at the table. Calvin came to me and dabbed at my face with a wet cloth. "It'll take a minute."

"She might not have a minute."

"There's nothing else to do right now but wait."

"Who the hell are you? How did you even know we were there?"

He pulled me up from the chair and held me pressed against him. I wished he could absorb my whole body, leaving nothing, no part of me, exposed to what was happening outside of his house, the room, that moment.

I pulled away and hurried to the bathroom. I held to the sides of the sink and gasped at the reflection of half my face scraped off, the other half normal, presenting a perfect picture of the two people fighting for existence within me.

My cell phone buzzed in my back pocket and made me jump.

"You really fucked up. You fuck with me again, and I'll kill her, you bitch," Jesse snarled.

"Is she alive? I want proof that she's alive." I heard rustling on the other end before Nareece's voice, robot-like, came on.

"Get the money, M. Get the money so he doesn't kill me. I don't want to die. I don't care about the money."

Jesse came back on. "I'll destroy everything precious to you, those precious little girls, the boy, your girlfriend. Get the money. I'll call back."

He clicked off. I called Dulcey.

"We're fine, the twins are fine, I'm fine," she said. "What's wrong?"

"Dulcey, listen to me. Take the girls to your sister's and call me when you're safe."

"We're safe right here."

"Just do it, Dulcey. I'm going to finish this, but I need to know you all are somewhere you can't be found."

When I came out of the bathroom, Calvin was talking to two men. I glanced from them to Calvin, wanting news about Laughton.

"Laughton will live, but Jesse's still nowhere, disappeared. Nobody's talking," one of the men said.

I went to the living room to check on Travis. He was sitting up on the couch with his head back, eyes closed.

I nudged his leg and said, "C'mon, we have to go."

I helped him up and guided him into the kitchen, where Calvin was at the door talking to the two men. He finished and closed the door.

"I need your car," I said.

"There's nothing to do but wait, Muriel, so get some rest."

"I want to take Travis home," I said, struggling for control. Calvin reluctantly gave me his car keys and said he would check in when he learned something.

When we pulled up to the house, Travis opened his door to get out.

"Stay here," I demanded, and took my gun from my pocketbook.

"I'm not letting you go in by yourself, so don't even waste your breath." Said like his mother's son.

After checking that everything in the house was as it should be, I waited for Travis to change clothes.

We left Calvin's car and drove mine to the family house in the West Mount Airy section of Philly, 7048 Lincoln Drive. Mount Airy was just outside Center City and host to Fairmount Park. Twenty minutes into the drive, which put us a few blocks away from the house, Travis said, "That guy, the one that has Aunt Nareece . . ." He stopped mid-sentence.

My hands were sweaty on the steering wheel. Heat rose up my neck. I kept my attention straight ahead.

"He said I resembled him, but that I looked more like my mother than I did him."

I pulled in the driveway of my parents' house, threw the handle in Park, and shut the car off. I took my gun from my pocketbook and checked it, then opened the car door.

"Ma, he said Aunt Reece was my mother."

I closed the car door and pushed Travis down in the seat as car headlights flashed by. When they passed, I checked around.

"We'll talk later," I said. "We need to do this right now."

"Do what, Ma? Whose house is this? Why are we here?"

"Just come with me. I'll explain later."

I gathered up the screwdriver and hammer I'd brought along and opened the car door. Inside the house, I closed and locked the front door. The last tenants had moved out a few months earlier, so the air was stale and smelled of urine and cigarette smoke, which probably meant some homeless folks had been living there.

No fond memories, sounds of peaceful laughter, or longing held me. Not that I didn't remember happy times in this house. I did, but the last memory was of Nareece being hurt, and that memory was the one that stuck.

I maneuvered my way around the house, turning on lights and checking the rooms and closets for intruders, Travis following my every movement. A broken window in the back family room let me know how squatters got in. When I was satisfied that we were the only ones in the house, I moved down the hall to the basement entrance and down the stairs.

The half-finished basement had wallboard in its natural state and charcoal-colored indoor-outdoor carpeting. Built-in storage bins ran the length of a side wall. I opened the center bin and found a Barbie doll's head in one corner, and a few red, white, and blue Legos piled in another. I knelt on the floor and tapped the sides, listening for a hollow sound. There were not any screw heads showing, so I pressed, but the side did not budge. A closer look revealed a slight differential in the corners of the right side panel. I scraped the spot with the screwdriver. Travis leaned over my shoulder.

"All this time, all these years, I looked everywhere. Never guessed it would be right here, somewhere in this house."

Startled, we jerked around to Cap, standing over us holding a .38. Travis stumbled back against the wall.

"Never once did you mention the money. I tried everything to get you to talk about it with me, but you never even hinted about it." He shook his head and smirked. In a snap, his face reverted to the soft, fatherly expression I knew. "I'm sorry about all this, Muriel. Things did not work out the right way."

"What're you talking about, Cap? What're you doing?" I had a difficult time believing Cap would shoot either one of us, but something about his facial expression, the hollow sound of his voice, made me nervous. I stood up and stepped sideways to block Travis.

"Cap, this doesn't make any sense. You can't be serious about this. I didn't even know about the money."

"Shut up, Muriel," he commanded. "I'm doing what I have to do to live. I've been watching your back for twenty years. Watching and making sure you, Nareece, and the boy had everything you needed." He wiped his brow with his forearm and then continued. "Yes, and at my own expense."

I must have looked confused. I *was* confused.

"Don't act like you're ignorant about what I'm saying. Or maybe you are. Maybe you ignored everything so you wouldn't have to deal. Well, I've had to deal with your parents' death, with your sister's pain, and with you. Now I'm going to deal with me and mine."

"You can't kill us. So what're you going to do with us?"

"I'm not going to kill you." He stepped in closer and eyed the panel. "Finish the job," he said.

I hesitated.

"Muriel, for once in your life, listen to me."

For a moment I reflected on how many times people had said that same statement to me in the past few days—Nareece, Laughton, and now Cap.

"I don't want to kill you, but don't think I won't if you don't do what I'm telling you. I didn't mean for all this to happen." He waved his gun in front of him and teetered back and forth, shifting his weight from one foot to the other, as though he was intoxicated. "Damn your father, always the good guy. Esther and Elliot's death is on my head. I've had to live with that for twenty years. I can't do this anymore. I gotta get away, far enough where they won't find my wife, where she'll be safe. Where I can set my kids up and no one will connect them to me."

"Cap, you're not making any sense. You can't just move your kids and their families . . ."

"I can do anything with enough money."

"And you think two million dollars is enough money?"

"No, but five million dollars is." He focused on Travis. "Boy, move. Get in there and get the money."

Now I was really confused. Nareece said there was two million dollars here, yet Cap talked about five million. What would he do when he found out the amount was less than he expected?

I turned to Travis and motioned for him to work on the screws. He knelt down and began scraping the paint away from the screw heads. Cap moved up behind me. I swung around at the same time Travis stood up, knocking me into Cap and sending him backward, his arm waving upward as the gun exploded. I rushed him. He recovered and smashed his fist into my face, sending me reeling back into the wall. Cap brought the gun around as I pushed off from the wall and kicked his arm away. The gun flew out of his hand and discharged again. Travis circled around behind Cap as he lunged toward me, his face contorted, teeth bared like a madman's. I side-kicked his stomach. As he bent forward, I punched upward to his jaw, sending him backward into Travis. His face flushed. He lifted one arm behind his head like he was reaching for something. Red-faced and wide-eyed, he fell forward into my arms, his weight pressing me to my knees. It was then that I saw the screwdriver protruding from his lower back, the screwdriver that Travis had put there. I rested him on the floor sideways and toppled over to a sitting position next to him.

After a few moments of silence while the dust settled, we got comfortable in our assumed positions, and our breathing slowed. I supposed I was in shock.

"I'm . . . I'm sorry," Cap said. "I didn't mean to hurt . . ."

"Shh," I said.

". . . your father . . . I'm the reason they killed him and Esther. Forgive me," Cap sputtered. "Jesse's out of control. He'll kill Nareece."

"Do you know where he's holding her? Are *you* Jesse's inside man?" I got down close to his face. "Did you tell him about us, about me and Nareece?"

"So many years passed . . . It got more messed up," he said.

"Damn, Cap," I said, whacking his shoulder.

"I couldn't get out. Bancroft Building." He closed his eyes and grunted out a long breath.

"Cap." I shook him, hard.

His eyes opened and he flashed a half smile. "I love . . ." He sucked in, released the breath, and flopped forward on my foot.

"Bastard," I screeched and pushed myself back against the wall, using him as leverage.

CHAPTER 24

"I killed him . . . I killed Cap," Travis stuttered between gasps for air.

I embraced him. I wanted to tell him the man he'd killed was not worth brooding over, but the words stayed lodged in my throat. Cap had been like a father to me and Nareece after my parents died. Of course, now I knew it was out of guilt, which seemed more palatable, since only a moment ago he would have killed me and Travis for money.

My body caught Travis's tremors as we rode the storm together. The weight of Travis's body, all six-foot-two, 180 pounds, leaned into me.

"Travis, Travis, baby, don't do this, not now." I guided him to the floor and leaned his back against the wall. I frantically checked him out and saw his arm bleeding as he slipped into unconsciousness. The shot Cap had squeezed off had hit his right bicep. I took off my overblouse, ripped it, and used it as a tourniquet. Travis fell sideways. Panicked, I laid him flat on the floor and checked his breathing.

"C'mon, baby, c'mon, baby, don't do this. You're all right." I rubbed his cheeks, I checked the tourniquet, and checked his breathing. I crawled to the bin to retrieve my cell from my purse and called for an ambulance, then settled on the floor next to him.

The floor creaked before the sound of footsteps came through. The timing was too quick and the rhythm too slow and deliberate for it to be the medics. My stomach and heart collided. I slid Travis's body to the side and gently let his head rest on the floor.

Cap's body and Travis were behind the stairs, out of view of anyone coming down the steps. I pulled my gun from its holster and moved to a small utility room to the left of the stairway. From where I hid, I had a good view of the steps.

When the door at the top of the stairs opened, I was totally chilled, as in frozen in place. I took a deep breath and slowly exhaled. The feet and legs of a man came in view, then his outstretched arms with hands clasped around the butt of a gun. The top half of his body was still out of view, as he switched around to either side, surveying the layout. After a few more steps, I recognized Jakes. Janey had the Dumbo ears. Or was it Jakes who had them?

I guessed and called out, "Jakes, Mabley here, I'm coming out. Don't shoot." I stepped from the shadows, lowering my gun.

I guessed right. Jakes lowered his gun and plodded the rest of the way down the stairs. Janey and his Dumbo ears appeared in the doorway at the top of the stairs still pointing his gun. "Clear," Jakes said. Janey lowered his weapon and went back in the darkness of the house. I quickly moved to check on Travis. He was dazed but conscious.

"We suspected the captain was the inside man for Jesse Boone," Jakes said, checking Cap's body for vitals.

"Nice had you shared," I said, helping Travis to his feet.

"Nice had you shared with the police about your sister being kidnapped. Mabley, we need to talk," he said, stepping sideways to block the way.

I stopped in front of him, holding on to Travis's arm.

"I'll call after I take my son to the hospital."

He stepped aside.

The ambulance showed up as we exited the house. It took Travis and me to Thomas Jefferson Hospital.

After surgery, the doctor reported Travis had lost a good amount of blood and was in shock, but that he would make a full recovery. It was hours before he was out of recovery and admitted to a room. I sat by his bed watching the slight movement of his chest, thankful that I still had my son with me. I woke to Calvin nudging me at 12:39 a.m.

"How'd you find us?" I whispered.

"It's not important. Only that you and the boy are all right."

He picked up my purse and pulled on my arm to get me up.

"What about Jesse? Did you learn anything?"

"We'll talk tomorrow. Right now, I'll drive you home so you can sleep."

I jerked away. "I can't leave."

"I checked with the nurse. He'll be out until morning. There's nothing more you can do here."

"I can be here when he wakes up."

"You will be."

I let him lead me out. When we got outside the room, Calvin nodded to one of his men, who took up a position by Travis's door. Calvin half-pulled, half-carried me through the corridors to the hospital parking lot. He put me in his car and directed another man to follow in mine.

Next thing I knew, light bounced up and down on my lids, seeping inside the cracks and burning my corneas. I sat up in a start. My head spun. A check of the clock on the cable box said 6:08. I fell back on the pillow and covered my eyes until the spinning stopped. A laugh gurgled its way to tears. "Laughton . . . Cap . . . Oh God, thank You for Travis," I blubbered, unable to keep from dribbling spit and snot down the sides of my face and into my ears. A backhanded swipe and a few snorts to suck it up and I was settled enough to call the hospital. Travis was still sleeping and probably would not wake for another few hours, the nurse said.

I stumbled into the shower and let the hot water ease the knot in my neck and clear my head. I got out and dried off, every muscle and joint in my body screaming at me. When the steam from the mirror cleared, I cringed at the black and blue around my right eye and the thin film of dried blood serum that coated my cheek, the result of Cap's rebellion. Cap. I felt like my brain was exploding. Then I remembered Cap's last words. *Bancroft Building.*

I dressed quickly, pulled my hair back in a ponytail, dabbed some A & D ointment on my cheek and headed out, first to the hospital. Travis woke up just as I arrived.

"I guess I'm official now," he whispered in a raspy voice.

"Yeah, I guess you are."

"Ma, that guy . . ."

"Don't worry about anything. You just rest now. Everything's going to be fine."

"Ma, you can't keep me out of this, away from the 'ugliness,' as you call it. You can't keep blinding me. I'm not a little boy anymore. You'd be surprised what I've seen, the things I've done."

"I think you'd better stop there."

"Why, so you can go on thinking I'm your perfect son?"

"No, so you can go on living. Now, get some rest. We'll do this later." I was stung but determined to keep Travis bound, at least until Jesse Boone was in custody.

I stayed with Travis until the nurse came in, gave him some meds, and he was knocked out again.

Jakes ushered me into an interrogation room at FBI headquarters. I had it straight now. Janey, who had the Dumbo ears, was absent. Jakes sat across the table from me.

"You understand what happened to you, your sister, your parents? It didn't come together until Jesse Boone started his killing spree. The captain made sure of that." He pushed two large files to my side of the table. "The captain's been under Jesse Boone's thumb for years. Jesse blackmailed him and threatened to kill his wife, daughter, and grandkids, his whole damn family." He got up and moved to the door. "Jesse Boone's all that's left now, and we'll get him." He gestured to the files. "You got twenty minutes."

I flipped open the first folder. Reports described the Black Mafia and named Sam Christian as the head and others like Eugene "Bo" Baynes, Ronald Harvey, Robert "Nudie" Mims, Donnie "Pork Chop" James, Richard "The Pistol" Boone, and Frank "Big Daddy" Mann Johnson, with photos of them as young men. Other photographs showed Nareece, young, beautiful, and laughing, with her arms around Jesse Boone, Dad and Mom coming out the front door of our house, Dad and Mom's dead bodies, me hugged up to Daddy Mann, grinning like a damn Cheshire cat. I remembered the event, but I didn't remember having a picture taken. I stood on one side of Mann, his arm draped over my shoulders and Jesse Boone on the other. He had been there, and yet I had no recollection of him back then. The last photograph was of me in a hospital bed with death's face on. I was looking at the photograph, but I could not believe that Jesse Boone and I were so close and yet never knew each other, or was it that I had blocked him out years ago?

The second folder had a recent picture of Cap with Jesse at an unfamiliar location. There were photos of me and Laughton on several investigations, going into and out of my house, pictures of Nareece, John, and the twins. The last photo showed Kelvin Boone the way he looked before his transformation to

Laughton. Kelvin Boone's face mirrored Travis's. Heat grew to a boil inside, forcing sweat from every pore until I had achieved wet T-shirt status. I left before Jakes returned.

Uncertain why Jakes had decided to be so forthcoming with the files and all, I was sure it wasn't because he'd suddenly found me likeable or needed to satisfy any guilt feelings. I doubted he possessed the capability to feel guilt. I was bait.

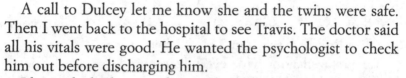

A call to Dulcey let me know she and the twins were safe. Then I went back to the hospital to see Travis. The doctor said all his vitals were good. He wanted the psychologist to check him out before discharging him.

I lay in the bed next to him and cuddled his head against my chest. "We'll get through all this." I pressed his head closer to my chest and stroked his arm, as dampness from his cheek registered against my skin.

"Ma?"

"Yes, baby."

"Are you my real mother?"

I did not stumble. I could not stumble. "If you mean did I give birth to you, no."

"It's cool, Mom. I want to know the truth."

The truth, the whole truth, and nothing but the truth, so help me God. I had gone over it in my head a thousand times, *the truth* that I would tell him when he was old enough. My heart thumped, I cooled, and the knot in my gut released. Travis sat forward and hugged me with all his might. My cell phone buzzed, disturbing the moment. A check of the screen showed Nareece's name. I started to move off the bed to go into the hall away from him to answer, but Travis grabbed my arm.

"You got the money?" It was Jesse.

"Let me talk to Nareece, make sure she's still alive before we talk money."

"Muriel, don't come. He'll kill you. Don't believe anything he—" I heard wrestling on the other end, and Nareece screamed.

Then Jesse came on again. "She might not stay breathing if you don't come through. I know you're the whoring bitch Big Daddy and all the other niggers did. I woulda done your ass, too, woulda been the best you'd ever had."

"You can't do anybody's ass, Jesse. You aren't equipped to do a damn thing because nobody can get past your stench. You have to kill women so you can do them."

"Shut up or I'll do her right now. Be at the Bancroft Number Five Building, two a.m." He clicked off.

Travis stared at me wide-eyed, I supposed, because he never heard me talk so bad. I also guessed he'd only heard one side of the conversation. I guessed wrong.

"You're not going to meet him alone?"

When I didn't respond, he moved to get up.

"I'm not going alone. Laughton . . ." I sighed. "I mean, Calvin will be with me." I helped him back to bed and pulled the covers over him. "You stay put. I don't need to worry about you, too. Calvin and I will get Aunt Nareece."

I drove back to my parents' house to get the money. Police tape was still across the front door. Children playing down the street stopped to watch as I tore away the tape and entered. I locked the door and moved quickly through the house, checking closets and behind doors. Paranoia aside, I did not want any surprises. By the time I got to the basement, I was breathing like I had just run a marathon. I knelt beside the bin, unscrewed four screws, and pulled the panel back—to an empty space.

CHAPTER 25

I fell back onto the floor, not knowing what my next move should be. Without the money, Nareece was dead.

I thought about the possibilities. Jakes and Janey could have been upstairs longer than they presented. They could have heard everything and learned about the money, then come back later and found it.

The previous tenants had moved out rather suddenly two months ago. The Williams family included two little girls who probably played down here like Nareece did. My fingers moved at lightning speed, finding Mr. Williams's number in my cell and dialing. A recording on the first ring said no incoming calls were being accepted.

Short of freaking out, I got up from the floor and looked in the cubbyhole again, then reached inside as far as my arm allowed. Nothing. I scanned the basement for something, anything, to smash apart the panels with. On top of the hot water heater was a hammer. Bashing in the panels required extreme effort. The money had to be here. By the time I got to the last panel I was swinging the hammer like a Hank Aaron wannabe. Still no money.

One other possibility came to mind. Dad had built storage bins in our bedroom. Maybe Nareece meant those bins. I raced up the stairs and banged out the panels. Nothing. I sat back on the floor and stayed awhile thinking, until my backside protested the punishment of hardwood against butt. And then Calvin called.

"Where are you?"

"I'm . . . wait, why? What's up?"

"The money's at my place."

The entire drive to Calvin's, my brain was popping with unsavory thoughts about him. I never told him about the money, where it was hidden, nothing. I felt bedeviled by yet another man. Anger seeped in.

When I got to the club, he was waiting in the doorway. I breezed past him and sat at the bar. Neither of us spoke until he had poured two glasses of ginger ale and set one in front of me. I sipped the drink.

"Seems we're at an impasse," he said.

"How the hell did you know about the money?"

"I didn't until Jakes called me. So I sent one of my guys to that house to find it because I knew you'd try to do this thing alone."

"All I care about is getting Nareece back, and if giving Jesse the money is necessary, no problem."

"I took the money because you can't do this thing by yourself."

"How am I supposed to trust you? I don't even know who you are anymore."

"I'm the guy who wants to make sure you get through this alive."

"You need to be straight with me right here, right now, before I can even attempt to trust you again."

"If I tell you, I'll have to kill you," he said with a slight laugh.

"You asked me to trust you. You have to trust me. Who are you? You told me you didn't know where Jesse's brother was, that you thought Kelvin Boone was dead, and that Laughton was Laughton."

"I'm a consultant of sorts for the FBI when necessary. Helps keep the neighborhood quiet. People around here don't ask for much. They want to live their lives and realize an expectation of safety."

"And you're the man to see that their expectations are satisfied?"

"I'm able to, so yes. The Black Mafia has morphed into a much tamer but still lethal form. I mean, these young dudes are selling their junk, running numbers and such, but they keep it on the hush, not like the old days. If they aren't the ones selling and running, some other gangbanger looking to make a name will step in. Right now it's just about getting Jesse Boone off the streets. Laughton contacted me and asked for my help. That's when I found out he was Kelvin. I did tell you Kelvin and Jesse were brothers."

"How does Cap fit in exactly?"

"Are you ready to hear this?"

"I'm sure I can handle it."

"Captain Butler worked inside for the Mafia for years. He was good, always above suspicion somehow. Your father and the cap came up under Sam Christian before the whole Black Mafia thing got crazy."

"Yeah, Laughton filled me in there. He also said my parents were murdered. Nareece thinks she's responsible."

"And you think you're responsible."

244 / CARRIE H. JOHNSON

I hung my head and closed my eyes, trying to deny his words.

"You played a big role in bringing down the whole organization and you got messed up. The Feds should have taken better care of you, but they didn't give a damn. They figured you were expendable. What happened to your parents had nothing to do with what you were doing."

I could not hide my surprise over the scope of his knowledge about me and my past.

He read my face. "I have my own sources. Your parents' murder had little to do with Nareece, either, and everything to do with Captain Butler making a choice: his family or your parents. I guess he figured he'd make it up by watching over you two, until the money thing came up."

"Cap confessed to being the inside man. He also said he caused my parents' death."

"Now Jesse with his craziness wants to muscle back in on the narcotics business of the black underworld and move in on the Italian families, which are so far out of his league. On the flip side is his insanity over your sister. The money means a lot to him, but your sister is his downfall. His problem is everybody's turning away from him and he's pissed. He thinks he can do anything he wants and get away scot-free. His entire life he's been handed a free pass."

Calvin went on for about another half hour about Jesse and Kelvin, Laughton, stuff Laughton had already told me. I listened anyway. By the time he quieted, I trusted him and told him about the phone call from Jesse.

"If I don't go alone, he'll kill her and God only knows who else by the time he's through."

"Jesse will kill you both anyway. You'll give him the money and he'll make you beg for your life first, then kill you." He walked around the bar and stood in front of me. "Jesse's a psychopath, a serial killer. He's responsible for the deaths of at least a dozen women, and this is the first time the FBI's evidence is solid." He fingered a strand of hair hanging in my face and pushed it behind my ear. I slapped his hand away.

"You keep interfering and messing with their program."

"Jakes and Janey, you mean."

"Yes, Jakes and Janey."

"They don't know where Jesse is."

"But you do." He sat on the stool next to me. I faced the bar and kept my gaze fixed on my reflection in the mirror above the shelves of liquor. "I'll help you before Jakes and Janey step in, but you need to trust me."

I checked my phone for the time. Five o'clock. A long night remained, waiting for the 2:00 a.m. hour Jesse connived.

"You only think you can do this alone," Calvin told me. "And if I interfere and things go bad, he'll kill her. I'm telling you, he's going to kill her anyway."

"Who's yanking your chain . . . besides me, I mean?"

"Whoa." He laughed and rose from his stool, backing away with both hands up like he was being arrested. "I'm solo, woman. No ties here."

"You're a regular double-oh-seven, huh?"

Ignoring my questions, he said, "C'mon, let me seduce your palate."

"Calvin, where's Laughton?"

"Laughton's good. I had him taken to a doctor friend. He'll come around."

I did not press for more. The idea that two men I loved were somehow connected at the hip caused a rift in my heart the measure of which I was not ready to embrace.

He helped me off the stool and into his arms. "I won't lose you on this," he said.

We took an elevator to the third floor. Calvin's condo seemed a zillion miles from the nightclub scene and rank streets below. A modern, open loft-like layout was complemented with a brick accent wall and a wall of glass. Antique collections and contemporary furnishings included an ultra-soft leather sofa I melted into. I watched as Calvin whistled through clanking pots and pans, running water, chopping—a symphony concert.

I called the hospital to check on Travis. They were releasing him the next day. I chitchatted my way through growing anxiety, until he said the nurse was there to check his vitals and we hung up.

What if something happened and I never again had the chance to ruffle his hair? What if I never had the chance to tell him the truth about who he was or how much I loved him?

I struggled to push back the worst-case scenario and concentrated on our family being together again: Nareece, Travis, the twins, and me. I fell asleep.

Seemed like I had been asleep for a full night when Calvin nudged me to consciousness. In reality, it was only an hour.

He placed a tray with a plate of pasta, salmon, and red sauce on my lap and sat next to me. I devoured it.

Calvin held his hand out for my empty plate.

"The only solution for me is Jesse Boone dead," I said.

He kissed my forehead. "I know."

CHAPTER 26

Dulcey swore to whale the twins' behinds if they did not settle down. Her threats fell on their deaf ears and nearly blew my eardrums out before she said hello. The twins' screeches faded as I supposed Dulcey left their presence.

"I should be your backup, girl," she said.

"You should be right where you are. As long as I know the girls are safe and Travis is safe in the hospital, I can operate. Besides, I got Calvin watching my back."

"You sound so calm." Dulcey sighed in approval, then continued, "Can't remember when you've sounded so clear. It's almost scary, girl."

"I'm clear on what I need to do to get Reecey back."

"You want to talk to the girls?"

"Enough talking will be going on when this is over." My body heated up with every word. "Damn these flashes."

"I told you, embrace them, girl. It'll make the journey a lot smoother."

"Ain't nothing smooth about the journey I'm on right now."

After I clicked off from Dulcey, I went outside on Calvin's deck off the kitchen area, which offered a magnificent city view.

I lingered rail-side admiring Philly from above before turning my attention to Calvin. He straddled a lounge chair with his head back, stargazing. I sat at the end of the chair and followed his gaze.

"Big Dipper," he said, pointing skyward. "Bear." He put his arm down and pulled me back so I rested against his chest. The strain of what lay ahead fell away.

"I told you Jesse always had this rotten fish odor stuck to him. Well, his daddy constantly belittled him, as did everybody else—except Kelvin. Kelvin fought anyone who messed with the boy, 'cept his daddy. Jesse hated Kelvin"—he hesitated—"Laughton . . . because Mr. Boone took Laughton as the favorite. An old story for a different family."

"But you said you didn't know Laughton before now."

"I didn't know Laughton was Kelvin Boone, so I didn't know Laughton, I knew Kelvin. Lives splinter, folks go their ways, come back, go another way. Kelvin acted crazier than Jesse. Kelvin always kept his killer expression on. He killed a boy with his fists behind Jesse's mess, Maxwell Perry, the schoolyard bully. One day, Perry was relentlessly picking on Jesse and would not pay attention to Kelvin's threats. Kelvin knocked me out when I tried to stop him from beating Perry to death. Daddy Boone sent him away to boarding school, or so the story went. And, well, Jesse grew up to be Jesse."

"And you?"

"I had my own demons. I went into the service at seventeen to get away." His voice became low and hard. "They trained me."

"Special Forces?"

"Nothing special about being trained to kill."

"You'd think the past, after so long, wouldn't have such a strong hold on you. Years pass, you'd think it would turn you loose, turn me loose," I said.

"The past doesn't let you go, baby. You gotta let the past go. Deal with it and move on."

I sat up and turned to face him. "My dad used to say, 'Every-thing comes out in the wash.' It's such a cliché, but spot-on."

"Your problem is, nobody ever told you the truth, or you shut the truth out."

"I guess it's more about me shutting it out." I twisted back around and rested against his chest again. "I figured it'd be worse than lies. All these years, Reecey's been holding every-thing in and I've called what I've been doing 'helping her.' We've been so close and so far apart at the same time."

"You can't blame yourself."

"I shoulda known about Reecey's troubles. Instead, I got hung up in my career. I shoulda had Laughton's back. Instead I stopped trusting him. I shoulda stayed on John until he told me what he knew. I shoulda told Travis the truth. I shoulda seen through Cap. I shoulda faced my own demons."

"Stop." Calvin squeezed me. "You did what you could. Now you're going to do what you can." He stood up and swung his leg over my head. "C'mon," he said, pulling me up.

I followed him into his bedroom and into a walk-in closet about a quarter the size of the bedroom. He tapped four times on the upper corner of the back wall and it slid sideways, ex-posing another smaller room. A variety of weapons hung on three walls and a large black metal footlocker took up most of the floor space. He twirled the knob of the combination lock on the footlocker back and forth and lifted the top. First, he handled a Glock Model 22 and set it on the floor. Then he pulled out a shoulder holster and slid in a Smith & Wesson Bodyguard .38 and tossed it to me.

"They'll search you, take your gun away. He'd suspect some-thing if you walked in naked." He smiled.

Other weapons in the footlocker included an AK47 7.62X39MM with a thirty-round magazine, Bushmaster, XM Basic Tactical Turbine, S & W MP, 308 Win gas-operated, twenty-round capacity, Heckler & Koch MP 5 9 mm sub-machine gun that fired in single shots or three-round bursts or full auto at eight hundred rounds per minute. This machine gun was developed especially for the Navy Seals, as it fired from a closed bolt-barrel 8.85 inches long. All "badass" impressive. Weapons on the wall included a collection of antique pistols, some revolvers, and some single shots.

"Impressive."

"I'm a weapons specialist of a different sort." He closed the lid and pulled me to him. "I'll show you mine, you show me yours."

His lips glided over my neck, cheeks, eyes, and nose. He leaned back and let his finger dance over my lips. I reached up and pressed him closer, wanting his lips, his tongue, and fighting the lions of guilt because of it.

"I can't."

He touched his finger to my lips, then lifted me up and carried me to his bed. I lay nestled in his arms, listening to his heartbeat and absorbing courage.

"Jesse will be waiting with four or five men. He'll try to blindside you, make you powerless so he can brutalize you, then make you beg for your life and your sister's life . . . if she's still alive."

"She's alive."

"Baby, you have to be prepared for all of the possibilities."

"She's alive."

Three hours later I drove down Broad Street in North Philly pass the Uptown Theater and made a right to West Fifty-first Street. The Uptown Theater was a major venue for the chitlin' circuit from about 1951 to 1978. Comedians such as Redd Foxx and Flip Wilson performed there, as did just about every R&B

group of that era, including James Brown, Ray Charles, Stevie Wonder, and The Supremes. I had not been to this side of Philly in years and was shocked at the change. What once had been a center of black culture and music, also frequented by jazz greats like John Coltrane and Stan Getz, was now one of the most dangerous areas in Philadelphia.

The address at American and Susquehanna Street was a five-story abandoned brick factory building. A DUNGAN, HOOD, AND COMPANY sign, though barely readable, still hung across the top of the building. The names of old industrialists, such as Gratz, Poth, Bouvier, and Schmidt, still adorned many of the signs on other empty buildings in the Kensington Mill District, once the world's largest manufacturer of textiles and the pride of Philadelphia. Now it had the distinction of being the haven of junkies.

A brisk wind whipped street signs around. Dark thunderclouds glided across the sky, and the early hour colored everything gray. In my head, I heard Rod Serling's drone, "You have just entered *The Twilight Zone.*" I parked across the street from the Dungan, Hood Building and waited, trying to detect any movement in the building or outside area. I checked my gun, sucked in a deep breath, and got out. The hum of my breathing and the swoosh of my Nike Air Maxes every time I stepped down on the pavement heightened the eeriness. I carried sneakers in the trunk for special occasions such as this.

I stopped at the door and checked the surroundings to catch sight of Calvin. He was nowhere to be seen. He said he would be watching, ready. I whispered a short prayer before pushing on the heavy metal door. It did not budge. I applied a full-body push on the second go-round. The scraping of metal on metal and the door banging the inside wall from the force of my weight foiled my planned surprise approach.

Inside, my eyes took a few moments to adjust to the dark,

but not before my nose caved to the smells of funk, urine, mold, and crap. It made me gag, then forced me forward, giving up Calvin's luscious salmon meal. My Nikes caught much of the splatter.

Though it was earlier than the 2:00 a.m. designated time, I expected one of Jesse's men to be on the lookout. I moved around the lower level until I pushed open a door that led into a large, open area, the main factory floor for textile goods.

A swishing noise made me spin around with my gun drawn—and then blackness.

Jesse's voice poked at me, bringing me to consciousness.

"Some rescuer." He spat and I felt the wetness on my arm. He pressed his foot into my rib cage, willing me fully awake. "Well, well, here we are again. Where's the money?" He shoved harder with his foot and turned me over.

My head was blazing. Blood coated my fingers when I took them away from where he or one of his men had clobbered me. We were in a large room with no windows. I caught sight of Nareece, lying facedown on a dirty mattress in the far corner of the room. She was half-naked and bloodied, her hands and feet bound. Jesse followed my gaze.

"She's alive. Now, where's the money?"

"She's bleeding. Let me go to her."

"Go ahead. Take your ass over there and check her out." He motioned to one of the two men who were in the room with us. The man moved toward me and grabbed me by the hair to pull me up.

I kicked him in the groin on the way up. He released my hair and bent over, grabbing himself. An uppercut to the jaw sent him reeling backward and moaning on the floor.

I heard the trigger cock on the other man's gun.

Please, Calvin, come now.

"Don't shoot," Jesse yelled. "Not yet." He laughed and motioned for me to go to Nareece. "Move." He followed behind me. "She's good for nothing . . . never was . . . but she's alive. I said I wouldn't kill her. Didn't say I wouldn't make her wish she was dead," he scoffed.

When I turned her over, I saw that Nareece was bruised over her face and body and reeked of Jesse's fish smell. She was barely breathing.

"Now, where's the money?"

"It's in my trunk."

"Give him the keys." He motioned toward another man, whom I threw my keys to. "Now, sit," Jesse said, waving his gun toward me. "Leave her be."

I ignored him and untied Nareece's hands and feet. I checked her breathing again, then took off my jacket and covered her.

"It didn't have to be like this. She coulda had everything," he snarled, waving the gun in Nareece's direction. "She just couldn't get over that I ordered your old man hit, simple bastard."

His words pierced my senses.

"What did my father do to you?"

"He threatened me—told my father to *make* me leave his little girl alone. I hated my father all my life and you're going to tell on me? Like I gave a fuck. And this stupid bitch wants to punish me by stealing junk and cash that belongs to my old man. As much as I loved her, if word got out that I let her get away . . . He stayed on me, and stayed on me, till I couldn't take his bullshit anymore. I enjoyed killing my old man." Jesse paced, still waving the gun around. "Where the hell is Mumford? Check it out," he commanded another man.

I got up.

"Sit down!" Jesse yelled.

"She needs water."

"You don't go anywhere until they get back with the money. Now, sit down." He rushed up on me and pushed me back against the wall, the gun jammed in my throat.

I grabbed his wrist and twisted him around, causing him to drop the gun. He raised his fist and aimed for my head. I ducked and jabbed him in the solar plexus, sending him back and to the floor. I fell to my knees adjacent to him and punched his face, until I fell forward and needed both arms to keep from falling on top of him. I got up and stumbled to the corner where Jesse's gun had landed, stumbled back and aimed it at his head. My hand shook. I used my other hand to steady my grip and pulled the trigger.

I pulled the trigger again, and again. Jesse Boone's eyes flew open as he rose up from the floor snarling and swinging. Only then did I realize the gun had misfired, too late. His fist slammed the side of my head and sent me flying. I hit the floor face-first and slid into a wall.

Nareece's whisper echoed in my ear, "Muriel, get up." Her voice grew louder until she screamed, "Get up, Muriel!"

I turned over as Jesse Boone lunged toward me, spit streaming from his mouth with each swear he slung. I struggled to push myself out of his path, but my arms, my legs, were like putty.

He grabbed me by my hair, pulled me across the floor, and slammed my body into the wall, stepped back, and swung me around the other direction in a circular motion. I held his arm, trying to lessen the pull on my head. With each turn, I saw Nareece crawling along the floor away from us. Boone slammed me into the wall again, which stopped the action for a moment before he swung me in a circle, all the way booming, "You bitch. You think you can go up against me? I will fuck you up.

Make you wish you were dead. I'll cut your ass up and feed you to the animals."

"Bastard!" Nareece screeched and pulled the trigger of the same gun I had used. She shot again and again until the gun emptied. At the first shot, Boone released my hair. I lay sprawled on the floor, covering my head. When the firing stopped and I looked up, Jesse Boone appeared suspended upright for a few seconds before he fell to the floor and landed on top of me. I scrambled like crazy to free myself, his stench fighting back to hold me. The clicking sound of the gun continued until I managed to get up and take the weapon from Nareece and she crumpled into my arms. I fell back against the wall as Jesse's other three men rushed into the room, guns blazing. I fell to the ground and covered Nareece with my body as gunfire exploded. When it stopped, Laughton and Calvin stood over us. After the smoke cleared and they'd confirmed that Nareece and I were all right, Jesse Boone was gone, as in left the building. Laughton ran out to find him.

CHAPTER 27

I screamed, "There's no way he's still walking around. Reecey shot him, four, five times. There's no way." Fear crept up my spine for this man, Jesse Boone, who had walked away from multiple gunshot wounds. I rushed over to where he had fallen. "He fell right here. Fell out, dead."

Calvin came over and put his hand on my shoulder, the weight of which nearly drove me to my knees. "Calm down, Muriel. He couldn't have gotten far. The guys and Laughton will find him."

I shook him off and went back to tend to Nareece. She was barely conscious. Her eyes flitted around as she grabbed hold of my arm. I wanted to tell her there was nothing to be afraid of, that everything was good, that Jesse Boone had no reach to her anymore. I wanted to . . . I could only squeeze her hand.

Calvin perused the room, picked up my bag and a torn piece of clothing, and double-checked that there was nothing else revealing left behind. Fact was, there were no sirens in the distance. No one really cared in this part of Philly. The bodies of the men would be found in a day, maybe two, maybe not for a few weeks or months. There would be some investigation, since the men would be identified as known associates of Jesse Boone's, and Jesse would be sought for questioning. Maybe. That would be that unless Jakes and Janey got involved.

Calvin carried Nareece to his car.

"I'll follow you to the hospital in my car," I said. I locked eyes with Reecey, who gave a slight nod, then I walked away too fast for Calvin to respond.

I felt the underside of the fender for my spare car key and got in. A check of the flap mirror showed my face scratched up and swollen, my eye still blackened, and my hair standing on end—literally. My hands were shaking. When I started the car, the light came on and a bell sounded indicating the trunk was open. I got out and slammed it shut. Boone knew the money occupied a different space, not my trunk, as I said. I knew he would go to where he thought the money was. At least that was what I thought I knew. I called Laughton.

"Where are you?"

"I'm trying to pick up Jesse's trail."

"I think I know where he went—to get the money. He's gone to my parents' house."

There was silence. "Laughton? You there."

"I'm here."

"Nareece told Jesse where she hid the money. That's where she sent me to get it, my parents' house. It's not there anymore, but I'm thinking that's where he'll go to check. I'm on my way there now. I'll meet you."

"How's Carmella?"

"She's going to be fine. She'll need some time."

"I'm sorry we left so many things unsaid."

"Laughton, you don't have to say anything. We all had a part in this . . . this . . . tragedy. We were all hiding. Everything is out in the open, and while it stinks like hell now, when it clears it'll be a new day and we can all get on with our lives, for real."

"You and your damn philosophical bullshit." He chuckled. "Meet you in a minute."

I wished we had kept talking until we got there. The quiet left me thinking, Jesse could be waiting there, thinking that sooner or later I would come and he could kill me; or we could miss him. Boone could have gone there, found the bins broken up and empty, and left already, with a big head start. What the hell would life be like if Boone disappeared? A staple of fear and uncertainty shoved down my throat: constantly checking over my shoulder and over the shoulders of my family members, and being afraid to let them from my sight. In that case there would be no new day. The stench would linger for God knew how long.

The thought made me gag. I pulled over, opened the door, leaned out, and puked.

I parked a few houses down from my parents' house. Laughton drove up a few minutes later and parked behind me. We got out of our cars, checked our weapons, and crept up to the door. The street was deserted. It did not appear anyone was in the house, either. It was dark and quiet—the kind of quiet that causes ringing in your ears. Jesse certainly would have had someone standing watch outside.

I tried the front door. It was open.

I pushed it open, and Laughton and I moved in with weapons drawn. The basement door was down the hall to the right. No light shined up from the basement. Laughton moved right around through the living room; I went left through the dining room. We came together at the basement door.

It was dark, but the smell of rancid fish and funk settled in. I pinched my nose and Laughton nodded.

Laughton flicked the switch on the wall leading down into the basement. "Jesse, we know you're down there. Give it up, man. It's over."

There was no response. Going down the stairs meant leaving ourselves open for target practice.

"I'm coming down. I just want to talk."

I motioned to Laughton not to be stupid. How do you motion "stupid"? you might ask. With a lot of whispering, arms
flailing, mouthing of swears, waving of a gun, and bending
from the knees up and down. Laughton put his hand up for me
to stop.

Sweat dripped into my eyes, down my arms, off the tips of
my fingers.

Laughton started down the stairs. "I'm lowering my weapon, Jesse. Don't shoot."

Silence.

I followed in Laughton's steps, ready to shoot, ready to blow
Jesse Boone's head off.

At the bottom of the stairs, Laughton turned around to see
the entire room. He stopped halfway around and was still, staring. I continued down the stairs and stopped at the bottom,
following his gaze. Jesse Boone sat upright on the floor, leaned
up against the back wall of the basement with a gun pointed
directly at Laughton. I aimed at him. He twitched, I fired.

CHAPTER 28

Jesse Boone dead felt good, but not like I expected. If I could smack him back to life and shoot him again, and smack him back to life and shoot him again . . . fifty, one hundred times, each time making him aware of what was coming . . . maybe then.

No matter how many times we killed him, the damage would remain the same, though. Nareece stared blindly into space, seemingly unaware of her surroundings, or her husband's funeral going on right in front of her.

Rose and Helen stood beside me at their father's graveside memorial service crying so hard their bodies shook as though freezing from cold. I held them close, one on each side. They blessed me with drippy nose wipes on my black paisley suit. And Travis stood soldier-like behind Nareece's wheelchair, stone-faced and white-knuckled from gripping the handles.

John's gravesite was in Fairview Cemetery in Hyde Park, Massachusetts. The burial had taken place weeks ago, but the twins had wanted a graveside service for their dad. The gravestones glistened in the June sun, which had already pushed the temperature to 85 degrees at 11:00 a.m. Ama's moans drowned out the preacher's final blessings. The moment the preacher stopped talking, Jerry and Debbie whisked their mother away without even a look across the gravestone at us, the only attendees besides Dulcey and Bates. Rose and Helen were crying too hard to care, thank goodness.

As Jerry's car pulled away from the curb, I focused in on Laughton's silhouette in the distance, the sun at his back and in my eyes. I shaded my eyes to see better, but he was gone. Maybe it was my imagination?

On the way to the car, Bates stopped me. I sent the twins along with Dulcey.

"There's bound to be some fallout behind all this," he said. "Like I told you, Boone had business in Boston, too. This whole thing has more to do with drugs and weapons and money than your sister. I suspect Boone left some things hanging."

"Much appreciated, Bates, but I really don't give a damn about Boone anymore or anyone connected to him."

"You're not hearing me, Muriel. Your sister might still be a target. Does she talk at all?"

I watched Travis half-lift Nareece into the van.

"No. She doesn't do anything anymore."

"I'll be in touch. You take care," he said, kissing my forehead. "You need for anything, you know I'm your man." He chuckled lightly.

"Thanks, Bates."

I drove down I-95 in a rented Caravan, back to Nareece's house. The twins unbuckled their belts and opened the vehicle's door before I had fully stopped in the driveway.

"We're home," they said with a hint of excitement.

A Realtor met us at the door, ready to finalize the deal of selling the house. Inside, the twins raced up the stairs to their bedroom for one more look, one more check in case something important was left—one piece of paper, one manila folder, one pencil, or one clue to any of the cases employed by the Twofer Detective Agency.

"We can't let our clients down," they quipped. Rheumy eyes contradicted their bouncy demeanors.

The warmth once exuded by Nareece's eclectic decorative style was now ripped away. Now the décor consisted of rolled rugs, gleaming wood floors, stark white walls, boxes of every size stacked against them, and furniture pushed together at the center of the living room like a fortress prepped to thwart the movers' assault the next day.

Our footsteps echoed, and voices bellowed in the emptiness.

A half hour later, we sped down I-90 toward Philly, the twins huddled in the far back of the van watching a movie, Nareece and Travis asleep in the midsection, and Dulcey driving. I worked on wrapping my brain around what lay ahead, a much happier prospect.

I embraced raising Rose and Helen in the house where Nareece and I had grown up, where we'd once lived as a happy family. I took a breath, whisking away the bad memories determined to whittle their way front and center. Today they lost the battle. New day, new memories.

Plans for remodeling the family house were underway. They included redesigning the kitchen and bathrooms, painting inside and outside the house, refinishing the wood floors and replacing carpets. Other plans included building an addition for a live-in nurse to care for Nareece and a shed-sized outhouse in the backyard for the twins' detective agency. Between me and Nareece, we had plenty of furniture and household goods to outfit the place.

I decided to rent out rather than sell my house. For now, it was where we would live until the renovations were completed at the family house.

I took leave from the department, unsure whether my road to happiness spelled retirement. Fifty years rested on my shoulders, asking the question: *What do you want to be now that you're all growed up?* Summer first, I decided.

Seemed like a lifetime ago I was tripping about being old, menopause-old, and not having accomplished a damn thing, and being alone. Menopause pummeled me at full throttle and sent me deep within *God, help me* territory, but I realized my saviors were upon me. The twins squawking double-time, Nareece needing everything from dribble wipes to ass wipes, and the prospect of telling Travis the truth, actually cooled the sweats and backed my moods into a dark room, slamming and locking the door after them. Crazy. Crazy.

My worst fear was still about Travis's reaction when he learned his true identity and that his whole life echoed regurgitated lies. The good news was that the past was the past for now and evermore—banished, handled, resolved, and done. At least it would be done after Travis learned the truth.

Next thing I knew, Dulcey was waking me up as she pulled curbside in front of my house. It was 9:30 p.m. Travis went to unlock the front door, while I got the twins out of their seat belts and guided them up the walkway and up the stairs to Travis's room. Travis went back and got Nareece. He carried her into the house and up the stairs to my room. Dulcey walked behind him the whole way with her arms out in case they stumbled and she needed to catch them. Then they would all be goners, for sure.

I settled Nareece in my bed, while Dulcey settled the twins in Travis's bed. I would sleep on the living room couch, and Travis would sleep downstairs in the basement.

"Girl, it has definitely been a journey," Dulcey said, trudging down the stairs. I followed behind her.

"It is not over yet."

"It's over for me, girl. I'm about beat to a frazzle. What's left is left for you." She stopped at the front door and said, "Now, Missy M, ain't nothing blocking your way but what you put there." She squeezed my hand and left. I watched her get in the car and drive off, before I closed the door and held on to the doorknob, contemplating running away—far, far, away. Then I went into the kitchen to put some water on for tea.

Tomorrow was a new day. There was Mr. Kim to check out, since I had not seen or talked to him since he'd left the note in my door. He wasn't answering his phone and seemingly had not been home since I went there after receiving the note. A tinge of concern stayed in my gut, even though I knew Mr. Kim was quite capable of taking care of his own.

There was the money, two million dollars, not five, as Cap had said, but still, two million dollars in drug money hidden away for twenty years—now a curse or a treasure? Calvin had returned it to me, and all I could think was, who else knew about it? Would there be others coming for it? I decided that when Nareece was better, we would figure out what good we could do with it, because she certainly did not need the money.

Turns out I never knew exactly what John did for work because he did not do much of anything. At twenty years old, he had invested in Microsoft and made a small fortune, then invested some of that and made more. He and Nareece were set for life. Now Nareece and the girls were set. I was good, too—content with what I had, with no desire to profit from drug monies.

And then there was the matter of my heart. Calvin. That was going to be either a long-ass conversation or a very short one. No matter, I was ready, able, and pumped. "Bring it on."

Travis snuck up behind me at the kitchen sink and kissed my cheek. "Talking to yourself, huh? You know what they say about people who talk to themselves? They got issues, ain't all there."

"That sounds about right."

He spun me around and hugged me tight enough to send my brains shooting out the top of my head. He turned me loose and kissed me again. I tousled his hair and scratched his beard. He slapped my hand away.

"I know, I know, I need a haircut and a shave," he said.

We laughed.

"Sit down, son. It's time we talked."

HOT FLASH

Carrie H. Johnson

About this Guide

The suggested questions are included to
enhance your group's reading of
Carrie H. Johnson's *Hot Flash*.

Discussion Questions

1. It is said that a strong woman loves, forgives, walks away, lets go, tries again, and perseveres, no matter what life throws at her. Do you think Muriel is a strong woman? Why or why not?

2. Do you like Laughton and/or Calvin? Do you think the author intends for us to like them? Why or why not? Who do you think is the man Muriel should end up with?

3. Both men in Muriel's life—Calvin and Laughton—lied to her about who they are and other important information. Yet in the end, when it came to going after Jesse Boone, she trusted them to help her. Would you have made the same decision? Why or why not?

4. What is Dulcey's role in the book? Why do you think the author wrote her as Muriel's "other sister"? Is she a likable character? Why or why not?

5. Muriel holds a lot of guilt for what happened to Nareece when she was only sixteen. Since then she has made it her life's priority to be there for Nareece. Do you think her guilt is justified? Do you think her being there at Nareece's every whim helped or hurt Nareece?

6. Do you like Travis? Did you think he was a strong character despite being a mama's boy? How do you think he will handle finding out he is Jesse Boone's biological son?

7. It is said that "God made us sisters, but love made us friends." Is Muriel and Nareece's relationship a "typi-

cal" sister relationship? How does it compare to your relationship with your own sister or someone you know? Would you have done things differently if it were your sister in Nareece's situation?

8. Nareece has acted poorly toward Travis to the point where Travis never wanted to visit her with Muriel. How do you think Travis will deal with Nareece now that he knows she is his real mother?

9. Do you believe Laughton would have killed his brother Jesse if he had found him before Muriel did? What kind of feelings do you think Laughton had about Jesse? From the way the author describes Laughton and his actions, do you think Laughton might be more like Jesse Boone than we would like to believe?

10. Were you satisfied with the book's ending? Why or why not? What do you think the future holds for Muriel, Travis, Nareece, and the twins?

Don't Miss:

Bad Blood by Mary Monroe

Seth Garrett's family taught him that anything less than the best simply isn't an option. Now he's out to prove he can be the most successful Garrett—and Rachel McNeal fits the bill. She's pretty, hard-working, good in bed—and willing to finance his dreams. He thinks she's perfect wife material—until he meets her relatives and discovers they're far from perfect. No problem, Seth's got a replacement lined up to give him the good life he's entitled to . . .

Steady and sensible, Rachel always believed the best about people. She thought Seth was the man of her dreams. But she can deal with the hurt and move on. Until she discovers the true reason Seth dumped her—and just how deep his contempt for her runs. She's done forgiving, much less forgetting. And taking his world apart piece by piece is only the beginning of her long-game payback . . .

The Score by Kiki Swinson

Identity theft mastermind Lauren Kelly has always had a taste for the finer things. With her lover and accomplice, Matt Connors, by her side, there's nothing she can't buy or steal. But she's not the only one. When their partner, Yancy, stumbles onto a tycoon's multimillion-dollar bank account, Lauren expects the latest scam will go smoothly—until she discovers Matt and Yancy are planning the ultimate betrayal. Fortunately, Lauren is one step ahead of Matt. Once she disappears with every last dollar, they'll have no doubt they chose the wrong woman to deceive. But all three of them chose the wrong target . . .

DON'T MISS MURIEL MABLEY'S NEXT THRILLER

When Muriel's nine-year-old niece is critically wounded in a drive-by and her best friend's husband gets involved in a dangerous situation, Muriel is forced to step outside the law she has sworn to uphold . . .

Coming in Summer 2017

DON'T MISS

THE STRIVERS' ROW SPY by Jason Overstreet

Stunning, suspenseful, and unforgettably evocative, Jason Overstreet's debut novel glitters with the vibrant dreams and dangerous promise of the 1920s Harlem Renaissance, as one man crosses the perilous lines between the law, loyalty, and deadly lies . . .

Coming in September 2016

CHAPTER 1

Middlebury College, Vermont
Spring, 1919

It was graduation day, and the strange man standing at the top of the cobblestone stairwell gave me an uneasy feeling. It was like he was waiting on me. With each step I climbed, the feeling turned into a gnawing in my stomach, gripped me a bit more, pulling at my good mood.

I glanced at my watch, then down at my shiny, black patent leather shoes. First time I'd worn them. Hadn't ever felt anything so snug on my feet, so light. Momma had saved up for Lord knows how long and had given them to me as a graduation gift.

Again I looked up at him. He was a tall, thin man, dressed in the finest black suit I'd ever laid eyes on; too young, it appeared to me, to have such silver hair, an inch of which was left uncovered by his charcoal fedora. Even from a distance he looked like a heavy smoker, with skin the texture and color of tough, sun-baked leather. I had never seen any man exhibit such confidence—one who stood like he was in charge of the world.

I finally reached the top step and realized just how imposing he was, standing about six-five, a good three inches taller than I. His pensive eyes locked in on me and he extended a hand.

"Sidney Temple?" he asked, with a whispery-dry voice.

"Yes."

"James Gladforth of the Bureau of Investigation."

We shook hands as I tried to digest what I'd just heard. What kind of trouble was I in? Was there anything I might have done in the past to warrant my being investigated? I thought of Jimmy King, Vida Cole, Junior Smith—all childhood friends who, God knows, had broken their share of laws. But I had never been involved in any of it. The resolute certainty of my clean ways gave me calm as I adjusted my tassel and responded.

"Good to meet you, sir."

"Congratulations on your big day," he said.

"Thank you."

"You all are fortunate the ceremony is this morning. Looks to be gettin' hotter by the minute." He looked up, squinting and surveying the clear sky.

I just stood there nodding my head in agreement.

He took off his hat, pulled a handkerchief from his jacket pocket, and wiped the sweat from his forehead. "You can relax," he said, "you're not in any trouble." He put the hand-kerchief back in his pocket and replaced his hat. He stared at me, studying my face, perhaps trying to decide if my appear-ance matched that of the person he'd imagined.

He took out a tin from his jacket, opened it, and removed a cigarette. Patting his suit, searching for something, he finally removed a box of matches from his left pants pocket. He struck one of the sticks, lit the cigarette, and smoked quietly for a few seconds.

Proud parents and possibly siblings walked past en route to the ceremony. One young man, dressed in his pristine Army uniform, sat in a wheelchair pushed by a woman in a navy blue dress. He had very pale skin, red hair, and was missing his right leg. Mr. Gladforth looked directly at them as they approached.

"Ma'am," he said, tipping his hat, "will you allow me a moment?"

"Certainly," she said, coming to a stop. She had her grayish-blond hair in a bun, and her eyes were some of the saddest I'd ever seen.

"Where did you fight, young man?" asked Gladforth.

"Saw my last action in Champagne, France, sir. Part of the Fifteenth Field Artillery Regiment. Been back stateside for about two months, sir."

"Your country will forever be indebted to you, son. That was a hell of a war effort by you men. On behalf of the United States government and President Wilson, I want to thank you for your service."

"Thank you, sir."

"Ma'am," said Gladforth, tipping his hat again as the woman gave him a slight smile.

She resumed pushing the young man along, and Gladforth began smoking again—refocusing his attention on me.

"I don't want to take away too much of your time, Sidney," he went on, turning and exhaling the smoke away from us. "I just wanted to introduce myself and tell you personally that the Bureau has been going over the college records of soon-to-be graduates throughout the country.

"You should be pleased to know that you're one of a handful of men that our new head of the General Intelligence Division, J. Edgar Hoover, would like to interview for a possible entry-level position. Your portfolio is outstanding."

"Thank you," I said, somewhat taken aback.

"I know it's quite a bit to try to decide on at the moment, but this is a unique opportunity to say the least."

"Indeed it is, sir."

He handed me a card. "Listen, here's my information. We'd like to set up an interview with you as soon as possible, hopefully within the month."

He began smoking again as I read the card.

"Think about the interview, and when you make your mind up, telephone the number there. We'll have a train ticket to Washington available for you within hours of your decision. Based on the sensitivity of the assignment you may potentially be asked to fulfill, you can tell no one about this interview.

"And, if you were to be hired, your status in any capacity would have to remain confidential. That includes your wife, family, and any friends or acquaintances. If you are uncomfortable with this request, please decline the interview because the conditions are nonnegotiable. Are you clear about what I'm telling you?"

"Yes, I think so."

"It's imperative that you understand these terms," he stressed, throwing what was left of his cigarette on the ground and stepping on it, the sole of his dress shoe gritting against the concrete.

"I understand."

"Then I look forward to your decision."

"I'll be in touch very soon, Mr. Gladforth. And thank you again, sir."

We shook hands and he walked away. Wondering what I'd just agreed to, I headed on to the graduation ceremony.

I picked up my pace along the cobblestone walkway, thinking about all the literature and history I'd pored over for the past six years, seldom reading any of it without wishing I were there in some place long ago, doing something important and history-shaping. I may have been an engineer by training, but at heart, at very private heart, I was a political man.

I wondered, specifically, what the BOI wanted with a colored agent all of a sudden. I was certainly aware that during its short life, it had never hired one. Could I possibly be the first? I thought it intriguing but far-fetched.

"Don't be late, Sidney," said Mrs. Carlton, one of my mathematics professors, interrupting my reverie as she walked by. "You've been waiting a long time for this."

"Yes, ma'am." I smiled at her and began to walk a bit faster. I reminded myself that Gladforth hadn't actually mentioned my becoming an agent. He'd only spoken of an interview and a possible low-level position.

"It's just you and me, Sidney," said Clifford Mayfield, running up and putting his hand on my shoulder, his grin bigger than ever.

"Yep," I said, "just you and me," referring to the fact that Clifford and I would be the only coloreds graduating that day.

"The way I see it," he said, "this is just the beginning. Tomorrow I'm off to Boston for an interview with Thurman Insurance."

Clifford continued talking about his plans for the future as we walked, but my mind was still on the Bureau. Working as an engineer was my goal, but maybe it could wait. Perhaps this Bureau position was a calling. Maybe if I could land a good government job and rise up through the ranks, I could bring about the social change I'd always dreamed of. I needed a few days to think it through.

Moments later I was sitting among my fellow classmates, each lost in his own thoughts inspired by President Tannenbaum. He stood at the podium in his fancy blue and gold academic gown, the hot sun beaming down on his white rim of hair and bald, sunburned top of his head.

"You are all now equipped to take full advantage of the many opportunities the world has to offer," he asserted. "You have chosen to push beyond the four-year diploma and will soon be able to boast of possessing the coveted master's degree. . . ."

Momma had told me from the time I was five, "You're going to college someday, Sugar." But throughout my early teens I'd noticed that no one around me was doing so. Still, I studied hard and got a scholarship to Middlebury College. My high school English teacher, Mrs. Bright, had gone to school here.

"It seems," Tannenbaum continued, "like only yesterday that I was sitting there where all of you sit today, and I can tell you from my own experiences in the greater world that a Middlebury education is second to none. . . ."

I'd left Milwaukee, the Bronzeville section, in the fall of 1913 and headed here to Vermont. I had taken a major in mechanical engineering with the goal of obtaining a bachelor's and then a master's degree in civil engineering. I would be qualified both to assemble engines and construct buildings. Reading physics became all consuming, and I'd spent most of my time in the library, often slipping in some pleasure reading. Having access to a plethora of rich literature was new to me.

"I want you to hear me loud and clear," President Tannenbaum went on. "This is your time to shine."

As I looked across the crowd of graduate students and up into the stands, I saw Momma in her purple dress, brimming with joy. She was so proud, and rightfully so, having raised me all on her own. For eighteen years it had been just the two of us, Momma having happily spent those years scrubbing other families' homes, cooking for and raising their children. But now that I had turned twenty-five, I would see to it that she wouldn't have to do that anymore.

It was time for my row to stand. As we progressed slowly toward the stage, I became more and more painfully aware of my wife's absence. I'd first laid eyes on Loretta in the library four years earlier when she'd arrived at Middlebury, making her the third female colored student here.

I'd approached her while she was studying, introducing myself and awkwardly asking her if she'd like to study together sometime. She'd just given me an odd look before I'd quickly changed my question, asking instead if she'd like to have an ice cream with me sometime in the cafeteria. She said yes and it was easy between us from that day on.

"Sidney Temple!" called out President Tannenbaum, the audience politely clapping for me as they had for the others. I walked onto the stage, took my diploma from his hand, and paused briefly for the customary photograph. I looked at Momma as she wiped the tears from her eyes.

I longed for Loretta to be sitting there too, witnessing my little moment in the spotlight. Before coming to Middlebury she'd spent one year at the Pennsylvania Academy of the Fine Arts and another at Oberlin College. But she'd finally found her collegiate home here and earned a degree in art history.

Her graduation, which had come three weeks prior to mine, had been a magical affair. Unfortunately, that celebratory atmosphere had come to an abrupt halt. Today she was grieving the loss of her father and was back home in Philadelphia arranging for his funeral. His illness had progressed during the last year, and he'd rarely been conscious the last time we'd visited him together. I'd figured that would be the last time I'd see him and had said my good-byes back then. Still, it was comforting to know that Loretta had insisted I stay here and allow Momma to see me graduate.

With the ceremony over and degree in hand, I headed to the reception the engineering department was having for a few of us. My mind raced to come up with a good reason for visiting Washington, D.C.—one that I could legitimately tell Momma about. As I arrived at the auditorium, she was waiting outside. We embraced.

"I'm so proud of you, Sugar."

"I couldn't have done it without you. I love you, Momma."

The pending trip to Washington crept into my mind even during that long motherly hug.

A week later I was standing in the train station lobby in downtown Chicago on my way to the nation's capital. I'd said my good-byes to Momma back in Milwaukee earlier that morning. My "good reason"? I'd told her I'd been asked to interview for a position on the Public Buildings Commission, a government committee established in 1916 to make suggestions regarding future development of federal agencies and offices. It was the first time I'd lied to her, and the guilt was heavy on me.

The Bureau had sent an automobile to pick me up at Momma's place in Milwaukee and drive me to Chicago. It was a wondrous black vehicle—a 1919 Ford Model T.

When my train was announced, I headed to the car where all the colored passengers were sitting. Unlike the South, here in Chicago there were no Jim Crow cars I was required to sit in, but I guess most of us just felt comfortable sitting apart from the whites, and vice versa. Was the way things were in public. But it was a feeling I never wanted my future children to have.

All the folks on the train were immaculately dressed, and I felt comfortable in my cream-colored three-piece suit and brown newsboy cap. We gazed at one another with curiosity, they probably wondering, as I was, what special event was affording us the opportunity to travel such a distance in style. The car was paneled in walnut and furnished with large, upholstered chairs. It was the height of luxury.

I began studying the brand-new Broadway Limited railroad

map I'd purchased. Ever since my first year of college, I'd been collecting every map I could get my hands on. It had become a hobby of sorts, running my finger along the various lines that connected one town to another, always discovering a new place various rails had begun servicing.

The train passed by West Virginian fields of pink rhododendron, then chugged through the state of Virginia as I reflected on its history and absorbed the landscape with virgin eyes. This was the land of Washington and Jefferson I was entering.